W9-BRW-210

RUDD HAD HEARD ENOUGH . . .

The way we love, he thought, as he walked to the car, is as much a conditioned process as any other human activity. It was only the popular songs that made it sound romantic, a question of losing your heart to the right person.

A man and a woman. The ancient duality. But the question was what sort of man and woman? Roles that seem separate and yet the boundaries are a lot less fixed than we imagine. And it was when those boundaries became too fluid that people like Jess Lambert went under, victims of a habit of loving that could end only in tragedy . . .

THE HABIT OF LOVING
June Thomson

Bantam Books by June Thomson

DEATH CAP
THE HABIT OF LOVING

THE HABIT
OF LOVING

JUNE THOMSON

All of the characters in this book
are fictitious, and any resemblance
to actual persons, living or dead,
is purely coincidental.

*This low-priced Bantam Book
has been completely reset in a type face
designed for easy reading, and was printed
from new plates. It contains the complete
text of the original hard-cover edition.*
NOT ONE WORD HAS BEEN OMITTED.

THE HABIT OF LOVING

*A Bantam Book / published by arrangement with
Doubleday & Company, Inc.*

PRINTING HISTORY

*Doubleday edition published January 1979
Published in England by Constable Publishers as*
DEADLY RELATIONS, *1978*

Bantam edition / April 1980

*All rights reserved.
Copyright © 1978 by June Thomson.
Cover art copyright © 1980 by Bantam Books, Inc.
This book may not be reproduced in whole or in part, by
mimeograph or any other means, without permission.
For information address: Doubleday & Company, Inc.,
245 Park Avenue, New York, New York 10017.*

ISBN 0–553–13322–5

Bantam Books are published by Bantam Books, Inc. Its trademark, consisting of the words "Bantam Books" and the por-
trayal of a bantam, is Registered in U.S. Patent and Trademark
Office and in other countries. Marca Registrada. Bantam
Books, Inc., 666 Fifth Avenue, New York, New York 10019.

for Roy

The Habit of Loving

1

Chris's arrival, exactly a week before the murder, seemed to serve as a prelude to the events that followed; or so Maggie Hearn was to see it afterwards, although that was only with hindsight. At the time, everything seemed ordinary enough. It was a Monday in late July, with nothing special to mark it out except there had been a heavy atmosphere in the air all afternoon, presaging a storm.

It broke towards evening, with a preliminary low rumble of thunder in the west where dark clouds were already beginning to bank up against the dying sun which lit them from behind, giving them a nimbus of dull gold. The wind began to rise, too. Maggie could hear the branches of the trees in the orchard creaking as she crossed the yard to shut the hens up for the night. Coming out of the stable, where the chickens had already gone to roost in an improvised henhouse in one of the loose boxes, she was startled to see him coming towards her in the windy dust, the rucksack on his back seeming too heavy for his thin shoulders.

He was young, she noticed, not more than nineteen or twenty, with dark brown hair and a long head, the sort she always thought of as intellectual, and a mouth that was too vulnerable, too easily given to betraying his feelings. There was something languid about him, too; a pallor that wasn't altogether natural.

You've been ill, my lad, Maggie commented silently.

"Excuse me," he was saying. "I wonder if you could help me?"

His voice was educated, light for a man, and hesitant. In fact, his whole manner expressed diffidence.

"Yes?" Maggie replied encouragingly.

For some reason that she couldn't explain, she was

drawn to him immediately. Perhaps, at that very first moment of meeting, he brought out some protective instinct in her. She wanted to look after him. Perhaps, too, she saw in him the son she would have liked to have if she had married: dark, clever, sensitive. Certainly, she was aware that he responded to her. When she answered him, he seemed to relax, as if he were ready to put himself in her hands.

For his part, he had been passing the house when he saw her cross the yard and he had stood hesitating at the gate, wondering whether to enter and speak to her or go on up the road. It was only anxiety about the coming storm that made him walk down the drive towards the back of the house. He was glad now that he had done so. She didn't look like an ordinary, middle-aged housewife who might be annoyed at being accosted by a stranger. She looked— well, he had to admit it—a bit odd, although interestingly so, standing there at the stable door, her hair, which was bundled up anyhow into a loose bun beginning to come down at the back; one long, dark coil, like a tail, slowly unwinding over the blue and white gingham blouse she was wearing loose over slacks, the cuffs of which were sprinkled with little pieces of chaff and straw. She was strongly built for a woman, with broad hips and backside, but the features were good; handsome, with a lot of humour in them. He was particularly attracted by her eyes, long-lidded and of an extraordinary colour, light grey with dark flecks in them which put him in mind, for some reason, of stones at the bottom of a clear stream, although there was nothing hard in their expression. On the contrary, there was something ingenuous about her that was almost childlike in its simplicity and frankness. He felt he might be able to trust her.

"I was looking for somewhere to camp for the night before it comes on to rain," he explained, "and I thought, as this was a farm . . ."

As he spoke, the first drops began to fall, as heavy as bullets, pitting the fine dust that overlaid the cobblestones and drumming on the corrugated iron roof of the cowshed.

"Come on!" Maggie cried and made for the house. After a moment's hesitation, he followed, coming behind her into the kitchen where she switched on the light. The room sprang into brilliance, cosy and cluttered, with the long deal table that took up the centre of the room strewn with sewing and a black cat with white forepaws sitting on the tiled floor in front of the Aga, above which a string of tea towels was airing off below a high mantle shelf crowded with objects, among which he noticed a pottery pig decorated with blue polka dots and a George V coronation tea caddy. A crocheted kettle holder shared a hook with last year's calendar from a seed merchant.

He liked it. It was different from the kitchen at home that was always hygienically clean and tidy, and it stirred in him images of some idyllic childhood that he had never had; of running free among fields and coming back at dusk to the warmth and safety of a room like this where there would be huge farmhouse meals and laughter. Even the cat dozing in front of the stove, with its eyes squeezed shut and its tail neatly folded, was part of the setting.

"Take that thing off your back and sit down," Maggie was telling him, indicating the rucksack. He obeyed her, giving her an odd, shy smile as he did so.

"Well, one thing's certain, you can't put a tent up in this lot," she continued, nodding towards the window. Beyond the darkened glass, spattered with rain drops, they had a refracted view of the yard and its surrounding buildings, drenched with water, the roofs glossy, and above them the clouds closing down, quenching the last of the light. "You'd better stay here till it stops. Hungry?" she added hopefully. He looked as if he needed feeding up.

"I am rather," he admitted.

"Then I'll get some supper. Will a fry-up suit you?"

"Please, you mustn't go to any trouble."

"Oh, it's no trouble," Maggie assured him airily. "I'd have to cook for myself, anyway. One more won't make any difference."

It wasn't quite true. If he hadn't been there, she would have made do with a piece of cheese or a couple of boiled eggs.

"What can I do to help?" he asked.

"You can clear the table if you like," she told him. "Bung it all on the dresser."

While the frying pan heated up she watched with concealed amusement as he folded up the sheet she had been doing sides to middle and carried it over to the dresser, returning for the sewing basket into which he carefully placed the scissors and the reel of white cotton, threading the needle into the little flannel book. It was all done with such solemn care, his thin hands moving with a delicate precision that fascinated her. Suddenly he looked up and caught her glance. Without intending to, she found herself laughing. It was a laugh of pure pleasure as well as amusement; not unkind but certainly indulgent. For a moment, he stood quite still and then he laughed too.

"As you can see, I'm house trained," he remarked.

The shared laughter seemed to finalise a bond between them although, later, Maggie was to blame herself for not paying enough attention to the second's silence that preceded it.

"It's daft," she said, "but I don't know your name."

"It's Christopher. Christopher Lawrence."

"I'll call you Chris. You don't mind, do you? Christopher's a bit of a mouthful."

Too posh, she really meant. Too privileged. Chris was better. There was a dark, crisp taste to the name that seemed to suit him.

"No, I don't mind," he replied, although he felt a small shock on hearing it. But Maggie, oblivious, was chatting on.

"Mine's Margaret Hearn, but call me Maggie. Everyone does. What do you do?" she added, putting sausages into the pan and watching them stretch and then curl up in the hot fat.

"I'm a student."

"Student of what?"

"English."

"You mean poetry and stuff like that?"

"Yes, stuff like that."

It was his turn to sound amused.

"I suppose you're on holiday now?"

"Yes, I would normally be. I mean, the term's over but I've been away ill."

So I was right! Maggie thought triumphantly. He has been ill.

"Is that why you're camping?" she asked.

"Yes, partly. I wanted a change and I'd been told to get plenty of fresh air."

And rest, he added wryly to himself. Christ, if only they knew!

She was watching his face closely. The vulnerable look had come into it again; a closed, secret expression that told her she had gone too far.

"You mustn't take any notice of me," she said quickly. "I'm a bit nosey."

"It's all right," he assured her. "I don't mind at all."

But he did mind, although he was too polite, too well schooled in social niceties to say so. Besides, his illness was too close for him to want to think about it, let alone discuss it with a stranger, although he could see her interest was well meant.

My illness! he thought suddenly, with one of those bursts of inward rage that he still hadn't learned to anticipate or control. Why the hell must I go on covering it up, even to myself? I wasn't ill in the way she means; I had a bloody nervous breakdown.

He put up his hand to hide the spasm that he knew always twisted his mouth on these occasions. But, mercifully, Maggie hadn't noticed. She was shovelling sausages, eggs and bacon onto plates and carrying them over to the table. By the time he sat down opposite her, the rage had passed and he was able to talk naturally.

"Do you run the farm yourself?" he asked, partly to steer the conversation away from himself, partly because he was genuinely interested in her; a good sign, he felt. Two months ago he wouldn't have given a damn about anybody. He had been so locked up in his own little cell of self-pity that no one outside it had any interest for him or any real separate identity.

"Not any more," Maggie replied. "It used to be a working farm when my father was alive but it got too much for me after his death. I still keep a few chickens and I sometimes rear a half-dozen pigs or heifers for market. But most of the land's let out now to tenants. I make a living from it that way."

As she spoke, she was surprised to find how little guilt remained, although, at the time, the decision hadn't been an easy one. The farm had been her father's whole life and she had felt a keen sense of betrayal when she had begun to let it go, field by field, as if she were slowly killing off everything he had worked for. But she had already betrayed him, she realised, from the day she was born and hadn't been a son.

She found herself explaining this to Chris in a way she couldn't have done to anyone else; not even people in the village who she had known all her life. Perhaps, she decided, it was the quiet, listening look in his face that made it easy and the feeling that he was sensitive enough to understand.

Although Chris was touched by her confidence, he was disturbed by it as well. Until that moment, he had seen only the positive side of her nature, her warm-heartedness and generosity. Why else had she asked him in and given him supper? Now he was aware of other qualities in her that alarmed him: her loneliness, her need to be wanted and understood.

I have nothing to give you, he wanted to warn her. It's all burnt out of me. There's no affection or warmth left anymore. All I want to do is sleep and forget.

All the same, he felt he could at least listen to her and for Maggie it seemed to be enough.

It was eleven o'clock before it stopped raining and it seemed then too late to expect him to put up the tent.

"Besides," as Maggie pointed out, "the ground'll be soaking wet. You'd better stop here for the night."

She saw him glance towards her left hand, which wore no wedding ring.

"I don't mind camping out in one of the barns," he offered.

"All right," Maggie agreed, touched by his concern for the conventionalities. Personally, she didn't give a damn but it was considerate and rather charmingly old-fashioned of him to think of them. "There's a room over the stable. It's warm and dry. You can sleep up there if you like."

It was quite an adventure, rummaging about in the attic for the camp bed, carrying it across the yard, the light from the hurricane lamp reflecting in the dark puddles and casting long shadows up the wall as they mounted the wooden steps to the loft, with the hens shifting about below on their perches, muttering and grumbling at being disturbed.

They emerged through the trap door opening into a large upper room under the eaves, its sloping walls, following the angles of the roof, boarded in pine. There was a pleasant smell of wood and straw, although Maggie wrinkled up her nose at the sight of the cobwebs that hung in dusty festoons in the corners and the old whitewash that was dropping off the walls in big, brittle flakes.

"It could do with a good clean-up," she remarked, as she helped him put up the camp bed.

"It's all right," he assured her. "It's only for the one night."

"Yes. Well," Maggie replied in a noncommittal voice. "I'll go and get you some blankets and a pillow."

She clumped off down the steps before he could explain there was no need: he had his sleeping bag.

Stripping the spare bed, she came to a decision. She'd ask him if he'd like to stay.

Why not? she argued with herself. It'll be company for me and it needn't be for more than a few days. Besides, he looks in need of a rest.

She couldn't rationalise the decision beyond this point, knowing that any arguments she might make would be outweighted by her overwhelming desire not to see him leave the following day.

Chris, waiting in the loft room for her return, had guessed that this was in her mind. Her tone of voice had given her away. It had been too carefully casual.

Should he stay? He didn't know.

The effort of making up his mind one way or the other was beyond him. It was easier to drift. And yet he felt in some strange way that the decision had been made for him three days before when he had walked out of the private nursing home. Since then he had been on the move, stopping nowhere for more than one night, putting as much distance as he could between himself and the past. Running away, in fact, as he admitted with a small, wry smile. Now he had landed up here, in this loft room that, with its bare wooden walls and floor, offered some kind of refuge.

Should he stay? He looked about him in the light of the hurricane lamp that Maggie had left standing on the floor. Through a skylight in the back slope of the roof, he caught a glimpse of the branches of trees, outlined against a sky from which the clouds were beginning to clear, revealing a few stars.

Another window overlooked the yard. Crossing the room, he looked out of it. The rear view of the house faced him: safe and solid with its warm, brick façade and old, tiled roof.

The kitchen window shone back at him. He could see the bunch of marigolds that Maggie had placed in a jam jar on the sill, close against the glass, and the white-faced clock with the black hands and Roman numerals hanging on the opposite wall.

Then Maggie's figure crossed the room and he drew back, anxious for some reason that he couldn't explain not to be seen.

She glanced up at his window as she walked across the yard to the stable, her arms full of bedclothes. The yellow light of the hurricane lamp shone out faintly.

Would he stay?

Well, I can but ask, she thought as she climbed the stairs.

"You'll be off tomorrow then?" she asked, as she unfolded and tucked in the blankets. "Where are you making for?"

"Nowhere in particular," he replied. He put the pillow in place and pushed the bed back against the wall.

Maggie felt her face go hot. Suddenly she heard herself saying, "You could stay on here for a bit, if you want to."

There! She had said it, but not at all in the way she had intended. Her voice sounded gruff and awkward, as if she were offering the hospitality grudgingly. But it was this very awkwardness that made him decide.

How could he refuse, he thought, when it had obviously embarrassed her so much to ask?

"Thank you," he said quickly, almost without thinking. "I'd like to. I'll pay, of course."

"You'll do no such thing!" Maggie cried warmly.

"But I must . . ."

It was turning into one of those polite arguments about money that she couldn't bear, at least not with him, although she enjoyed haggling with her tenants over the rents for her land.

"I'm not taking any payment and that's an end to it," she said. "But I'll tell you what you can do in exchange—a few odd jobs about the place for me, a bit of gardening, things like that."

"Of course," he agreed. "If you're sure it's enough?"

"It'll suit me," Maggie replied with a businesslike brisk-ness, content that he had accepted and finding her old assurance again. "You can have a lie-in in the morning. You look as if you need it. I've got to go out anyway, but I'll leave the back door open so you can make breakfast for yourself if I'm not back when you want it. Well, I'll get off to bed," she added and, turning abruptly, went down the steps before he had time to thank her.

So it was decided, he thought, as he undressed and got into the camp bed. In some ways, he was glad. At least it solved one problem for the time being, for he couldn't go on tramping about the countryside indefinitely. Sooner or later, he'd have to make up his mind to go home or return to the clinic and he didn't want to do either. Now that decision was postponed. He could remain here, in a pleasant state of limbo, committing himself to nothing. Besides, if it didn't work out, he could always leave.

Chris! She had called him Chris.

Well, it didn't really matter, although her use of the shortened form of his name had startled him with a sense of ominous familiarity. Someone else had called him Chris but he preferred not to think of her.

All of that, though, was in the past that he had hoped to leave behind. Here, in this bare room, there was the possibility of starting again; perhaps of finding a new personality for himself, someone less vulnerable, better equipped at dealing with life, better armoured against its slings and arrows.

A quotation from *Hamlet*, of course, and although, to use the psychiatrists' jargon, there was some similarity between their case histories, like Eliot's Prufrock he had never aspired to be the Prince of Denmark.

But it served to illustrate the drawbacks of a literary education, he thought sardonically, that gave you all the language and imagery of passion, only at secondhand. When he had been faced with the real thing, he hadn't known how to deal with it and had gone to pieces.

The thought wakened the sick, swooping sensation in his stomach that was one of the physical symptoms of his breakdown.

Oh, Christ! he thought wearily.

Getting out of bed, he fumbled in the pocket of the rucksack for the bottle of tranquillisers.

Only one, he told himself. They've got to last.

Swallowing the tablet painfully with a mouthful of spittle, he got back into bed and lay with his arms folded behind his head, staring up at the oblong of night sky above him, waiting for the black tide that would presently come sweeping up and carry him away.

2

The morning following the storm was perfect; a clear, cloudless day with the sky a pure, washed blue and a brilliance to everything, as if each twig and blade of grass had been outlined with light.

The same brightness touched Maggie as she laid the breakfast things on the table ready for Chris when he woke up, before fetching her bike from the barn and setting off for the village.

He would be there when she got back, she told herself. The reality of his presence already seemed a settled thing and her thoughts ran happily on, planning a future that included him.

I'll do a ham salad for lunch and a chicken casserole for supper. He looks as if he could do with feeding up. I can stop off at Ellis's in the village for the meat on the way back from seeing Ken.

Ken Aston, who owned the market garden on the far side of the village, was one of her tenants. He was already renting one field from her and was thinking of leasing another, the terms of which she wanted to discuss with him that morning.

The road led in a long, downhill slope to the village centre, a scattered rectangle of houses and a few shops strung out behind wide grass verges, with the school at one end, the Rose and Crown facing the village hall in the centre, and the church, a little aloof, tucked away behind trees at the far side, where the road began to rise again in an upward incline.

Halfway up, Maggie dismounted and began to walk, passing the entrance to Bateson's farm on her left, another of her tenants. On the crown of the hill, a finger post pointed to a footpath that led across the fields to the next village, Dearden.

Just beyond it, Aston's market garden came into view, with its five long greenhouses glittering in the sun and the sprinklers working in one of the fields alongside, revolving slowly and throwing leisurely arcs of bright water drops over the rows of lettuce.

Leaving her bike just inside the gate, she went in search of Aston and found instead Vi, Aston's wife, in the packing shed behind the greenhouses, shoving lettuces into cardboard crates with a speed and efficiency that was due as much to bad temper as long practice. She was a big-boned woman, only in her middle thirties, but already round-backed and heavy-footed from too much stooping and standing. When she could be bothered or could spare the time, she went into Watleigh to have her hair bleached but it had been some time since her last visit for Maggie noticed at least half an inch of new, dark growth close to the scalp. Maggie, who had known her all her life, remembered her when Ken had first started courting her—an upright, well-made girl, with high, firm breasts and a loud laugh.

"Ken's out," she replied in answer to Maggie's question. "Don't ask me where because he didn't say."

"Do you know when he'll be back?"

"Can't tell you that either," Vi said shortly. "He cleared off straight after breakfast although he knew we'd got this bloody order to make up by dinnertime."

She completed a crate and shoved it out of the way down the bench before jerking out another flattened box from the pile beside her which she assembled with a few quick movements.

"Want some help?" Maggie asked. It was early yet to go home. Chris was probably still asleep and, besides, the packing shed, cool and smelling of moist earth and the crushed, discarded outer leaves of the lettuces that littered the floor under their feet, attracted her. She felt sorry for Vi, too. Being married to Ken couldn't be easy. She wondered if he'd been after another woman again. It was usually the reason behind Vi's anger. Anyway, she'd find out sooner or later. Vi would bottle it up only for so long and then it'd come pouring out—the suspicions, the frustrations, all the accumulated bitterness of fifteen years.

Although she didn't encourage these confidences, Maggie knew why she received them. Vi had as good as told her.

"You've been through a lot of it yourself," she had said. "You know what I'm talking about."

Not the faithless husband bit, of course. But, like Vi, she had known what it was to do hard, outdoor work, man's work, and get damn-all back in the way of gratitude; except in Maggie's case it was her father who had taken her for granted.

But Maggie had gotten out and, for that reason, Vi admired her and turned to her for advice and consolation, seeing her as someone older and wiser and stronger than herself; shrewd, too, and a good businesswoman and that counted for a lot in Vi's estimation. Anyone who had the sense to let out her land instead of breaking her back trying to farm it must know a thing or two about life.

But not about men, Maggie thought, as she rolled up her sleeves, revealing sturdy forearms, and took her place beside Vi at the bench. There had been only two: a farmer from Gossbridge, whom her father had wanted her to marry, and Alec, an insurance agent in Watleigh, whom she had loved but who already had a wife. The farmer had bored her, with his fumbling attempts at lovemaking and his everlasting talk about pigs and the price of feed stuff. As for Alec—perhaps, in the end, she had bored him. She had always felt gauche and awkward in his presence, like a big, clumsy schoolgirl, too anxious to please. Finally, he had gone back to his wife, whom he hadn't really left in the first place. The two women worked in silence for a time, Vi not yet ready for a full confession; Maggie absorbed in the task of packing, finding pleasure in handling the lettuces, each one a carefully made-up bouquet of green leaves, with a dense, secret heart. She had to give it to Ken, she thought. He knew what he was about where growing crops was concerned. It was all good quality stuff.

Any chance of intimate conversation was, anyway, restricted by the presence of Lambert, Aston's foreman, who came into the shed from time to time to pile the completed crates onto a trolley which he wheeled away to the loading bay outside the door to await the arrival of the lorry.

He was a short, powerfully built, grey-haired man who never had much to say and who merely nodded in acknowledgement of Maggie's greeting when he first came in. She saw Vi give him an odd look, hostile and suspicious, but she didn't think much of it, except to assume

Vi's anger included him. Vi had never liked the man much anyway, resenting the fact that, when Aston was away, he took charge.

"What did you want to see Ken about?" Vi asked when Lambert had gone away with a trolley load.

Maggie hesitated, reluctant to explain to Vi that Ken was thinking of renting another field from her, knowing that he had probably not discussed it with her. It was one of Vi's complaints against him that he didn't confide in her where business matters were concerned.

"Oh, nothing much," Maggie replied casually. "I was just wondering when he was going to put the pickers into that currant field just up the road from me, that's all."

Vi shrugged.

"It's no good asking me. Ken never tells me anything. I get fed up sometimes . . ."

She broke off as Lambert came back with the trolley.

"That the lot?" he asked gruffly, picking up the last of the crates.

"Yes, we've finished," Vi told him.

He turned to go and she shouted after him, "What about them tomatoes?"

"Packed," he said shortly, without bothering to look back at her.

"Surly bugger," Vi commented, loud enough for Lambert to hear. She glanced at her watch. "We've finished in good time, thanks to your help. What about coming up to the house for a cup of tea? I could do with a sit-down. I've been on my feet since seven this morning. Look at my bloody ankles!"

"All right," Maggie agreed, not very enthusiastically. She guessed Vi would take the opportunity to confide in her and she wasn't sure that she wanted to listen. It would be a shadow on an otherwise perfect day. On the other hand, Vi had no one else to talk to.

They walked up to the house, which lay behind the packing shed in the middle of a shaggy lawn. Vi, opening the door, let them into the kitchen, expensively equipped but, as always, in a mess because Vi never had time for housework and Ken refused to help. It was another of her grievances.

"Look at the place! It's like a bloody pig sty," Vi remarked by way of an apology. Then suddenly, without any preliminary, she began to cry, sitting down at the table and propping her elbows among the dirty breakfast dishes.

Oh, God! thought Maggie. Here we go again.

Aloud, she said briskly, "I'll make the tea, Vi," adding, over her shoulder as she washed cups and emptied the pot of its stale contents, "What's the matter? Is it Ken?"

Vi nodded, wiping her eyes and blowing her nose.

"Yes, the sod."

"What's he been up to this time?"

"Need you ask? What he's always up to. Mucking about with someone else."

"Are you sure?"

"Course I am! And don't ask me have I seen them together, because I don't need to. I know him of old. Forever combing his hair and going round grinning to himself the whole time. I know the signs. *And* he's bought himself some new shirts. It's not bloody fair, Maggie! I work Christ knows how many hours in that bleeding market garden of his, while he's pissing off whenever he thinks my back's turned. I'll scrag the pair of them if I catch them at it!"

"Do you know who it is?" Maggie asked, setting out cups and pouring the tea.

"I've got a bloody good idea," Vi said darkly. She looked into Maggie's face with an expression that was meant to be casual. "Have you noticed him going past your place much recently?"

What on earth is she getting at? Maggie wondered. As a matter of fact, she had noticed Aston's car going past the house on a couple of occasions over the past few days but had thought nothing of it at the time, assuming he was on his way to look at the currant field he rented off her which was a little further up the road, or was driving into Gossbridge, the next village, on business. But she had no intention of mentioning any of this to Vi.

"He might have done," she replied cautiously. "Not that I'd take all that much notice. I'm in the kitchen most of the time, or the yard, and I can't see the road from there. But who could he be seeing up that end of the village? There's only . . ."

She stopped abruptly, realising who it could be.

"That bitch of a daughter of Lambert's," Vi said, voicing the thought for her.

"But that's crazy," Maggie protested.

"Is it?" Vi asked. "Why?"

Why indeed? Maggie thought. There was no real reason why it shouldn't be Jess Lambert. She was young and pretty and it wouldn't be the first time. There was a baby to prove it. All the same, she felt she had to argue against it.

"Well, she's too young, for a start."

"Nearly eighteen," Vi answered back.

"And she's his foreman's daughter. He wouldn't want to get mixed up with her."

"Why not?" Vi seemed determined not to be convinced she might be wrong. "I can't see that stopping him from running after her. All the better, in fact. He knows where Lambert is during the day, down here at the greenhouses, so he's safely out of the way, and Ken's got a good excuse for going up your end of the village, keeping an eye on that currant field. It's a perfect set-up. Besides, I reckon that's why he kept Lambert on all this time—he fancied *her*."

But this time she really had gone too far.

"Now that's not fair," Maggie protested, feeling the injustice of the remark. "I know for a fact that Ken thinks he's good at his job. He told me as much himself."

Vi was quick to seize the opportunity.

"What else did he say? Anything about her?"

"Not much and what he did say was over a year ago, just before they moved into the bungalow. All he said was Lambert had had some personal trouble and that's why he was giving up his old job and starting work here. And Ken only told me that because they'd be living just up the road from me and he thought I might like to know. He's not said anything since. It wasn't all that long before anyone could tell what the trouble was—the daughter was pregnant so it's common knowledge now, anyway."

"Common's the word," Vi replied, ignoring the rest of Maggie's explanation. "The little tart! Do you see much of her?"

"No, I don't," Maggie said sharply. She felt sorry for Vi but she was beginning to resent this cross-examination. "I've got better things to do with my time than worry about what Jess Lambert gets up to. Anyway, I'm sure you've got hold of the wrong end of the stick," she added more gently. "Ken wouldn't be such a fool."

"Don't you believe it," Vi retorted. "He's got no sense

where women are concerned and I'm getting fed up with it, I can tell you. One of these days, I'll pack up and walk out and then that'll show him."

They were on safer ground now; the old complaints and threats that Maggie knew the responses to.

"Don't be daft, Vi. Where would you go?"

"I don't care. Anywhere."

"But you know it doesn't mean anything. If I were you, I'd sit tight. He'll soon come running back."

"I'm not sure I want him back."

"You know you dont' mean it."

"This time it's different," Vi said, in a new, hard voice. "If it is her, then I tell you, Maggie, I won't stand for it."

So she isn't absolutely sure, Maggie thought. She only suspects. She wondered, too, if Vi's bitter resentment wasn't because the girl was Lambert's daughter. Vi did nothing to conceal her dislike of Aston's foreman.

"Leave it," Maggie advised her. "Try to put it out of your mind."

She wondered whether to change the subject by telling Vi about Chris and then decided against it. Of course, sooner or later, the village would get to hear of him but, absurdly, for the moment, she wanted to keep him to herself. Besides, to speak of him in the present bitter, tense atmosphere would somehow spoil it. Suddenly she wanted to go home.

"I've got to go, Vi," she said, getting up from the table. Vi looked up at her, her face blotchy with tears and twisted into an expression of angry grief that gave Maggie a small shock of fear; not exactly a premonition of disaster but a realisation that Vi had passed beyond the point where the usual, comfortable platitudes meant anything to her.

It was a relief to Maggie to get on her bike and cycle away from the place although the shadow seemed to follow her and didn't disperse until, entering the yard, she was just in time to meet Chris coming out of the stable.

"Slept well?" she asked him.

"Like a log," he replied, smiling.

She looked him up and down critically.

"You look better for it."

He certainly seemed more relaxed. Even his smile was less tense. It had lost that stretched, brittle brightness.

Indeed, he did feel better. For the first time in months,

he had awakened without the heavy, overhung feeling that the tranquillisers usually gave him, opening his eyes to a huge oblong of dusty sunlight shining through the skylight in the roof into the bare, empty room that held no memories of the past, no residual guilt or responsibilities.

It was going to be all right, he thought. He felt he had come home.

The feeling continued and strengthened over the next few days. Although Maggie had suggested he help about the place in return for his board and lodging, she made no great demands on him and it was largely through his own initiative that he did anything at all.

"Oh, don't bother," she told him casually when he suggested a job he might do for her. "It'll keep."

All the same, he did the tasks, finding pleasure and satisfaction in the physical work. After weeks of inactivity, he preferred to keep busy. Most of the time he occupied himself in the kitchen garden, secluded from the house behind high brick walls, with a wooden door in one of them that led into the yard. Here he felt alone and unobserved. The heat was trapped inside it and he worked in shorts, stripped to the waist, feeling the sun burn into his skin like an analgesic. There was no need to think. Instead his body took over from his mind and he hoed and dug with a steady, automatic rhythm. All the weeks of mental anguish that had gone before seemed to be burned out of his body, leaving it dry and empty.

In the afternoons, he went for walks, exploring the fields and woods that lay round the farm, but the evenings he devoted to Maggie, guessing at her need for company and knowing that, by doing so, he repaid her for her hospitality more satisfactorily than all the odd jobs he did.

For Maggie, the evenings were the best part of the day. She felt she had Chris to herself. For the rest of the time, it was enough to know he was about the place, to hear the lawn mower chirring in the front garden or the regular chock-chock of the axe as he chopped kindling in the barn. She rarely bothered him, sensing a need in him for solitude.

He's been ill, she told herself. He needs a bit of time to himself.

But the evenings were different. After the supper things

were cleared away and he had helped her to wash up, she made a fresh pot of tea and they drank it, sitting opposite each other at the table, and talked. Or rather, she talked, encouraged by his questions; stories and anecdotes mostly about people in the village; discussion about her tenants; her plans for the future. It was a long time since anyone had listened to her with such attention.

All the time, though, she was aware of an unspoken question that seemed to hang between them. When would he leave? He made no mention of it and neither did she, frightened that, if she put it into words, it might become a reality.

It was the only shadow on her happiness. Even the anxiety about Vi receded until Maggie almost forgot about it. She saw nothing more of Vi during the next few days and nothing either of Lambert or his daughter. Nor did Ken Aston put in an appearance until the Friday morning, three days before the murder.

He arrived in the yellow pickup truck, which he parked in the yard entrance before coming into the kitchen, looking pleased with himself, as Vi had mentioned. Maggie decided to say nothing about her visit to the market garden or her talk with Vi, however casually.

Instead, they discussed the field that he wanted to rent from her and, after an hour's bargaining, he agreed to her terms.

"I'm on my way to have a look at that currant field," he added, as he rose to go.

"Oh, yes?" Maggie replied, carefully offhand.

"I was reckoning on putting the pickers into it on Monday. You don't happen to know anybody who'd be interested in a few days' work? The rates'll be good."

Maggie shrugged.

"There's only the usual crowd," she replied.

Finding casual field workers was always a problem. Most of the women who were free to go out to work were either already employed by Aston or went into Watleigh where they could get jobs in the shops or one of the light engineering firms that had been built in the new industrial development on the outskirts of the town.

"What about that young man of yours?" Aston asked, grinning.

"Oh, so you've heard about him?" Maggie said. "It

didn't take long, did it, for the news to get around? He's not my young man, anyway. He's camping out for a few days in the stable loft, that's all. But I'll ask him if you like. He's a student so he might be interested in earning a bit of money."

Going to the door, she began shouting for Chris, who presently emerged from the door in the garden wall.

"Ken Aston wants to know if you'd like to do a few days' currant picking for him next week, starting Monday," Maggie told him.

Chris looked at the man who was standing at Maggie's side and felt an immediate return of the old defensive withdrawal that had been one of the characteristics of his breakdown. Only with Aston, there was the added feeling of male inadequacy. Aston was a tall, strongly built man; good-looking if you liked his type of coarse, obvious attractiveness; deeply tanned with light brown, curly hair that he had allowed to grow in long boards down the side of his face. More than that, he exuded a masculine assurance that made Chris feel small and slight in comparison.

"The rates of pay aren't bad," Aston was saying. "You could knock up quite a few quid if you're prepared to work hard."

Chris looked from him to Maggie.

"I don't know," he said uncertainly. "It's up to Maggie."

For both of them, Aston's offer opened up the possibility of postponing for a few more days Chris's decision to leave.

"You could try it for a day and see how you get on," Maggie suggested, with pretended indifference. She was anxious not to appear too eager in front of Ken.

"All right," Chris agreed with equal indifference.

Aston's grin broadened. During this exchange, he had looked from one to the other of them, seeming to sense out something in their relationship that amused him.

"That's fixed then," he said to Chris. "You start Monday at nine."

He walked away to where his truck was parked with an easy, jaunty stride, leaving them standing behind in the yard, both of them feeling oddly diminished by this encounter.

"He's getting a damn sight too big for his boots," Maggie remarked sharply and, turning away, went back into the house, finding it impossible to meet Chris's eyes. Aston's grin had made her see, for the first time, what an outsider might think of herself and Chris and the knowledge made her self-conscious and embarrassed, although she didn't know exactly why.

"Not that I give a damn," she said out loud. She had nothing to be ashamed about. Chris was a pleasant young man and it was company for her to have him around the place. That was all. But deep down, she knew there was more to her feelings about him.

But, anyway, what about Aston himself, come to that? she argued defensively. He's a fine one to grin! Looking at the currant field, my eye! I bet I know where he's really off to.

She glanced quickly out of the window. Chris had gone, presumably back to the kitchen garden, for a tall pillar of white smoke was visible over the top of the wall where he had lit a bonfire. Letting herself out of the back door, she walked rapidly across the yard to a gap at the far end of the outbuildings that led to the orchard and the fields beyond.

At the far side of the orchard, she climbed on to the second rail of the fence. From there she had a view across the meadow that Aston had just agreed to rent from her to the farther field, also rented by Aston, that was planted with currant bushes. From that elevated position, she could see his yellow truck parked in the gate opening but of Aston himself there was no sign, although the bushes were too low to conceal a man. A little farther off still, the slated roof of Lambert's bungalow poked up from above its surrounding hedges.

It looked as if Vi might be right, Maggie thought, not that she'd say anything to her although Maggie couldn't help feeling a certain sense of satisfaction at catching Ken out.

He's a fool, though, she added to herself, climbing down and walking back across the orchard. Sooner or later, someone was bound to talk and then there'd be trouble.

The feeling of threat in the air returned to her more strongly and now it seemed to touch herself and Chris. It was stupid, of course, to take it so seriously, but later,

when she was to look back, she came to heighten this
moment into an experience of genuine premonition, as if
she were already aware of the links in the chain that
bound all of them together and that were to lead to the
final tragedy.

3

But had she really known what was going to happen, she would have done something to prevent Chris from going to the currant field on the Monday morning.

As it was, she sent him off cheerfully, preparing a flask of coffee and a packet of sandwiches for him in case he felt hungry by midmorning, animated by her new role of getting him ready for work. Like the breadwinner, she thought, although the idea struck her as preposterous at the time. The field was only ten minutes' walk up the road.

"And I've done your box for you," she added.

"Box?" he asked, bewildered.

"To sit on, of course, while you pick," Maggie explained, scornful at his lack of knowledge.

It stood in readiness in a corner of the kitchen—a stout, upended beer crate, padded on top with a bit of old blanket.

She even walked with him as far as the gate, waving good-bye to him as he set off. He waved back a little awkwardly, exasperated by all the fuss, although he tried not to show it. She was beginning to remind him of his mother and he didn't want to think of her. She was a ghost from the past that he thought he had laid to rest, although ever since Aston's visit Maggie had begun to act more and more like her. Something had happened to their relationship since that Friday. Maggie was trying too hard, smiling too much, coming into the garden to find him at odd times during the day with unnecessary offers of cups of tea or simply to see how he was getting on.

Chris didn't understand why it had happened. Even Maggie wouldn't have been able to explain it adequately, had he asked her. She only knew that the ease and spontaneity had gone out of her relationship with him. Having once seen herself and Chris through the eyes of an outsider, she no longer found it possible to return to the old familiar footing.

Chris didn't meet the girl straightaway. When he arrived at the field, she wasn't among the small crowd of women, some of whom had young children with them, who were already gathered round the lorry that, with its tail board let down, was parked just inside the gate.

"You're from Maggie's, aren't you?" the man in charge of the lorry asked as Chris approached. "Mr. Aston said you'd be joining the pickers."

He was a pleasant, smiling, fresh-faced young man, with an air of cheerful mateyness about him that Chris liked. Of Aston there was no sign, to his relief.

"Yes, that's right," Chris replied. "I'm staying with her for a few days. What do I do?" he added. "I've never done any currant picking before."

"Take one of these," Reg told him, handing him a double-sided cardboard basket from the pile in the back of the lorry, "and find yourself a row. When you've filled it, bring it back here to be weighed and I'll give you a chitty for it, saying how much you've picked. You can cash them in at the end of the morning, if you like, or wait till the picking's finished."

Taking the basket, Chris walked away down the edge of the field looking for an unoccupied row, and, finding one, he set the crate down firmly on the dry, crumbly earth in front of the first bush and parted the leaves.

They gave off a hot, pungent smell in the sun, distinct but not unpleasant. The black currants hung between the leaves in clusters, richly dark, each fruit a tight, glistening globe, bursting with ripe juices. At first, he picked slowly, but as time passed he became more adept at stripping off the bunches. Soon a rhythm built up, as mindlessly satisfying as digging Maggie's garden. With the sun hot on his back, his world was reduced to the leafy foreground of the bush immediately in front of him, the only sound the occasional high-pitched shouts of the young children playing along the rows or the grass verges as their mothers worked and the women's voices shouted back at them.

It was only when his basket was full and he rose to carry it back to the lorry to be weighed that he realised how stiff he was. His back and shoulders ached with the effort of stooping.

"That your first?" Reg asked with a grin.

"I'm afraid so," Chris admitted. "I'm not very quick at it yet."

"You'll improve," Reg assured him. "It takes a bit of getting used to."

As he turned to walk away, Chris noticed a pram drawn up on the grass under the shade of the hedge in which a baby lay asleep on its back, in such an attitude of abandoned slumber that he smiled as he passed it. Small children rarely interested him, but this one, with its eyelids sealed up and its skin flecked with tiny scraps of sunlight as they fell through the leaves, lost to the conscious world like an animal, touched in him some regret for lost childhood; not its innocence—that was generally overrated, mere adult sentimentality—but for its complete self-absorption and total disregard for anything outside the immediate now, the present, living moment.

He wondered vaguely who its mother was. She hadn't been there when the baskets were first handed out so she must have arrived later, after the other women had dispersed across the field.

He didn't meet her until eleven o'clock when there was a general move back to the gate for a midmorning break. Seeing the women coming down the rows and trudging past, Chris hesitated before joining them. He knew nobody, except Reg, the lorry driver who had spoken to him earlier, although he had been aware of the curious glances the other pickers had given him on his arrival. There would be conversations in which he couldn't join. And then he thought, why not? He felt in need of a break himself and it might seem stand-offish if he remained apart. All the same, he felt a little self-conscious as he approached the small groups of women who were seated on the grass like families on a picnic outing.

He noticed the girl immediately, sitting on her own, cross-legged beside the pram, the baby that he had seen earlier propped negligently in her lap while she held a plastic drinking cup with a little spout to its mouth. She was young, not more than seventeen or eighteen, dressed casually in jeans and a blue T-shirt, her long brown hair caught up in a pony tail with an elastic band. Yet, despite her youth and contemporary clothes, there was something oddly old-fashioned about her: a ripeness and a fullness that suggested to him one of Hardy's country girls or a shepherdess from a pastoral.

"Sorry. Excuse me," he apologised as he reached past her to get his bag containing the flask and the sandwiches, which he had left in the shade of the hedge.

"Can you reach it?" she asked. "I can shift if you want."

"No, please don't bother. I can manage," he replied.

With the bag in his hand, he stood looking round, wondering where to sit. The girl made up his mind for him.

"You can sit with me, if you like. The others are all with their mates."

There was a faint tone of bitterness in her voice as if she resented being left out and he wondered why she was being excluded in this way.

"If you're sure you don't mind," he replied, sitting down beside her. "I don't know anyone here to talk to."

"No more'n I then. I know most of them by sight but that's about all."

"Haven't you lived here long?" he asked, thinking that this might be the reason for her isolation.

"Not all that long. Just over a year, that's all. But I don't live right in the village, see, so I don't get to know people."

He was surprised how easy it was to talk to her. Usually he was self-conscious with girls. But there was a directness and a lack of sophistication about her that reminded him, in a strange way, of Maggie, although physically they had nothing in common.

"You're staying just down the road, at the farm, aren't you?" she asked, watching while he opened his packet of sandwiches.

"Yes, at Maggie's," he replied and smiled. "I've only been there a week but people seem to know about it already."

"They would. You can't keep nothing private in a place like this for long."

Again, there was a resentful note in her voice.

"My dad told me about you, as a matter of fact," she went on. "He works for Ken Aston down at the market garden. You're a student, he said. Is that right?"

There was a quality of cross-examination in the question that he didn't much care for. It reminded him too much of the kind of scrutiny he had been subjected to in the past.

"Yes, that's right," he replied a little shortly. If she was aware of his defensiveness, she didn't show it. The baby had finished drinking and she sat the child upright in her lap, wiping its mouth with the bib it wore round its neck. Its round, blue eyes gazed about it with a look of dazed curiosity. Getting to her feet, she swung it round so that it straddled one hip before she put it back in the pram, propping it up against the pillow. There was an easy, almost careless assurance in the way she handled it, more like a she-cat with a kitten, and the child seemed to respond in the same way, with the passive docility he had seen in young animals.

The other women were beginning to move, too, gathering up their bags and flasks and straggling back to the field.

Chris stood up. He was half inclined to wait for the girl and walk back with her but some of the women as they passed gave him amused, knowing glances and, feeling embarrassed, he set off alone.

He couldn't put her out of his mind, however, and every time he stood to move the crate to the next bush farther along the row, he looked across the field, hoping to catch sight of her. Once he thought he caught a gilmpse of her blue T-shirt but it was too far away for him to be certain.

At half-past twelve, he decided to pack up and go back to Maggie's for lunch. Walking back towards the lorry, he was pleased to see her again, obviously on her way home, too, for she was struggling to push the pram across the rough grass towards the gate.

"Wait a minute!" he called. "I'll help you."

Dumping down the basket he was holding, he ran across to her.

"It's better to carry it," he told her. "You take the handle. I'll lift it this end."

Between them, they picked up the pram and carried it out onto the road, where they set it down on its wheels.

"Thanks," she said briefly. She looked tired and flushed and he felt a sudden protective surge of tenderness towards her. Standing in the road, pushing back her hair with one hand, she seemed defenceless and vulnerable and, for that reason, she aroused in him a sexual desire that he hadn't felt since his breakdown.

"Have you got far to go?" he asked, aware that his voice sounded odd, louder than usual. His face, even his eyes, felt hot.

"Only up the road a bit."

She jerked her head in the direction of a bungalow that he could see standing behind a hedge about three hundred yards away.

As she spoke, Aston drove past them in his yellow pickup truck, parking it in the gateway immediately behind the lorry. Chris heard the door slam and then Aston's voice speaking to Reg.

"How's it gone this morning?"

"Not bad."

"Let's have a look then. . . ."

Their voices grew less distinct as they moved away to the back of the lorry to inspect the baskets of currants.

"I've got to go now," the girl was saying hurriedly. "I've got to get the baby his dinner."

"Will you be coming back this afternoon?" Chris asked.

"I don't know. I've got things to do."

"Tomorrow?"

"Maybe."

She seemed anxious to go, her hands grasping the pram handle in readiness to set off.

Chris found himself saying, "Look, I'd like to meet you again."

She gave him a quick glance up and down that seemed to encompass the whole of him. Then she shrugged faintly, a mere stirring of her shoulders that expressed indifferent acquiescence.

"All right, if you like," she replied.

"When?" he asked eagerly.

"I don't mind."

"Tonight?"

"If you want to."

"Where?"

"There's a footpath just up the road from my place. I could meet you there," she suggested, without much enthusiasm. "Half-past seven suit you?"

"Yes, that's fine," Chris agreed quickly.

Behind them, Aston's voice could be heard saying,

"When do you reckon we'll clear the field by, Reg? Wednesday?"

"I've got to go now," the girl repeated and started to walk away rapidly up the road.

As he turned back to retrieve his basket, Chris found Aston leaning on the side of the lorry watching his approach with a sardonic grin.

"Been chatting her up?" he asked.

"I helped her carry the pram onto the road," Chris replied stiffly.

"Oh, I get it. Doing your good deed for the day," Aston remarked sarcastically, and then, deliberately ignoring Chris, he turned back to Reg and announced, "I'm off to look at that other field of Maggie's. See you later."

He sauntered off towards the gate.

"Are you cashing your chitties in now?" Reg was asking. Something had happened to annoy him. His face yas set and disapproving. It was probably Aston, Chris thought, for Reg followed him with his eyes as he walked away.

"I'll cash them later," Chris replied and, stuffing the latest chit into his back pocket, went over to the hedge to collect Maggie's bag containing the flask.

By the time he got out into the road, both the girl and Aston had disappeared; the girl into the bungalow, presumably; Aston to look at the field, wherever that might be; not that Chris much cared. All that mattered was that the road was now empty and there was nothing to stop him from walking past where she lived.

It was a ridiculous, juvenile wish, he realised, and one that he couldn't rationalise. It was partly curiosity to find out more about her. Part of it was a need to put off going immediately back to the farm and meeting Maggie, knowing that, in her present mood, she would start asking him questions about the morning's currant picking and he didn't want to face that. He had already made up his mind to say nothing to her about the girl or the arrangement to meet her again that evening.

But mostly, as he admitted to himself, it was a leftover of desire for her that made him want to prolong the contact with her, however remote it might be.

Taking a quick look over his shoulder, he saw that Reg was no longer on the lorry and none of the pickers were in sight either so he set off up the road with a rapid, guilty

pace, keeping his head averted until he was directly opposite the bungalow and then allowing himself only a hur-
ried, sideways look at it as he drew level.

It was a small, squat building of ugly, dark-red brick,
not at all romantic or attractive, with a central door under
an arch and two bay windows of mean proportions on
either side of it. A long, dense hawthorn hedge ran in front
of it and it was placed squarely on a narrow plot with fruit
trees and a lawn on one side and a vegetable garden on the
other.

The next moment, he had passed it and there was
nothing he could do except walk as nonchalantly as he
could a little farther up the road before retracing his
steps.

He had been mad to come, he told himself as he
walked back again. Supposing she saw him? It was then he
realised that he didn't know her name, not that it mattered. He could ask her when he saw her again that
evening. Meanwhile, he was content to think of her as "the
girl," an anonymous figure in a rural setting; milk maid,
shepherdess, it wasn't important.

Drawing level with the bungalow once more, he gave it
another brief, covert glance. There was still no sign of *her,*
although he thought he saw a shadow pass behind the net
curtains of the right-hand window. But he couldn't be sure
because it had gone in an instant. All the same, he walked
more rapidly, feeling foolish and exposed on the empty
road.

On the other side of the net curtain, Jess Lambert
paused in the act of taking off her bra and watched him
walk past the gateway. She knew why he was there. She
had seen it in his face when they had stood together in the
road.

They're all the bloody same, she thought contemptuously, out to get one thing; although she had to admit to
herself that it was nice to be fancied. A sodding sight
better than being like some of the girls she'd known at
school, the ones with fat legs and glasses, sidling up to the
boys, their tongues practically hanging out, dying for a
touch.

This one, though, Maggie's camper, was a cut above the
others, posher, better-educated. In spite of the fact that
he'd been working in the currant field, she knew this by his

voice and the way he'd treated her with a polite, considerate, formal air that she'd found touching and yet, at the same time, slightly ridiculous. She didn't know how she'd kept from laughing, what with the look on his face and Ken Aston standing only a few yards away, not that Aston would suspect anything. He was too bloody sure of himself for that.

Behind her, Aston was trampling down his trousers in his eagerness to get them off.

"Come on! Get a move on!" he was urging her. "I've only got a bloody half hour and I'm supposed to be back home."

But she got her own back. Seconds later, while he bucked and sweated on top of her, she lay quite rigid, knowing this would rile him.

He treats me like a bloody tart, she thought resentfully.

"What the hell's the matter with you?" Aston asked when he finally rolled off her.

"Nothing. Why should there be?" she asked.

"You lie there like a bloody sack . . ." he began. He wanted to add that even Vi was better than that but he didn't dare.

"What do you expect!" she shouted back, suddenly angry. "You turn up here when it suits you. What am I supposed to do? Say 'Thank you very much, Mr. Aston, sir'? You've got a nerve!"

"What else do you want?" he asked in genuine surprise. "You know I can't manage it any different."

"Yes, and we know why, don't we? It's your bloody wife you're thinking of. *She* mustn't find out. But me, I don't matter. I'm just dirt."

He was silent for a moment and then he turned away, muttering, "I'm sorry."

He had aplogised but it didn't seem enough.

"It's easy enough to say sorry. That's just words."

"I'll stop seeing you if it makes it any better," he offered.

It was probably best anyway, he thought. He didn't fancy her much now that the first excitement was over. Besides, it was stupid to go on. Sooner or later people would start talking. Reg suspected something already. There had been a look on his face today, when Aston had left the truck in the currant field, that he hadn't much cared for. And, once the crop was cleared, it would be difficult finding an excuse to keep coming up this end of the village.

"Oh, that'd suit you," Jess was saying. She had scrambled off the bed and was grabbing up her clothes. "You're not dropping me as easy as that."

"What do you mean?" Aston asked quietly.

She hadn't meant much except bitterness and resentment at the way he had treated her but the implied challenge in his reply made her go on.

"You watch out someone don't tell your wife, that's all, if they haven't already."

"Meaning who?"

She began to laugh.

"That's got you scared hasn't it?"

He looked her up and down with contempt before going to the door.

"You're a right little cow," he said as he went out.

"You watch out!" she shouted again but it was a waste of time. He had already gone, slamming the door behind him.

Did Vi know? he wondered, as he parked the truck in the driveway of the market garden and went into the house. It wasn't easy to tell. She was in a bad mood, he knew that, greeting him with an indifferent "Oh, so you're back?" as he entered the kitchen. But she was often like that.

"Dinner ready?" he asked with forced cheerfulness.

"It's in the oven. I'll get it." She dumped the plate down in front of him. "I've eaten."

"I'm not late, am I?" he asked, deciding to brazen it out.

"It's a bloody quarter to two."

"Christ, is it!" He looked surprised. "I got held up at the field."

"Oh, yes?"

Her reply could have meant anything, although there was a note of sarcasm in it that he took exception to.

"I was talking to Reg. Don't you believe me? You can ask him, if you like."

It was a dangerous line to take. She might do just that.

But all she said was, "There's a trifle in the fridge. Help yourself to it," before going out.

Another bloody stupid cow, he thought to himself but he was convinced she didn't know anything; not yet anyway.

4

Chris ate his midday meal, watched surreptitiously by Maggie. There was something odd in his behaviour that she couldn't exactly put her finger on; an edgy quality that was possibly due to tiredness, but not entirely. He had a furtive air about him as well and he quickly became impatient when she asked him who had been in the field that morning and if he'd talked to anybody.

"I don't know their names, Maggie. And I didn't speak to anyone at all, except the man in charge of the lorry."

She wanted to go on and ask what the man looked like—it was probably Reg Deakin—but she didn't like to.

She was aware that he was drawing away from her; aware, too, that it was mostly her fault. She couldn't be natural with him anymore. And the greater her anxiety to please him, the more exasperated he became. She had done the same with Alec till she had finally driven him away.

Would the same happen with Chris she asked herself. Perhaps, in the end, she destroyed all relationships that really mattered to her, killing them inch by inch with too much attention.

All the same, she couldn't help putting one more question to him.

"Did Ken Aston turn up?" she asked.

"Not for long," Chris replied shortly. "He was there for about ten minutes then he left saying something about looking at a field of yours."

"Oh?" said Maggie. It sounded like an excuse to her but she didn't want to say anything more about it to Chris. She guessed from the tone in Chris's voice that he didn't much like Aston, an animosity she could understand. As men, they were as different as chalk and cheese. More than this, though, she didn't want to involve Chris in the tangle of realtionships between Aston, Vi and Jess Lambert in which, despite herself, she seemed to have become implicated.

After lunch, Chris returned to the currant field, relieved to get away from Maggie. He knew he had disappointed her but he couldn't help it. His thoughts were full of the girl and his coming meeting with her that evening. Besides, he felt guilty, knowing he would like to tell Maggie about it. It had happened before, for much the same reason.

Why the hell can't they leave me alone? he thought bitterly. And he felt his stomach churn with the familiar, agonising nausea of anger, guilt and desire.

For this reason, he was glad to find, on arriving at the field, that the girl wasn't there. He wouldn't have been able to talk to her naturally, not in his present state of mind.

I've got to calm down before I see her again, he told himself. I must make myself think about something else.

He picked doggedly all afternoon, trying to steady his thoughts and centre them on nothing more than the immediate present: the leaves, the sky, the distant, calling voices, the dark juice of the currants that stained his hands.

At half-past four, he packed up. Most of the younger women with children had already gone. The older women began to leave, too, to be home in time to prepare evening meals for husbands and sons. Chris took his last full basket back to the lorry where he cashed in the day's chitties. Walking out of the gate into the road, he gave only a glance in the direction of the bungalow. He had no desire to walk past it, as he had done in the morning. That madness, at least, was over.

Maggie was in the yard when he got back to the farm, bringing in some washing from the line. It was impossible to avoid her.

"You look tired," she said.

"I am a bit," he admitted.

He looked more than tired, she added to herself. He seemed exhausted and ill. The pallid, languid look that she had noticed when he first came had returned, shadowing his face.

"Perhaps you've got a touch of the sun," she went on, although she knew it wasn't just that. "I'll make you a cup of tea."

"I'd rather lie down, Maggie."

"You'll want some fluid inside you first, if it's heat stroke," she told him. It was only partly for his benefit, though. She wanted to have him near her, to fuss over and see to his needs.

He followed her reluctantly into the kitchen where she put the kettle on.

"I don't think you ought to go picking tomorrow," she added, setting out cups. She could see he was exasperated by her concern.

"I'll probably feel better tomorrow."

"All the same, you don't want to knock yourself up."

"But it's ridiculous!" he protested. "Some of the women are quite elderly and yet they manage to put in a full day's work."

"They're used to it."

"Meaning I'm soft, some kind of pansy?"

It was bordering on a quarrel. Maggie looked at him with anxiety.

"I didn't mean that, Chris. Field work's hard. I know. I've done it. You've got to go at it slowly to begin with."

"Yes, I know. I'm sorry, Maggie."

"Drink your tea and then have a bath and a rest before supper," she said gently.

On this occasion, she was glad to see him go. His moody irritability distressed and saddened her.

He'll leave soon, she repeated over and over again, as she washed lettuce and sliced up tomatoes for the evening meal. A steady despair had settled on her, as it had when Alec left. Her body went on working, performing necessary tasks, but her mind was quiescent, curled up in its own grey, sick misery.

He came in later, without being called, just as she was laying the table.

"Anything I can do?" he asked with a terrible, false cheerfulness.

"It's done," Maggie said. "You can eat."

They sat down opposite each other.

"I thought I might take tomorrow afternoon off and go into Watleigh," he remarked, after a silence.

"Yes, why don't you?" Maggie replied.

"I might go to the cinema if there's anything on that's worth seeing."

"It'll be in the local paper."

We're talking across a void, Maggie thought, two strangers, signalling to each other with words. Presently, he'll turn and walk away. She could almost see him retreating from her, his rucksack on his back, silhouetted against a great, white sky.

After supper, he helped her wash up and then said that he was going to his room for an hour to read.

"You don't mind, Maggie?" he asked.

"You please yourself, my lad," she replied, with pretended indifference. "I've got my accounts to do anyway."

"I still feel a bit tired," he explained. "But I'll come back later and we can talk."

She knew instinctively that he was lying even before she went across the yard later to shut up the hens for the night and, calling up to him, got no answer. The loft room was empty when she went up the steps to look, the bed tidy, his rucksack propped up in one corner.

He had already been gone for nearly an hour, climbing out of the back window of the stable, so that Maggie wouldn't see him, and making a wide circuit through the fields to emerge finally onto the road at the far side of the currant field, a little distance from the bungalow and not far from the place where he had turned to walk back earlier that morning.

The bungalow was just visible and a light was on somewhere at the back for he could see it shining out from behind the hedge, even though the sun had not yet set and the evening was still bright.

It came from the kitchen, dark even at midday, where Lambert had been eating his supper. He had worked late that evening, as he looked like doing for several days, checking the weight of the baskets of currants and getting them ready for despatch the following morning.

He didn't mind. There was a morose, dogged persistence about him which was one of the reasons why Vi Aston disliked him. He never took time out to joke and chat with her as the other men did, making her feel important as the boss's wife and also as a woman. He simply got on with his work, speaking only when the job demanded it, and this aloofness exasperated her.

Lambert was aware of her hostility and didn't much mind that either. He accepted it and didn't expect her to change her attitude any more than he intended adapting his own ways to suit her. He had no high expectations of life or people, anyway. At the market garden, all he wanted was to be left to get on with his work; at home, a modicum of comfort. His leisure hours he spent tending the garden, watching television, occasionally going out rough-shooting with Bateson, a local farmer or drinking quietly by himself most evenings at the Rose and Crown, where he made no effort to start up a conversation and spoke only if others addressed him first. Mostly, though, they left him alone, sensing his preference for solitude.

But, about once a month, the silence and loneliness would gather in his chest like a heavy weight which he would carry about with him for a few days until he could bear it no longer. Then he would open a bottle of whisky and drink himself into a stupor.

He had felt it gathering again recently, although, so far, he had been able to contain it. It was a matter of pride in him not to give way too soon.

Coming home that evening, he found his supper laid out on the table but no sign of his daughter, Jess.

He called her name, going to the door that led into the narrow hall. Her voice came back from the front bedroom that she shared with the baby.

"Stop shouting! I'll be out in a minute."

Satisfied at her presence, he went back to the table and began to eat, a copy of the *Daily Mail* that he hadn't yet had time to read propped up against the pickle jar in front of him.

Presently she came into the tiny kitchen, squeezing past the end of the table to put the kettle on for tea. He watched her in silence over the top of the paper. She had changed into a dress and done her hair differently than its usual style, with a little coil on top and the rest of it loose, so he knew she was going out. It wasn't this question, however, that he put to her first. At the best of times, their conversation was brief and laconic.

"Been currant picking?" he asked. He had finished his main course and, pushing his empty plate away, reached across the table to help himself to stewed apple and custard.

"I went up there for a bit this morning," she replied. "But I didn't bother going back this afternoon."

"Good few pickers, were there?"

She shrugged indifferently.

"Not bad. I suppose."

"Mr. Aston reckons he'll have the field cleared by Wednesday."

She didn't reply, intent on making the tea.

After a short pause, he went on, "Going out this evening, Jess?"

"I might do. I haven't made up my mind yet."

"Where to?"

"I told you, I don't know! For a walk, perhaps. What else is there to do in this dead-and-alive place?"

"I was hoping for a drink down the Rose this evening," he said offhandedly.

"Well, go then. There's nothing to stop you."

"What about the kid?"

"It's asleep. It won't come to no harm."

She saw the anger settle in his face, giving it a hard, mulish expression. But his voice was still quiet when he answered.

"I've told you before, I won't have that child left alone in the house."

"All right! All right!" she shouted. "I'll come back. I'll bleeding well have to, won't I?"

"Half-past nine," he said heavily, getting up from the table and, taking his cup of tea and the paper, going into the living room.

She stuck out her tongue at his retreating back, knowing further protest was pointless, and a few minutes later she slammed the back door on her way out, to show her contempt.

It was gone half-past nine and getting dusk before Chris came back. Maggie, who had been waiting in the kitchen with the curtains still drawn back, heard him in the yard and ran to the door. The light, streaming out, caught him in its brilliance, his face white as paper and a crouched tension in his body like a wild creature, illuminated by a car's headlamps, gathering itself up to turn and flee. She was startled by his wild appearance, although she tried not to show it.

"Chris? Is that you? Are you coming in?"

He entered the kitchen reluctantly.

"I'll make some tea," Maggie continued, putting the kettle on the hot plate of the Aga. With her back to him she added, "Had a good walk?"

For what seemed like a long time there was silence and when she turned round, she saw him looking at her with a

helpless, guilty expression that he didn't bother to conceal.

"Why did you lie?" Maggie continued in a conversational voice. She kept her hand on the handle of the kettle. Its
warmth and strength seemed to steady her.

"I—I changed my mind," he said.

"Did you?" The dull anger that had been smouldering in
her all evening came to the surface. "I don't think you did,
Chris. I think you'd already intended to go out. Of course,
it's none of my business . . ."

She meant to add that she hated anyone lying to her,
she had had enough of that with Alec, but he didn't give
her time.

"No, it isn't any of your business!" he said, his voice
rising. "Christ! You don't own me, Maggie, although you'd
like to, wouldn't you? Like my bloody mother! Clean socks
and a hot meal twice a day in exchange for my soul. That's
why I lied to you. You didn't give me any alternative."

Now he had said it, he saw the truth in it. Not his guilt
but theirs. Relief made him cruel.

"You don't want me whole, any of you!" he shouted.
"All you want is some mild, tame, castrated creature,
bellowing after you, that you can fuss over and cherish.
But it's not love. You're incapable of love. It's not in you."

He saw that she had backed away from him, her mouth
fallen open, and he was suddenly afraid of what he had
done. Turning, he ran blindly away from her, across the
yard and up the steps to the loft where, in the faint light
still coming in through the window and the skylight, he
began snatching up his belongings and cramming them into
the rucksack.

"Chris! Chris! Come back!" he heard her shouting.

She was in the yard when he came out of the stable,
only her pale face and light-blue blouse visible in the dusk.
She took a few steps towards him.

"Get away from me!" he shouted, flinging up an arm.

It caught her on the cheekbone, just below the right eye,
knocking her off balance. By the time she had picked
herself up, he had gone.

Maggie went slowly back into the house. The blow had
dazed her and for several minutes she could do nothing
except sit in a chair, staring in front of her, one hand
covering up the place where he had struck her as if hiding
a disfigurement.

Had he meant to hit her? She wasn't sure, although his anger had frightened her. She hadn't thought him capable of violence, not Chris. It had been like confronting a menacing stranger in a dark alleyway. She couldn't get out of her mind the image of his arm lifted, fist clenched, dark against the sky.

After a while, she got up from the chair and, going to the sink, began patting cold water onto the bruise, which, she could see in the mirror hanging on the window frame, was beginning to show through the swelling.

Better if it comes out, she told herself, and then, catching sight of her own eyes in the square of glass, big and round with shock, she began to cry, quietly at first, the tears pouring noiselessly out, and then with greater abandon, as Vi had done, in ugly, gulping sobs.

It's not bloody fair! she told herself. Vi's words. I do everything for him, treat him like a son, and what do I get back?

But it didn't work. The comparison with Vi shamed her and, wiping her face on the roller towel behind the back door, she went out to the barn and fetched her bike.

At the gate, she hesitated. Which way had he gone? Instinct told her that he hadn't made for the village where there were lights and people. She knew that whatever had happened to him, a breakdown, some kind of nervous collapse, caused by God knows what, she hadn't had time to think about that part of it yet, he would keep to the darkened roads where no one would see him. He must have turned right then, towards Gossbridge, and, mounting her bike, she pedalled off, the lamp on the front wobbling and lighting up alternatively patches of tarmac or grass verge.

Aston drove up to the house soon after Maggie had left, parking the car in the yard. Seeing the lights on and finding the kitchen door unlocked, he assumed she was at home and was surprised to find the room empty when he went in. Nor did she seem to be anywhere in the house. He looked briefly into the downstairs rooms and shouted up the stairs but she was obviously out.

It both puzzled and annoyed him. It was unlike Maggie to go out at night leaving the house unlocked. Besides, he was hoping for a talk with her about Vi. After an unnerving evening at home, when Vi had hardly spoken to him, he had come reluctantly to the conclusion that something was up, although exactly what he wasn't sure. In the end he had retreated, announcing that he was going down to the pub for a drink. It was half in his mind, had Lambert been in the Rose, to go round and see Jess and try to talk her out of causing any trouble, perhaps even offer her money, although the thought of being beholden to her in any way made him angry.

But Lambert wasn't in the pub although Reg Deakin and Fraser, another of his employees, were in the public bar and, after a few beers in their company and finding it embarrassing, for Reg was clearly ill at ease. Aston made an excuse and left. Reg knew something. Aston was convinced of that now. Fraser, he thought, didn't. But it was an unpleasant foretaste of what might happen if that little bitch opened her mouth.

Coming out of the pub, he hesitated, uncertain what to do next. Lambert was probably at home, so talking to Jess was out of the question, not in front of her father. That really would put the cat among the pigeons. If the truth came out, Lambert's anger was one of the things Aston dreaded most; more even than Vi's. And he'd lose a bloody good foreman into the bargain.

It was while he stood hesitating, unwilling to go home and face Vi's hostile silence, that he thought of Maggie. Maggie had a lot of common sense and Vi might have said something to her. He knew the two women were friendly. At least he'd know exactly how the land lay. Failing that, he could perhaps enlist Maggie's help in smoothing Vi down, if things ever came to a head, or even having a talk with Jess and persuading her out of doing anything stupid.

Out of a set of alternatives, none of which were very satisfactory, it seemed the best. At least he'd be doing something, and inaction, at that moment, seemed the worst of the lot.

His mind made up, he drove to Maggie's, only to be baulked there by finding her out. Backing the car out of the yard, he drove on to Gossbridge, where, in a mood of angry frustration, he stayed drinking in the White Hart until closing time.

He passed Maggie on the road, not that either of them noticed the other, their thoughts busy elsewhere. Maggie was on her way home, having turned back at the Automobile Association box at the crossroads, certain that Chris couldn't have got any farther in the time since he had left. He must, therefore, have taken to the fields. It was a hopeless task trying to find him in the dark but, all the same, she wheeled her bike, stopping at every gate to shine its front lamp through the bars and call his name.

At the last gate, she gave up and went home, where she made a pot of tea and sat drinking it at the kitchen table, thinking about Chris. All her former anger had gone. She felt inexpressibly old and tired and sad. What he had said to her about her not being able to love had hurt her the most. Perhaps he was right, she thought. Perhaps she could only love someone in that demanding and selfish way that took too much and gave too little.

Had it been like that with Alec? She wasn't sure anymore. She only remembered that, when he had been absent, she didn't seem to exist, as if something inside her dimmed and guttered, like a lamp running out of oil.

She felt the same lack of brightness now without Chris and, together with this emptiness, there was a terrible weight of responsibility that it was she who had caused his breakdown and driven him away.

How, she didn't know. She could make no sense of it and, in the end, she gave up trying. Her mind was too tired to go over it again. Going automatically through the ritual of closing the house up for the night, she finally dragged herself upstairs to bed.

Three heavy knocks startled her awake some time later. For a moment, she thought it was Chris come back and she got hurriedly out of bed and ran to the window. But the figure standing below in the yard was Lambert's.

"What do you want?" Maggie called out.

"Is Jess there with you?" he called back. His voice sounded slurred and he was unsteady on his feet.

"Jess?" she asked, bewildered.

"She's not come home yet," Lambert answered.

"But why should she be here?" Maggie demanded, although she knew the answer as soon as she asked the question. She'd been a fool not to see it before.

"Because that young chap that's staying with you has been mucking about with her, that's why."

"If you mean Chris, he's gone," Maggie replied coldly. "He left a long time ago."

Lambert muttered something that she couldn't hear and

then walked away round the corner of the house with a heavy, lurching stride.

"Come back!" Maggie shouted but he had gone. Seconds later she heard his van start up in the road and drive away.

She got dressed, her hands trembling as she put on her dressing-gown and slippers, noticing the time by the clock on the bedside table. It was nearly a quarter to twelve.

What in God's name was it all about? The knowledge that Chris had been meeting Jess Lambert made sense of his disappearance tonight when he had said he was going to his room to read. The lies and evasiveness she could understand now but the anger and violence still remained unexplained.

He's ill, of course, she told herself. He isn't responsible. But the girl? Where was she? What had happened to her?

Maggie had a sudden mental image of Chris caught in the light from the door, white-faced and crouching, like a terrified animal, and then his arm raised ready to strike her and, although the two events were distanced in time from each other, they seemed part of the same sequence, the implications of which she didn't dare consider.

5

It was easy enough to find the place. Straight through the village on the Gossbridge road, the local policeman, Cookson, had said, and there he was, standing on the grass verge beside his parked car, looking faintly alarmed as the convoy of official cars drew up alongside, as if it were his fault that all these men had been called out from headquarters.

Detective Inspector Rudd, fresh-faced and with the disarmingly frank and open expression of a countryman, got out of the first car and came forward to introduce himself and his Sergeant Boyce, a tall, bulky man with broad shoulders.

"The body's in there, sir, just inside the gate," Cookson explained in a quiet, respectful voice, like a sidesman in church. He led the way, keeping, Rudd noticed, to the grass tussocks at the side of the gate opening and away from the central area of earth the dry surface of which had been churned up by feet and the heavy tyres of a lorry.

The field beyond was a large one, sloping gently down towards the road and planted with black-currant bushes in neat rows.

The body lay to the left of the gate, close to the hedge, laid out on its back, its arms at its sides and its head turned a little as if to conceal the wound just above the temple, round which the light-brown hair was matted and dark with blood.

The features themselves were unmarked. She was, Rudd guessed, a girl of about eighteen; pretty if a little plump, with high, rounded cheekbones that in life would probably be flushed with healthy colour, and full lips that had fallen apart in a surprised, faintly stupid expression. She was wearing a light summer dress of green cotton, sprigged

45

with white leaves and flowers, and this combination of green and white, together with the long, abundant hair, suggested to Rudd a Persephone figure, a pagan sacrifice to spring.

He turned to Cookson, cocking his head inquiringly, and the constable, a youngish man but already running to middle-age spread round the waist and jowl, hastily transferred his fascinated attention from the dead girl to the inspector.

"It's Jess Lambert, sir. A local girl. Lives, or rather lived, just up the road. You can see the bungalow from here."

He indicated the slated roof that was just visible to their right.

"And the body was found this morning?" Rudd asked.

"That's right, by Reg Deakin when he brought the lorry up for the currant picking, although, as a matter of fact . . ."

It was obvious from the deep breath he took that he was about to embark on some long and complicated story. Rudd cut him short with a quick movement of one hand.

"Just a minute. Let's get a few things straight first. Is this exactly how the body was found? Nothing's been touched?"

"No, sir. According to Reg, he parked the lorry at the side of the road, got out to open the gate and saw her straightaway. He was just starting off to fetch me when I came past. You see . . ."

"Where's Deakin now?" Rudd interrupted him.

Cookson looked uncomfortable.

"He went home, sir. He was quite badly shaken up. But he only lives in the village so if you want to see him . . ."

He broke off lamely, anxious in case he'd handled the situation badly, that Rudd knew this, that more highly ranking officers did, too, perhaps even the chief constable himself, and it would go down on his file as a black mark against him, a permanent bar to his own modest hopes of promotion to sergeant.

But Rudd only nodded and, turning back to Boyce, said, "Get Henty and one of the dogs over here to see if it can pick up a scent before too many of us start trampling all over the place."

Boyce walked back to one of the parked vans where he spoke to a uniformed sergeant who was holding an Alsatian on a long tracking lead. The other men fell back as the dog and its handler moved forward towards the gate but it was clear in a few minutes that there was no chance of it picking up a trail. After the dog had cast about uncertainly both inside and outside the opening, Rudd swore softly under his breath and signalled the sergeant to take it away.

"All right, Henty, you and the other dog handlers can go back to the village," he told him. "Wait there. We may need you again later."

As Henty got back into the van and drove off, Cookson stepped forward, looking apologetic.

"I'm afraid the currant pickers started arriving soon after Deakin found the body," he explained. "They may have confused the scent."

"Well, it can't be helped," Rudd replied philosophically. It was a damn nuisance, though. If the dog had picked up a trail, it might have saved them a lot of work. He beckoned the other men forward.

"Right. We'll have to start from square one. Stapleton, if you and some of the men can start searching the area, McCallum can photograph the body before Pardoe examines it. Boyce, you and Kyle start making out the position of the body and measuring up and, while you're at it, have a look at the gateway, although I don't think you'll get much in the way of individual footprints. My guess is quite a few people have been in and out recently."

Cookson gave a small, modest cough and Rudd looked at him.

"Well?"

"The pickers were in the field all day yesterday, sir, clearing the currant crop. There was at least a dozen of them, I'd say, and the tyre marks are most likely from Deakin's lorry. He works for Mr. Aston, the man who rents the field."

"I see," Rudd replied. While they had been talking, the three of them had moved back the few yards towards the gate, where Boyce squatted down to examine the prints more closely.

"Well, we can try," he remarked without much enthusiasm, "but it's not much more than dust with a lot of scuff marks in it."

"Do your best," Rudd told him and, beckoning to Cookson, walked with him towards the cars.

"You've got something to tell me," he asked.

"It's a bit complicated," Cookson began apologetically.

"Never mind. Take your time telling it."

"It really started last night, about ten to twelve. I was wakened up by George Lambert, that's the dead girl's father, banging on the door. When I went down to let him in, he said Jess was missing and he was worried about her. He seemed to think that she'd had a date with a young man who's been staying at Maggie Hearn's. When she didn't come home, he'd called at Maggie's before coming on to me and she'd told him that this young man had already left earlier in the evening."

"Wait a minute," Rudd interrupted him. "Before you go on any further, I'd like a quick picture of these people. Let's start with George Lambert."

"He's in his late forties, I'd say; works as foreman down at Ken Aston's market garden; a quiet man, never says much but a steady, reliable worker, according to Aston. Widowed or possibly divorced; anyway, there's no Mrs. Lambert about. Like I said, he lives just up the road. The daughter kept house for him."

"I see. And Jess Lambert,"

"Young, pretty," Cookson said in a diffident voice that made Rudd wonder if he hadn't himself cast more than a casual glance in her direction. "There's a child," he added, with an embarrassed look at the inspector as if reluctant to pass on gossip, "but no husband that we know of."

"Who's the father?" Rudd asked quickly. "Someone from round here?"

"No one knows but it's not likely he's a local lad. The Lamberts moved here just over a year ago from Suffolk, I think, and she was expecting the baby then. It must be about eight months old now."

"No one outside the village known to call on her?" Rudd asked. It had occurred to him while Cookson was speaking that there was a possibility she might have kept in touch with the child's father. It was another line of inquiry that was worth following up.

"Not that I've heard of," Cookson replied.

"No strangers seen about?"

"No, nor any cars parked near the Lamberts' place,"

Cookson added, following the drift of Rudd's questioning. "I'm up and down this road a fair bit and I'd've noticed anything that looked at all suspicious."

"I see," Rudd said, commenting silently to himself that this fact didn't necessarily mean the inquiry was invalidated. "Go on about the girl. What was she like?"

Cookson pressed his chin down into his collar, a habit he had when thinking that was already giving him a double chin.

"It's difficult to say, sir. With the baby and her father to look after, she didn't go out much, as girls of her age normally do. There were no boy friends that I know of. I got the impression, too, that Lambert kept a strict watch on what she got up to. Perhaps he was scared she'd get pregnant again."

"But when Lambert came to see you yesterday, he seemed to think that she had a date with this young man, whoever he is?"

"His name's Chris, sir, and I don't know much about him, except he's a student and he was putting up at Maggie's, sleeping in the stable loft by all accounts. That's her house," he added, nodding in the direction of a tiled roof and chimneys that could be seen between the trees.

"Maggie—Miss Hearn, that is—owns quite a bit of land round here, most of which is let out. It seems the young man was looking for somewhere to camp when that storm blew up a week ago and Maggie offered to put him up. I only know that because I was down at the Rose and Crown the other evening and Aston was there. He'd evidently called on Maggie and met this young man. He was saying he was a bit on the posh side—well spoken and educated."

"You said Lambert had already been to Miss Hearn's and found out the young man had gone?" Rudd asked.

"So I gathered," Cookson replied. "Mind you, Lambert was a bit muddled in what he said. He was upset, of course, but he'd been drinking, too. I could smell it on his breath and he wasn't all that steady on his feet. It surprised me because he's never struck me as being a heavy drinker. I know he goes down to the Rose most evenings but I've never seen him put back more than a couple of pints of beer."

"Why had he come to you?"

"I'm not all that sure myself," Cookson admitted. "I

think he wanted me to go out looking for her. He was worried, too, about being left on his own with the child. It seems she went out earlier in the evening, presumably to meet this young man, leaving Lambert to baby-sit and promising she'd be home by half-past nine so that he could go down to the pub for a drink before closing time. When she didn't come home, he went out looking for her, first to Maggie's in case she was there and then on to me."

"Go on," Rudd said noncommittally. This account, learned at second hand from Cookson, would obviously have to be checked with Lambert. "What happened then?"

"I took him home," Cookson continued. "He'd come in the van and I didn't think he was in a fit state to drive back. I suppose I should have breathalised him, but under the circumstances it didn't seem . . ."

He broke off and looked sideways at Rudd, who merely nodded.

"Anyway, I saw him indoors and then walked back by the footpath to the village. It's a well-known spot for courting couples and I half wondered if I might find her somewhere along it."

"Dead you mean?" Rudd asked sharply.

Cookson seemed unwilling to commit himself.

"To be honest, I didn't know what to think, sir. It was clear something must have happened but it didn't strike me as very likely she'd run off and left the child. Besides, I only had Lambert's word that she even knew this young man from Maggie's and he wasn't being very coherent."

Presumably, though, Rudd thought, he'd be sober by now and ought to be able to give a better account of what had happened.

"You drove Lambert home," he said, encouragingly, reminding Cookson of where he had got to in his account. "What happened then?"

"I saw him into the house and waited while he checked to see if Jess had come home in the meantime but she hadn't, so I left and walked back across the footpath, like I said."

"And this morning?"

"I drove up from the village, intending to catch Lambert before he left for work and get a clearer story out of him of what exactly had happened last night. I half expected the girl had come back. You know how it is. Come the morning, a lot of drama goes out of a situation and I thought it'd probably blown over. I was passing the currant field and I saw Reg at the side of the road being sick so I stopped to see what was up. It was then he told me about finding the girl's body. I said to him, 'Have you touched it?' And he said, 'No.' He'd seen it from that gate and that'd been enough for him. He hadn't gone any nearer. So I told him to hang on where he was while I went up the road to see Lambert. I was so close to the bungalow, I thought it best to tell him first before putting in a report to headquarters. After all, it was kinder to him, in a way, to let him know the worst; put him out of his misery, so to speak."

"Go on," Rudd said, for Cookson had paused again as if expecting an official reaction.

"I found Lambert in the kitchen. He must have already fed the child because it was lying in the pram by the back door, awake but not crying, and there was a packet of baby cereal and one of those feeding cups on the table, so I suppose he'd managed somehow."

This concern over the child struck Rudd as unusual in the young constable, the cause of which was explained when he added, "I've got a youngster of my own and I've often wondered how I'd cope if the wife were taken ill, although her mother'd lend a hand, I suppose."

"How did Lambert take the news?" Rudd asked.

Again Cookson made the small, downward inclination of his head.

"It's difficult to say, sir. He was his usual self by then; sober, I mean, and not inclined to say much. When I told him, he just turned his head away and muttered something about he might have guessed."

"Meaning what?"

"Well, I took it to mean that, when she hadn't come home all night, he'd realised something had happened to her."

"Have you any reason to think, apart from Lambert's account, that she might have been meeting this young man?"

Cookson shook his head.

"No gossip in the village?" Rudd couldn't resist asking.

Cookson caught his grin and smiled back.

"Not that I've heard of, or the wife's mother. It's usually through her that I hear the titbits."

"Lambert will presumably know more," Rudd continued. "I can check with him."

"I'm afraid he's gone, sir," Cookson said hurriedly. "I was going to tell you about it. When I saw him this morning and told him about Jess, he said he couldn't go on looking after the child on his own and he'd have to take it to his sister's in Norfolk. As a matter of fact, he drove past me in his van when I was on my way back from reporting to headquarters so I assume that's where he was off to. I've got the address," he added. "It's a Mrs. Dunlop, of Eighteen Furze Road, Norwich."

"Did he say when he'd be back?"

"About six o'clock this evening, he reckoned. I said he'd be needed to make a statement. Maggie Hearn might know—about the young man, I mean. After all, he was staying with her."

"I'll check with her later," Rudd replied and, telling Cookson to join the others in the search, he walked back to the canvas screens that had been erected round the body where Pardoe was just finishing his preliminary examination of the body.

"I can't tell you much yet," Pardoe informed him in his usual brisk manner. "I'll have to have the body in for a proper postmortem before I can give you a detailed report. Judging by the degree of rigor mortis and the rectal temperature, she's been dead a good few hours, though; between nine o'clock and midnight, but that's only a rough estimate. I can be more precise when I've tested the stomach contents. And, for my money, it's murder. The wound on the side of the head is sufficiently serious to cause death. It was quite a savage blow and I can't see it happening accidentally. There's no other sign of injury that I can see and if she banged her head, say, in falling, she must have gone down hard enough to bruise herself elsewhere."

"Any idea of the type of weapon that may have been used?" Rudd asked.

"Not at this stage," Pardoe replied brusquely. "You'll have it all in my report later. There are a couple of things I can tell you though. She wasn't sexually interfered with in any way and the wound must have bled extensively."

Rudd thanked him and turned to McCallum.

"Have you finished?" he asked him.

The police photographer nodded.

"Then we'll have her taken away," Rudd added and, emerging from behind the screens, gave orders for this to be done before turning to Boyce.

"I'll leave you to carry on with the measuring and the detailed search of the area round the body," he told him. "If you want me, I'll be down the road at that house you can see behind the trees, interviewing a Miss Maggie Hearn."

"Possible witness?" Boyce asked nosily.

"Perhaps," Rudd replied and added, with a smile, knowing Boyce's dislike of being kept in the dark, "I'll put you in the picture later when it's a bit clearer to me."

He set off to walk down the road, edging past Kyle, who was squatting in the gateway with his paraphernalia, making plaster casts of the tyre marks and the few footprints that were clearly distinguishable in the dust.

The house had a closed air when he reached it, the front windows and door shut, and, after surveying it for a few seconds from the road, he crunched down the gravelled drive to the rear where the same closed, vacant air greeted him at the back of the house. He found the door locked when, having knocked several times and gotten no response, he tried the handle. Cupping his hands over the glass, he peered through the kitchen window and saw a long deal table with a cup and saucer and a teapot standing on it, a tea towel flung down beside them, and a dressing gown draped untidily over the back of a chair. Wherever Maggie Hearn had gone, it looked as if she had left in a hurry.

Rudd turned his attention to the outbuildings that faced him across the yard, remembering that Cookson had told him that the young man had been sleeping in the stable loft. The door of what he took to be the stable, with its half sections, was set open and, walking over to it, he peered inside. It seemed to be empty, apart from a hen sitting in a nesting box in one of the loose compartments that clucked angrily at being disturbed and watched him sideways with a suspicious and malevolent eye. Clucking back at it soothingly, Rudd mounted the wooden steps and emerged through an open trap door into the room above.

The sun was streaming in thought the skylight, throwing a great oblong of brightness across the bed and the bare boards of the floor. Standing at the top of the stairs while he surveyed the room, Rudd was struck by an odd make-shift quality about it. A camp bed, with a pillow and a blanket on it, was pushed back against one wall, while the rest of the room was furnished with the bits and pieces one might find rummaging about in an outbuilding. A wooden apple box stood in one corner on which were placed a small camping stove, together with a tin kettle and a white mug. A trestle top, supported on more boxes, was drawn up under the window that overlooked the yard, with a battered kitchen chair standing in front of it. Some paper-back books were lying on top of the planking, while nearby, pinned to the sloping wall, were some coloured photographs of mountain scenery that looked as if they had been torn from a colour supplement magazine.

The general effect was an amalgam of study and den, the sort of hideout that a young boy might arrange for himself in a shed or an attic to give himself the feeling of independence, a place of his own where he could read and brew coffee without any family interference.

Yet, despite the temporary nature of the boxes, Rudd got the impression that the young man who had occupied this loft room had looked on it as somewhere more than a mere place to sleep for a few days. Otherwise, why had he bothered to pin the pictures up on the wall?

And why had he gone, leaving behind his camping stove and his books? It seemed that he, too, like Maggie Hearn, had left in a hurry.

Rudd crossed the room to the table, and picking up the books, scanned their titles, wondering if they would give him some clue to the personality of Maggie's camper, as Cookson called him. All the inspector knew of him was that he was a student, young and educated, and a bit posh, if Aston's remarks about him were to be believed.

The titles of the books gave him not much more information. There were three of them. The first was a copy of Thomas Hardy's *The Well Beloved*. The second was a Penguin edition of D. H. Lawrence's *The Rainbow*. The third was an illustrated guide to the county, giving brief descriptions of places of historical interest to visit, some of which had been marked with a small pencilled cross as if they had been seen.

Rudd was just replacing the books on the table, no wiser than when he had picked them up, when he heard the sound of wheels on the gravel drive and, glancing through the window, saw a woman on a bicycle entering the yard.

He remained where he was, knowing that if he moved, she would almost certainly look up and see him, and he was intrigued also by this first glimpse of Maggie Hearn in those few intimate moments before she was aware of being watched.

She was middle-aged, he noticed, dressed casually in slacks and a cotton blouse, her hair bundled up anyhow behind her head. A good-looking woman, too, with a strong face—not beautiful, it was too distincly featured for that, the nose and chin particularly marked and the dark eyebrows a little too heavy. But it was an interesting face all the same, full of individuality and character that would normally, he felt, express a strong and positive personality. At the moment, it looked worn and defeated, with a weariness that he was sure wasn't its usual expression. He noticed, also, the dark area of bruising beneath her eye.

She came up the drive, riding the bike with the same tired heaviness that showed in her face, her shoulders bowed, her legs seeming almost unable to turn the pedals.

At the same time, although he wasn't conscious of moving, she became aware of him, glancing up as if instinctively, and he saw her expression change rapidly from one of delighted pleasure that almost immediately vanished to be replaced by suspicion and, he thought, fear.

He smiled and nodded to her reassuringly, indicating with a movement of one hand that he would come down to her, and, walking across the room, he began descending the stairs in time to meet her in the doorway.

6

Seeing the figure at the window, Maggie thought for one blinding moment of joy and relief that it was Chris come home. She had been out looking for him since first light, having found it impossible to go back to bed after Lambert's visit. Instead, she had sat in the kitchen, still in her dressing gown and nightdress, drinking cups of tea and dozing uneasily in a chair from time to time, her head resting on her arms on the table. At dawn she had gone out again, taking her bike and exploring every likely path, having come to the conclusion that he must have left the road and camped overnight in a field, but, although she cycled as far as the outskirts of Gossbridge, she hadn't found him.

Returning along the road, she had passed the currant field and guessed from the police cars drawn up alongside the verge and the men searching both sides of the hedge that something terrible had happened, although she hadn't the courage to put her fears into exact words. She only felt for Chris's sake an overwhelming sense of fear and danger.

Reassurance poured into her when she saw him at the window. It was all right! He had come back!

The next second, her vision cleared and she saw, with a sickening sense of returning fear and danger, that it wasn't Chris after all. It was a much older man who stood looking down at her with a watchful, interested look on his face and a hunch-shouldered stance that was casual and at the same time ominous. She knew without needing to be told that he was a policeman and he had come to find Chris. Quite self-assured, he nodded to her and then moved away from the window without any impression of haste or urgency but, even so, she barely had time to prop her bicycle up against the barn wall and compose her face before he had emerged from the stable door and stood confronting her.

"Miss Hearn?" he asked pleasantly.

"Yes?" Maggie replied, a little breathlessly. For a moment, she was disarmed by his voice and expression, which seemed so amiably bland until she noticed his eyes were observing her with a cool appraisal.

"I'm afraid you were out when I first called," Rudd began, but before he could explain the purpose of his visit she put in hurriedly, "Yes, I had to go in to Goss-bridge."

"I hope you didn't have an accident on the way," Rudd said gravely. It was clear she didn't understand and he added, "The bruise on your face, Miss Hearn."

Her hand flew up to cover it.

"Oh, that! No, I—I caught it on the barn door. The wind blew it open suddenly."

"I see." It seemed an acceptable enough explanation, although he had the impression it was merely an excuse, made up on the spur of the moment. However, it didn't seem all that important and he continued, "I understand a young man's been staying with you for the past few days?"

"Yes," Maggie said tentatively, afraid to say too much.

"Is he still here? I see his room's empty. By the way, I hope you didn't mind my going up to look? The door was open."

"No, he's gone. What did you want to see him about?" Maggie asked.

"Police inquiries. I'm Detective Inspector Rudd."

"Inquiries into what?"

She had recovered some of her spirit, Rudd noticed, although the underlying fear and caution were still there. He had the impression, too, that she was playing for time.

"A death, Miss Hearn."

He waited but she said nothing and he guessed that she already knew whose death he meant.

So it must be true, Maggie was thinking. Lambert's visit late last night and the presence of the police could mean only one thing. But it couldn't be Chris! she cried out passionately to herself. Not Chris! But, even as she thought it, the two images that had haunted her all night, Chris's face in the light from the door and his arm raised up to strike her, returned in all their nightmarish vividness.

"Come into the house," she said, turning away and crossing the yard, leaving him with no option but to follow. Finding the key in her pocket, going through the act of unlocking the door gave her a few precious seconds in which to fight down her rising panic.

"Whose death?" she asked, as they went into the kitchen.

Rudd noticed that she still didn't face him but busied herself in clearing the table of the used crockery, setting out clean cups and putting the kettle on to boil. Her face in profile as she bent over the stove was very pale and the bruise beneath her eye showed up with greater intensity.

"Jess Lambert's," Rudd told her. He had seated himself at the table, looking relaxed and at home, as indeed he felt in the big, sunlit room, full of homely possessions.

Maggie paused with the teapot lid in her hand. It would be useless to deny knowing anything, she decided. The inspector had probably found out quite a lot already.

"Her father was here last night, looking for her," she admitted.

"What time was this?"

"About a quarter to twelve. I'd gone to bed."

"Why did he come here?"

Rudd already had Cookson's version. It would be interesting to see what Maggie Hearn said about it.

She hesitated. It was the question she had been dreading. All she could do was play it down, try to make it seem unimportant.

"I'm not sure. He'd been drinking. At least, that's what it seemed like to me. Jess hadn't come home and he had some crazy idea she might be here."

"Why should he think that?"

"I've no idea," Maggie said quickly.

"Didn't he believe that she'd been seeing the young man, Chris, who was staying here?"

So he even knows Chris's name, Maggie thought. What else did he know? She tried to keep her hands steady as she poured the boiling water into the teapot and carried it over to the table.

"If he did, he had no reason to think it," she replied with a sharpness of voice that surprised herself.

"Chris said nothing to you about meeting her?"

That was easy.

"No," Maggie replied with conviction.

"Did he go out last night?"

"No, he was here all evening."

It was only a half-lie, she told herself. After all, Chris had said he was going to read. If she hadn't gone up to his room and found it empty, it would be the truth as far as she was concerned. All the same, it didn't come naturally to her and Rudd was aware of her growing unease.

"And a bit later on, he decided to leave," Maggie added, in a little rush of words. "He'd already stayed on here longer than he'd intended and he wanted to move on."

"What time was this, Miss Hearn?"

"Time?" she asked, as if she hadn't understood.

"Yes, when he left."

Oh, God! thought Maggie. What can I say? If I tell him the right time, he'll know at once that something was wrong.

"Just before eight o'clock," she said quickly, surprising herself at how quickly and convincingly the lie came to her lips. "I looked at the clock."

She glanced at it now as if to demonstrate how easy it was to see it and verify the time.

"Did he take his camping gear with him?"

"Oh, yes. He had the rucksack on his back with the tent and sleeping bag rolled up on the top."

"And did you happen to see which way he went?"

She hesitated for only a moment. It was obvious to her that she would have to lie about this for under no circumstances could she let Rudd believe that Chris had gone anywhere near the Lamberts' bungalow.

"Towards the village," she said firmly.

The story sounded plausible enough, Rudd thought, but he wasn't altogether convinced. The signs of hasty departure in Chris's room, the books and camping stove left behind, suggested a sudden, unplanned decision to move out. Maggie's distress and fear when he had first seen her in the yard also didn't square with this account. But he decided to leave it there for the time being. He could tackle her again later when he was more certain of the facts. Until he'd seen Lambert, for instance, and checked with him, he couldn't be sure that Chris even knew the girl. Besides, it might give him a psychological advantage if he left now, giving her the impression that he was perfectly satisfied with her account.

"Well, it all sounds quite straightforward," he said comfortably. "I'll have to find him, of course, and just check with him. Do you happen to know where he's gone?"

"No, I don't," Maggie said sharply. "He's camping. He could be anywhere. I don't think he had any exact plan."

"Just pleasing himself?" Rudd asked. "It's nice to be young and not have any ties. Could you tell me his full name?"

"Christopher Lawrence."

"And his home address?"

"I don't know."

"On holiday was he?"

Maggie hesitated before deciding to tell the truth, at least over this detail. It couldn't do any harm.

"In a way. I gather he'd been ill and had been told to get plenty of fresh air. He called here a week ago, looking for somewhere to camp for the night and then it started to rain. As he couldn't put his tent up, I suggested he sleep in the stable. It was my idea he stayed on for a few days, giving me a hand round the place."

"Very useful," Rudd agreed, thinking that this part of the story checked with what Cookson had told him. He was aware, too, of Maggie's eagerness to accept all the responsibility for the young man's presence at the farm.

"Could you give me a description of Mr. Lawrence?" he added.

"Well," Maggie began reluctantly, "he's young, only about nineteen or twenty. Dark brown hair and eyes. Rather thin-faced. Medium height. A bit on the slight side. He doesn't look very strong."

The last detail was true, although more especially of Chris when he had first arrived. She stressed it now in the hope that the inspector, with his honest, open face that, she had to admit, gave damn-all away, would get the impression of someone unlikely to commit a murder.

But who did commit murder? she thought a little wildly. Almost anyone, it seemed, judging by the papers. There had been a case only the other week of a retired bank manager in his seventies who had attacked a cantankerous neighbour with a pair of garden shears.

Rudd, who had been scribbling down the details in his notebook, glanced up and caught her expression. Her face, with its strong, handsome features, looked distressed.

"Yes?" he said quickly, convinced that she was about to say something.

She struggled to put her thought into words.

"Chris had nothing to do with it. He's not the type. I know him." She stopped, conscious that, by saying too much, she was only making matters worse. "Besides," she went on, trying to retrieve the situation, "how do you know Jess Lambert wasn't meeting someone else?"

As she said it, she tried not to think of Ken Aston, although a series of vivid images flashed into her mind: Vi, seated at the kitchen table, her face ugly with tears; Aston's yellow pickup van parked in the gateway of the currant field, within sight of the Lamberts bungalow.

Rudd was watching her with eyes that had an alert, bright look in them that disquieted her.

"You know of someone else?" he asked.

"Oh, no!" she protested too quickly. "Only she was young and pretty . . ."

She left it there, realising it would be dangerous to go on, and was reassured when Rudd merely nodded and smiled, as if in agreement, before getting up and making his way towards the door.

His thoughts, however, were busy with this last part of the interview and, on his return to the field, he sought out Cookson from the group of men who were searching the area and drew him to one side.

"Look," he told him, "I want to know if there's been any gossip about Jess Lambert and anybody from the village."

Cookson tried to avoid his eyes.

"Well, it wasn't much," he said reluctantly. "It was nothing more than an impression I got and I could be wrong."

"Out with it," Rudd insisted.

"It was the same evening at the Rose and Crown when Aston was telling us about the young man from Maggie's. A bit later on, the talk turned to the question of this field. Aston said he was thinking of putting the pickers in on Monday—that is, yesterday—and he was discussing the arrangements with Reg Deakin, who was going to be in charge. Halfway through, Ken got up to go out to the gents' and Reg said something to the effect that it was about time Aston made up his mind about the field; he'd been up and down the village all week looking at it and people might start getting the wrong idea."

"Meaning what exactly?"

"I'm not sure," Cookson admitted, "but I got the impression he was getting at Aston, not so much by what he said as by his tone of voice. It could be nothing at all but, as you can see for yourself, it's only a short distance from here to the girl's place and, if he'd been calling on her during the day, he'd be sure of finding her alone. Lambert's busy down at the market garden until gone six most evenings and he doesn't go home midday."

"And you think that's what Reg Deakin might have been hinting at?"

"I couldn't say for sure," Cookson confessed. "I might be reading more into it than I should."

"I'll have a chat with Deakin," Rudd said, half to himself. "You said he went home. Where does he live?"

"There's a pair of brick cottages next door to the butcher's. He lives in the one on the far end."

Rudd nodded, dismissing him as Boyce approached.

"They've completed the search of the immediate area," the sergeant announced, "and the body's been taken away. There's not much blood, by the way. Do you want to have a look for yourself?"

Together they walked into the field and behind the screens where Rudd stood looking down at the white tapes that outlined the shape of the dead girl's body. He saw immediately what Boyce meant about the blood. Only a small patch stained the grass, certainly not large enough to have come from the wound when it was first struck. As Pardoe had pointed out, it must have bled extensively.

As they stood there, they were joined by Inspector Stapleton, a tall, depressed-looking man whose years of stooping and bending over scenes of crime had left him round-shouldered and slow-moving, with a sharp eye for detail.

"We've found nothing here," he told Rudd. "Do you want the men to spread out and cover the rest of the field?"

"I suppose they'd better," Rudd replied, "not that they're likely to find much. It's my bet the girl was killed somewhere else and brought here afterwards."

"You mean the small extent of the bloodstain?" Stapleton asked. "I noticed that."

"Yes, and there's also the way the body is lying," Rudd pointed out. "It's too tidy. If someone struck her down with a blow on the side of her head, she'd've fallen in a heap, anyhow. So, whoever killed her must have either straightened the body out afterwards or carried her here and laid her down fairly carefully."

"Any takers so far?" Boyce asked, trying not to sound too inquisitve as Stapleton moved away and began organising the search to be extended.

"Yes, two possibles and a third that's worth following up. One's a young man, a student, who was staying just down the road at the farm," Rudd replied and gave Boyce a quick resumé of what Cookson had told him and what he had learned since from Maggie. "According to her, he was there until about eight o'clock when he left on foot towards the village. I'm not sure yet whether to believe her or not. There's a lot more to check on first. On the face of it, though, it doesn't seem likely that he'd set out for a date loaded down with camping gear. But the point is he's gone. All perfectly innocent, according to Maggie Hearn but I'm not so sure. He's left some of his stuff behind which makes me think he may have cleared off in a hurry. Anyway, we've got to find him, if only to check her story. It shouldn't be too difficult. He's walking so he can't have gotten all that far, unless he thumbed a lift. Start off with a house-to-house in the area, as far as Gossbridge on this side and Dearden on the other. You'd better take as many men as Stapleton can spare, including Cookson. He ought to know the district. And don't forget the farms. If that doesn't bring in any information about his whereabouts, then we'll have to spread the net wider and start searching the fields. You'll want a description," he added and, taking out his notebook, read out the one that Maggie Hearn had given him while Boyce wrote it down. "While you're about it, you might ask if anyone's seen a stranger about the village or a car parked under suspicious circumstances."

"Is that also to do with Chris Lawrence?" Boyce asked.

"No, but Cookson told me that Jess Lambert had an illegitimate child by someone presumably where the Lamberts used to live in Suffolk. As it's not all that far away by car, it's possible that the child's father was still visiting her."

"That's a bit of a long shot, isn't it?"

"Perhaps," Rudd conceded. But I want it checked all the same. It's a line of inquiry we can't afford to ignore."

"Will do," Boyce replied. "Where will you be if we pick Chris Lawrence up?"

"Interviewing Reg Deakin, the man who found the body. If I'm not at his house, then I'll have gone on to see a man called Ken Aston, who rents this field. According to Cookson, it's possible Aston had been seeing the girl, although it's only gossip so far. Meanwhile, if you find Chris Lawrence, take him to the incident room we're setting up in the village hall. It ought to be organised by then. Lewis has the arrangements in hand."

As they were talking, they walked back to where Rudd's car was parked at the side of the road. The inspector got into it and drove off towards the village.

Cookson watched him go. He guessed where he was making for—Reg's place and then Ken Aston's. He was beginning to regret passing on that bit of a remark he'd heard Reg make. It could mean nothing at all. After all, people make snide comments about their employers without it having any real significance.

He felt, too, obscurely resentful in a more general way at the intrusion of the men from headquarters onto his patch. All right, so it was murder and that was a serious crime, but it had taken him a long time to build up good relationships in the village and it meant a lot to him that he was acknowledged in the street or could drop in at the Rose of an evening and be sure of a welcome. Now that pleasant life would be disturbed and churned over by people like Rudd and his sergeant asking questions, prying into private lives, a process that, as part of the law himself, he'd be associated with. He could almost see the gulf widening between himself and the local people.

Rudd found Deakin's house without any difficulty. It was, as Cookson had said, next door to the butcher's, one of a pair of modest brick cottages with tiny front gardens which, on Deakin's side, had been carefully divided up with almost mathematical precision into oblong borders of blue lobelia and pink geraniums round a pocket-handker-chief-sized square of lawn. A concrete path led round to the back of the house where two small children were splashing about in a bright-red plastic paddling pool set out on another, larger square of lawn.

A youngish, sharp-faced woman answered his knock at the door, brisk and tidy, with a preoccupied air that quickly turned to one of hostile suspicion when he announced who he was and why he had come.

"Yes he's in, but he's sick to his stomach, what with finding that girl," she announced, as if it were all Rudd's fault. The expression "that girl" suggested some of her hostility might be directed at Jess Lambert as well, a point that Rudd hoped to take further if he got the opportunity.

"Well, you'd better come in, I suppose," she added a little grudgingly and, opening the back door wider, took Rudd through the kitchen, immaculate in blue and white and a tribute, he felt, not only to her skill as a housewife but to Reg Deakin's as a do-it-yourself expert, into a small living room that impressed him with the same attention to order and neatness.

"He's having a lie-down," Mrs. Deakin went on, and, going into the hall, shouted up the stairs, "Reg! It's the police come to see you."

It was not, Rudd thought, a very auspicious beginning to an interview and he tried to make himself look as inconspicuous and as friendly as possible.

Deakin came downstairs shortly afterwards, showing signs of having hastily dressed; a pleasant, chunky man in his thirties, suntanned and, Rudd guessed, normally affable and easygoing, but there was a subdued, strained air about him, occasioned not only by finding the body but by the whole business of the police investigation that he now found himself mixed up with.

Rudd having apologised for troubling him took him quickly through the first part of his evidence. It was much as Cookson had already told him. Deakin had taken Aston's lorry up to the currant field in readiness for the day's picking, had left it at the side of the road while he opened the gate and had seen the dead girl immediately. No, he hadn't touched her. He hadn't even gone up close. He could see all he wanted to from the gate, thanks very much, and that was more than enough. Yes, he guessed she was dead from the way she was lying and, yes, he recognised who she was.

"What happened then?" Rudd asked.

"I went back to the lorry," Deakin replied. "I thought it best to get back to the village and fetch Harry Cookson. Suddenly, I came over bad . . ."

"You always had a weak stomach," his wife broke in to comment. She was in the kitchen, with the intervening door between the two rooms set open, washing children's clothes in the sink. Deakin grinned at her in shame-faced agreement.

"Then, just as luck would have it," he continued, "who should drive past but Harry Cookson himself. He stopped and I told him what I'd seen. He took a look himself and then he told me to wait there while he went to Lambert, the girl's father. When he came back, he said to hang on a bit longer, because he had to go and phone headquarters and he didn't want the currant pickers arriving and trampling all over the place."

Quick thinking on Cookson's part, Rudd thought, although the request evidently hadn't met with Mrs. Deakin's approval.

"He should have let you come home there and then," she remarked. "He knew how sick you'd been."

"He was right, though," Deakin said judiciously. "The women started arriving soon afterwards and I wouldn't have wanted any of them to see her."

"Did you tell them what had happened?" Rudd asked. He was curious to know how much was known in the village about the crime.

"I said there'd been an accident," Deakin explained. "Then Harry Cookson came back and told them to get off home. 'You'll find out soon enough what's happened,' he said. And they did, too. It's all over the village by now."

"Not from me," Mrs. Deakin put in quickly. "I haven't said a word to anybody.

Rudd doubted the accuracy of this statement, not that it really mattered. News of any kind travels quickly in a small place; bad news even faster. Besides, it was bound to be talked about sooner or later.

"Then I came home," Deakin added. "I stopped off at the market garden to leave the lorry and one of the men brought me back in his car. He could see how bad I was."

"And he went straight to bed," Mrs. Deakin put in sharply, as if Rudd didn't believe the truth about her

husband's state of shock. "He wouldn't even ha
tea."

"Did you know Jess Lambert?" Rudd aske
both the Deakins in the question. It was, as
Mrs. Deakin who answered.

"I've seen her about the village but I didn't
she replied.

"What was she like?"

"Tarty, if you ask me."

Deakin, who looked shocked at this criti
dead, was quick to try to cover up his wife'
ness.

"Oh, come on, Phyl," he protested. "She
bad."

"Wasn't she?" Mrs. Deakin retorted. "Well
is you can't have seen her like I have, com
village in jeans and a sweater two sizes too s
all she'd got, pushing that baby in the pram
don't know what."

"She's young," Deakin replied, inadverte
present tense as if she were still alive. "Gi
dress like that. It don't mean nothing.
child . . ."

He broke off and, catching his wife's ey
mumble, "Anyone can make a mistake once."

His attitude seemed to be very much the same as
Cookson's—a subdued admiration for the girl and a kind
of pity. Had he, too, perhaps, quietly lusted after her in his
heart? Certainly, he didn't seem to share his wife's condemnation.

"Did she have any boy friends?" Rudd asked. He
directed the question over his shoulder to Mrs. Deakin,
although he kept his eyes on her husband's face and
noticed how Deakin immediately looked away, as if disas-
sociating himself from this part of the conversation. Rudd
thought he could guess why. Aston was, after all, the
man's boss and Deakin might very well prefer not to let
any gossip about him circulate too freely, especially as his
own wife seemed to have a sharp nose for scandal. It was
probably men's talk only, confined to the pub and then
limited to a wink and a nudge or a remark not intended to
be taken too seriously.

"Not that I know of," Mrs. Deakin was saying, wringing
out socks until her knuckles whitened. "Mind you, she

didn't have much time for gadding about with the baby and her father to look after."

Hinting that, without them, Jess Lambert might have lain half the men in the village, Rudd thought unkindly. But he was doing her an injustice. She came to the door of the living room, a bowlful of washing balanced on one hip, and added in a softer voice, "Poor kid! Now I come to think of it, it can't have been much of a life for her, stuck in that bungalow all day long, with not even a next-door neighbour."

She sighed and then almost immediately her old, brisk manner returned. "Well, I'd better get this lot out on the line."

Rudd waited until she had gone out of the back door before he turned to Deakin.

"I hear there's been gossip," he said in a quiet voice.

Deakin tried to bluff it out.

"Gossip? I don't know what you're talking about."

"About Mr. Aston and Jess Lambert."

Deakin looked down at his hands.

"Come on," Rudd told him encouragingly. "Are you going to tell me or do I have to go asking half the village before I get at the truth? He'd been seeing her, hadn't he?"

He saw the beads of sweat break out on Deakin's lip.

"For God's sake, keep your voice down," he said. "I don't want Phyl to know anything about it. It's only rumour, anyway; there's nothing definite. The fact is me and a couple of others noticed that he's been making excuses over the past week or so to keep going up that end of the village." He jerked his head vaguely in the direction of Lambert's bungalow and the currant field. "We had a laugh about it at first. Then yesterday . . ."

"Go on," Rudd said, for Deakin had stopped abruptly, half rising from his chair to take a quick look up the garden where his wife was still busy pegging out washing on the line and scolding the children.

"Well, yesterday," Deakin continued, "I was pretty damn sure it was true. Mr. Aston came up to the field at midday to check on how the picking was going, or so he said, although other years he's not bothered. We stood chatting for a few minutes and then he said he was going to look at another field he'd arranged to rent off Maggie Hearn. But the point is he walked *up* the road and the field's in the other direction, farther down towards Maggie's place."

"Did you see him go into the bungalow?" Rudd asked.

"No, I didn't. That young student chap who's staying at Maggie's came up to get his basket weighed and by the time I'd done that and given him a chitty for it, Mr. Aston was nowhere in sight. But I wasn't happy about it, I can tell you. For a start, I know Mrs. Aston and I like her. In a funny way, I like Mr. Lambert, too, although I know a lot of people don't get on with him ... ."

"Wait a minute," Rudd interrupted him. It was obvious that Deakin was trying to justify his attitude to Aston. Deakin was, after all, a decent man, a family man who, whatever his own private yearnings might be, would regard actual adultery as something to be disapproved of. But this wasn't what interested Rudd. "You say Chris Lawrence was working in the currant field yesterday morning?"

"That's right. According to Mr. Aston, he'd fixed it up with Maggie to take him on. She thought he might be keen to earn a few quid. Why?"

"Nothing," Rudd replied offhandedly. Indeed, it probably wasn't important. But Deakin was regarding him with a bright-eyed look.

"*She* was there, too," he said.

"You mean Jess Lambert?"

"Yes. Only the morning, mind. She didn't turn up in the afternoon. Perhaps she'd had enough of it."

"Did they meet?"

"Jess and the young man from Maggie's? Yes, they did. Mind you, I don't think they'd known each other before; at least, that's not the impression I got. But I saw them talking together when the pickers stopped for a midmorning break and later ..."

He broke off as his wife came back into the kitchen.

"Well, Mr. Deakin," Rudd said in a loud, cheerful voice, at the same time making a small nod of his head towards the garden, "thank you for being so helpful."

"I'll see you out," Deakin mumbled and they went guiltily through the kitchen past Mrs. Deakin, who regarded their departure suspiciously.

"Later?" Rudd reminded him as they reached the front gate. But Deakin seemed to regret his decision to talk.

"Nothing much," he said unwillingly. "At dinnertime when they were knocking off, I saw him helping her to carry the pram out into the road. She'd got the wheels stuck in the long grass. They stood talking for a few minutes . . ."

"Did you hear what they said?" Rudd asked eagerly.

"No, they were too far away and, anyway, it was then that Mr. Aston arrived."

"While Chris and the girl were still taking?"

Deakin gave a small, rueful grin, as if reluctantly admitting to the humour of the situation.

"Yes. It struck me, too, as a bit of a funny do at the time. There they were, the pair of them, and him with a look on his face so you could see he fancied her and then Mr. Aston turns up. She cleared off soon afterwards, seemed in a hurry to go and I'm not surprised, because it was obvious that Aston wasn't going to like it very much. When the young man came back to the lorry to have his basket weighed, Mr. Aston was quite sarky with him. 'Doing your good deed for the day?' he asked him or something like that. Then Mr. Aston walked off, like I said *up* the road and after I'd weighed the basket for the young chap, he left, too."

"Where did he go?"

Deakin shrugged.

"I didn't see. Back to Maggie's, I suppose."

Rudd was silent, thinking over the implications of what Deakin had told him. It was now evident that Chris Lawrence had met the girl in the currant field on the morning before she was murdered, a fact that Maggie Hearn hadn't divulged although, perhaps, to be fair to her, she might not have known about it. But it was a point he'd have to take up with her. In fact, her whole account would have to be checked over in more detail. But not yet, he decided. He'd leave her a little longer in her fool's paradise.

Aston, too, was well in the running as another possible suspect, for it seemed possible that he'd been meeting the girl, if not having an affair with her, and this might give him a motive for wishing her dead.

"Where's Mr. Aston's nursery garden?" he asked Deakin.

"It's on the right, straight through the village, past the church and up the hill," Deakin told him. "Look," he added in a worried voice, "I don't want to cause any trouble. Maybe I shouldn't have said anything. . . ."

"If I hadn't heard it from you, I'd've gotten it from someone else," Rudd assured him. "Besides, I shan't say who told me."

But it didn't seem to cheer Deakin up. When Rudd drove away, he remained standing in the tiny garden, his pleasant, round face haggard with new concern.

7

Maggie sat alone in the kitchen, trying to convince herself that everything would be all right. Rudd didn't really believe Chris could be guilty of the girl's death, she told herself. She was quite sure he'd accepted her account that Chris had stayed in his room until he left the farm for good. And yet, some niggling doubt remained. She didn't trust him, in spite of his friendliness and his pleasant smile.

The sound of car engines starting up farther along the road startled her. Running into the yard, she was just in time to see four of them pass the end of the drive, with uniformed policemen sitting inside. A purposeful air about the polished, official cars and their occupants filled her with dread. She could guess where they were off to—to look for Chris.

Rudd must have started a search, she realised, and she was suddenly struck with the thought that it might be something that he had found in Chris's room that had initiated this move. Some evidence, perhaps. A note from the girl, although that didn't seem very likely. A diary, then.

She went quickly up the steps to the loft. It was the first time she had been in the room since the previous evening and then it had been too dark to see much. Now, she felt a sudden pang at the signs of Chris's recent occupation. He had left some things behind, she noticed, although the significance of it didn't strike her in the same way as it had the inspector. She only felt for Chris's sake that he might need them, especially the camping stove. How on earth was he to manage about cooking food for himself without it? She'd have to find him somehow, warn him about the police inquiries and take him some provisions.

Having found nothing else that seemed important, she

picked up the stove and went back to the kitchen where she began making preparations. Having something practical to do steadied her. She found a plastic shopping bag and began packing the items carefully into it with the heaviest object, the stove, wrapped in sheets of newspaper, at the bottom. On top, she placed a flask of coffee, bacon, bread, a carton of eggs and packet of cheese sandwiches that could be eaten at once. In his abrupt departure last night, he had left some clothes behind, too, a shirt and a pair of socks that she had washed for him and that had been airing on the line over the Aga. Folding them lovingly, she laid them on the top.

I must keep calm, she told herself, as she locked up the house and, fetching her bike, put the bag into the basket on the handlebars. I mustn't forget to go over it all carefully so that he understands, including Lambert's visit last night and then the inspector coming this morning and what I said to him. If Chris sticks to the same story, it should be all right.

Her reasoning broke down after that. She knew too little about the other evidence that Rudd might already have in his possession. But if Chris was innocent, and that was a fact she had to hang onto in spite of everything, then nothing could happen to him.

At the gate she paused, wondering which way to go, hesitating to turn up the road because that would take her past the field where the girl's body had been found. Some of the police might still be there and see her go past. Besides, she had searched most of the fields that lay in that direction without finding him.

The other alternative was to ride down the hill towards the village, a route that she had dismissed last night because it led towards houses and people.

Now she wasn't so sure that her conviction had been correct. If Chris had gone up the road, then he would have passed Lambert's bungalow, and, whatever had happened last night, something had distressed him badly, something connected with the girl, she felt sure. In running away, he might very well not want to go past the place where she lived.

So it seemed likely to her now that he had turned towards the village and, mounting her bike, she rode off in that direction.

But what happened last night? she asked herself, as she

freewheeled down the long slope towards the houses. It was a question she had avoided until that moment. Every instinct in her cried out against the possibility that he might have killed the girl. Yet, she had seen his rage and, now that she was a little distanced in time from the looming images of his raised arm and convulsed face, she began to see a little more clearly the nature of his anger. It had been like a child's tantrum, translated into adult terms of force and energy, that had broken though the conventional exterior, revealing a dark centre of frustration and bitterness that she realised she should have been aware of. His tension and vulnerability when he first arrived ought to have warned her but instead she had convinced herself that he was happier and more relaxed under her care.

I was blind! blind! she told herself furiously. There I was, feeding him up, chatting on every evening about the farm, and I never saw that there was something else he needed that I didn't give him. Although what it was, she wasn't certain herself. She only felt that she had let him down by some fatal and overwhelming omission on her part.

She had passed the houses and was pedalling up the hill on the far side of the village. Halfway up, she dismounted and began pushing her bike. On the crest, a green-painted finger post with white lettering pointed out a public footpath to Dearden. It was the only path out of the village on this side and a route that Chris might have taken. Anyway, it was worth trying.

There was a stile but somehow she managed to haul the bike over it and, remounting, set off at a slow wobble along the faint track that ran across the grass. As she rode, she looked about her, searching for the orange blob of his tent against the background of trees and hedges.

At the far side, a gate led into a lane that ran between a long spinney on one side and a high hedge on the other. The ground here was too rough to ride on, churned up over the winter by tractor wheels that had since dried out into hard ridges, so she walked, pushing the bike and propping it up at intervals against the hedge while she searched the spinney. But there was no sign of him.

The belt of trees ended and, at this point, the lane forked, broadening out into a cart track, one arm of it turning to the left to lead back towards Bateson's farm, the other branch leading off downhill to the right, following the slope of the land and running between high hedges that cut off any view of the surrounding fields.

After hesitating again, Maggie set off along it, pushing her bike, her confidence beginning to seep away. She couldn't imagine Chris finding his way along here in the dark. Or did he have a torch? It was possible he had one in his rucksack. All the same, she felt committed to taking this route. There was no point in turning back.

I'll go as far as the old quarry, she told herself, surprised at remembering its existence. It was years since she'd been there; not since her childhood, in fact, when it had been one of the good places to explore on the outskirts of the village. It had seemed enormous to her then: a great, irregular bowl cut out of the ground, overgrown with bushes and small trees through which narrow paths led down to the bottom where, in wet weather, there was always a shallow pool of water, marvellous for sliding on in the winter.

It lay just off the path, in the corner of a field, its rim hidden by great, tangled heaps of blackberry bushes, trailing long brambles on which the hard, green fruits were already forming. Propping her bike up against one of them, she approached the edge and looked down.

It was smaller than she remembered and now almost filled to the brim with undergrowth, although it was still possible to discern the faint traces of paths that led downwards, following the contours of the quarried sides.

One of the paths opened on her left, a narrow gap between a hawthorn and another blackberry bush that had sprawled together, closing the gap.

But not quite. She noticed that some of the brambles had been lifted to one side, exposing the whitish undersides of the leaves.

Maggie looked quickly about her, making sure there was no one in sight. Going back to the bike, she retrieved the bag of provisions and then carefully inched herself sideways through the tiny opening.

It was only when she was halfway down the slope, slithering on smooth grass in places, hanging onto the low branches of trees to help her down the steepest parts, that she saw the orange flash of his tent between the leaves close to the bottom.

The sound of someone approaching awoke Chris. For a few seconds, he lay on his back in the sleeping bag, looking up at the orange canvas above him, bright with sunlight and spattered with the moving shadows of branches, wondering what the sharp crackle of breaking twigs could mean. The next moment, he was out of the bag and struggling to put on his shirt and trousers in the confined space. Unzipping the tent opening, he ducked outside just as Maggie, one hand on the ground to steady herself, clambered awkwardly down a bank of hazel scrub and emerged onto the flat shelf of grass where he had pitched his tent.

His appearance shocked her. He hadn't shaved and his face had a wild, dark, famished look.

"It's me, Chris," she said gently. She stood uncertainly, clutching the bag of provisions, knowing from his expression that she wasn't welcome.

"What the hell do you want?" he asked furiously.

His anger distressed and yet, at the same time, comforted her. If he had killed Jess Lambert, wouldn't his reaction more likely be one of fear?

"I've brought you some food and your camping stove," she explained. "I thought you might need them."

Squatting down on her haunches, she began to unpack the bag, laying out its contents on the grass in front of him, like some bloody peasant in a bazaar, he thought with exasperation. All the same, he was touched by the care with which she arranged them, first his shirt, neatly folded, then his socks, rolled one inside the other, then the food, lastly the camping stove, wrapped in newspaper, and the blue plastic thermos flask which he remembered taking to the currant field.

"Come on, eat," Maggie was telling him, opening a packet of sandwiches and offering them to him. But there was none of the usual authoritativeness in her voice. She seemed subdued and tired, as if the fire had died out in her. Her eyes had sunk back like a much older woman's and he noticed the dark bruise on her cheekbone and guessing how it had come there, he felt ashamed.

"I'm sorry, Maggie," he said humbly.

She knew what he meant and felt ashamed, too.

"It's all right, Chris," she assured him and, to cover up her embarrassment, flourished the packet of sandwiches. "Come on. Eat something. You must be starving."

"I am," he admitted and took one, thinking that at least food always made some sort of bond between them.

"How did you find your way here in the dark?" Maggie asked, looking about her. Now that the first tension of the meeting had passed, they were both more relaxed and ready to talk; but not yet, she felt, on the main reason for her visit. Anyway, she was dreading having to put it into words.

Death. And meanwhile the sun was making the leaves above their heads transparent and Chris was sitting cross-legged on the grass in front of her, eating a cheese sandwich and drinking coffee out of the blue thermos mug. It seemed perfectly natural to Maggie, only a more idyllic extension of their already established relationship, with the familiar act of sitting opposite him and watching him eat transported to another setting. It was the fact of Jess Lambert's murder that was crazy and incongruous.

"I didn't," he replied. "I got as far as the wood just up the lane and I slept there for the night. At least, I tried to. I didn't bother putting up the tent. I just got into the sleeping bag. As soon as it was light, I moved on here."

"But why?"

"Why?"

The question caught him off guard. "I don't know. I saw the bushes and thought it would make a good camping site. It was only when I walked across to it, I realised it was a quarry." He paused and added a little lamely, "It seemed sheltered."

Safe, he admitted to himself. He looked about him, acknowledging for the first time the true motives that had sent him clambering down the side of the quarry in the grey dawn light that morning. The psychiatrist would have something to say about it, he thought wryly. An animal going to ground. A return to the womb. An atavistic longing to penetrate downwards, below the surface, and cover yourself up with leaves. The old babes-in-the-wood syndrome. I'm a bloody fool.

"You'll have to come back," Maggie said abruptly. "They're looking for you."

He glanced up at her in surprise.

"Who are?"

She began to cry.

"Maggie?"

He scrambled round on his knees to her side and

touched her on the shoulder, feeling a sudden protective urge towards her. She's vulnerable, too, he thought with an angry pity that shocked him. She has no right to be, although even as he thought it, he knew he wasn't being fair.

"Oh, Christ!" Maggie was saying in a despairing wail, wiping her eyes inelegantly on the bottom edge of her blouse. She had meant to be calm and gentle, telling him what had happened in a controlled way, playing it down. Instead, it came pouring out in broken sentences, almost incoherently.

As he listened, she saw his expression change from bewilderment to disbelief and then, frighteningly, his whole face seemed to disintegrate. His mouth fell open and began to shake, his eyes squeezed up very small, their lids trembling, and a series of convulsive shudders ran through his whole body.

He scrambled away from her with an odd, rolling movement and, clutching his stomach, ran towards the bushes behind the tent where she could hear him vomiting.

Unable to move, she sat helpless, shocked and frightened by the violence of his reaction.

"Chris?" she asked falteringly after a few seconds. He half turned his head.

"There's a . . . bottle . . . tablets," he gasped out. "Front pocket . . . rucksack . . . in the tent."

Crawling inside the tent, she found the rucksack lying beside his sleeping bag. The straps fastening the pocket were stiff and she struggled with increasing panic and exasperation to get them undone. At last they yielded and, plunging her hand inside, she found a small glass tube containing white tablets. With it clutched in her hand, she emerged backwards on all fours out of the low opening of the tent.

Chris was sitting on the grass near where she had placed the contents of the bag, his arms folded across his knees and his head resting on them. He looked up as she approached, revealing a face that was greenish white, stiff like a mask, in which his two eyes stared at her with a dreadful, sick, helpless look, like an animal on the point of death.

She placed the phial in his hands, watching as he opened it and shook out two tablets, which he swallowed with the dregs of coffee in the plastic mug, throwing his head back to get them down, the muscles in his throat contracting painfully.

"Tranquillisers," he explained.

"You're ill," she protested. "You can't stay here on your own. You must come back with me, Chris."

"I can't," he replied. He lay back on the grass, his arms behind his head, staring up at the leaves. "I didn't murder that girl, Maggie, but they'll never believe me."

"Of course they will," she said futilely. "They'll have to. I said you stayed in your room yesterday evening."

Something like amusement glinted under his half-closed lids.

"Don't perjure yourself for me," he replied. "I'm not worth it. They'll find out I met her soon enough anyway."

They probably guessed it already, he thought. He couldn't imagine Maggie, with her almost obsessive regard for the truth, making a very convincing liar.

"Then come back and tell them what really happened," Maggie argued. "They'll believe you."

"Will they?"

"But if it's the truth . . ."

"The truth!" He laughed abruptly. "Oh, Maggie, dear Maggie, you don't understand. If I told them the truth about myself they'd be even more likely to believe I killed her."

She was silent, not knowing what to answer, realising for the first time how little she knew about him.

"Tell me," she pleaded.

He shook his head.

"I can't, Maggie. I'm sorry."

"Why not? Do you think I wouldn't understand?"

In her eagerness, she had crept nearer to him until she was kneeling at his side.

"It's not that," he replied. "I can't tell you; not yet. It's still too close. And, besides, I'm too ashamed."

The last word struck her as strange. Ashamed? Why ashamed? She searched his face but it had taken on that closed, secret look that it had worn when he first came to stay with her. His eyes were turned upwards, fixed on the leaves of the birch sapling above him with a curious, concentrated intensity, as if he were trying to penetrate their thin, green membranes, made translucent by the sun.

He was aware of her presence even though he wouldn't

look at her. She loomed beside him, just inside the circle of his consciousness, and he felt the concern and distress pouring out of her.

But, thank God, it was distanced, he thought. The pills had begun to work, gently circulating through his bloodstream, slowing down his reactions, dimming his awareness, so that he seemed to float in a pleasant, warm, muffled world, familiar from his days in the clinic where nothing much mattered anymore, except the leaves, with their fragile tracery of veins, and the little patches of blue sky he could see beyond them.

Maggie had begun scrambling to her feet.

"If you're not coming back . . ." she began.

"No, Maggie," he said slowly, slurring out the words.

"I'll go then."

He turned his head and looked at her.

"Thanks," he said.

"Take care," she added.

He watched as she walked away.

Poor old Maggie, he thought. A kind of tenderness came over him. She was struggling up the bank, hauling herself upwards by the low branches of the scrub, scattering leaves as she went, her broad backside stuck out, her hair tumbling down, her strong shoulders stretching the cotton fabric of her blouse almost to bursting point.

Ridiculous and lovable and loyal, he thought hazily. He wanted to call her back but he didn't have the energy to form her name out loud.

Then she had gone, although he could still hear her crashing her way to the top. After a few more minutes, there was silence and, rolling over on his side and putting his arms over his head, he dropped into oblivion.

Maggie reached the edge of the quarry and paused to look back, reassuring herself that there was no sign of his tent visible from above. Stepping sideways through the gap, she closed the brambles behind her, trailing them carefully over the opening. It was all she could do for him.

Retrieving her bike, she set off again along the lane, thinking distractedly, what will he do? The food she had brought would last, at most, two days. Would he move on after that? Or would he stay? If he stayed, there was a good chance that he would be found.

She knew she daren't return to the quarry. It was too

risky. She might be seen and unwittingly lead the police to his hiding place. On the other hand, it seemed unthinkable to return to the house and not know what became of him.

Reaching the fork in the lane, she paused. To return home by the way she had come seemed dangerous. Someone might see her climbing over the stile from the footpath and report it to the police, if they didn't themselves see her. The only alternative was to go straight on up the cart track that led into the back of Bateson's yard. Calling on Bateson would, at least, give her a reason for being out; he was, after all, one of her tenants and she could easily think up an excuse for her visit—the gate that needed replacing in one of the fields he was renting from her would serve as one. Even so, it involved a certain amount of risk. If Bateson saw her coming by the lane instead of the road, it might rouse his suspicions; not that she thought he'd say anything.

She was aware suddenly of the danger Chris was in and the futility of his attempt to hide. They'd find him sooner or later. They were bound to. She'd seen news pictures on the television of a police search: dozens of men spread out across an area, moving forward with a slow but deadly earnestness.

What should she do? Turn left or go straight on? She stood in an agony of indecision, frightened that, at any moment, a long, similar line of men might be working its way across the field towards her. Her own vulnerability occurred to her, too, for the first time. What would they call it? Harbouring a known criminal? Perverting the course of justice? There'd be some high-sounding phrase to describe what she was doing.

Strangely, this thought steadied her.

I don't bloody well care, she told herself briskly and made up her mind. She'd go straight on, call in on Bateson, chat with him about the gate, as if this were the reason for her visit. And if Rudd found out, she'd look him straight in the eyes and tell him so.

She began tidying up her appearance, bundling her hair up at the back and brushing pieces of torn leaves from her clothes. Then, seizing the bike firmly by the handlebars, she set off down the track towards the farm.

Luck was with her. Bateson was round at the back of the barn, gloomily peering into the engine of a tractor, and didn't notice her arrival. He was a small, energetic, dried-up man, closer to her parents' generation than her own, bow-legged from his days as an amateur point-to-point rider, and still preserving in the tweed hacking jacket and flat cap that he wore, a faint aroma of horses and stables. An odd kind of intimacy existed between him and Maggie. Although she had known him all her life, they rarely spoke to one another except on farming or business matters and it was from the gossip of others, not from him, that she found out about the deep bitterness that had soured his reationship with his only son who ran the farm with him and had tried every trick in the book to get old Bateson to retire.

Propping her bike up against the barn wall, Maggie walked casually across to speak to him.

He looked up, an expression of recognition and welcome on his face that quickly turned to one of embarrassed wariness.

"Oh, it's you, Maggie," he said. He sounded as uncomfortable as he looked.

Maggie had known him for too long to be anything but direct with him.

"Something's up, Will. What is it?"

"Nothing."

He pretended to be busy wiping his hands on a bit of oily rag.

"You might as well tell me," Maggie said firmly. "You've always been straightforward with me in the past."

"All right then," he replied. "It's best you knew, anyway: It's the police. They've been here, asking about that young man who's been staying with you. Doing a house-to-house inquiry, they said, right through the village and calling at all the farms."

It came as a shock to her even though she knew they'd be looking for him.

"When was this?" she asked sharply.

"About half an hour ago."

It was as much as she could do to stop herself looking back over her shoulder in the direction of the quarry.

"What did they want?"

"They asked if I'd seen anyone answering his description passing the farm or camping on my land. I told them no."

"So they've gone?" she said with relief.

"For the time being. They said they'd be back later and make a search of the fields." He made a helpless gesture with the hand that held the rag. "What could I do, Maggie? I had to agree even though . . ."

He broke off, unable to find the words to express his sense of loyalty that should have prevented him from giving his permission. His face was tuckered into long lines of concern.

Maggie, understanding, nodded quickly in reassurance.

"But there's nowhere much on your farm anyone could camp without being seen, is there?" she asked disingenuously, thinking that, if Bateson mentioned the quarry, she'd take the risk of going back and warning Chris.

Bateson shrugged.

"Not many places," he agreed. "There's the spinney but that won't take much searching. The rest of it's open fields. They'd spot anyone with a tent a mile off."

"It won't matter if they do find him," Maggie assured him, trying to sound off hand. "He didn't do it. He was . . ."

She was about to tell him the same falsehood that she had told Rudd, that Chris had been in his room the previous evening, but she couldn't bring herself to do it.

". . . he's not the sort," she finished lamely. "I know him. He could no more kill somebody than I could."

"Oh ah," Bateson said noncommittally, not wanting to be drawn into any partisan agreement. "But the fact is, Maggie, people in the village are going to think he did. It stands to reason they will. He's a stranger, an outsider. He turns up here, from God knows where, and then Jess Lambert's found murdered. What else are they going to make of it?"

"They think I shouldn't have taken him in?" Maggie asked sharply. For the first time she was aware that the local people were critical, perhaps even hostile, to her decision, an attitude that had been implied in Aston's grin.

"I dunno what they think," Bateson mumbled, although she could tell by the way he ducked his head that he knew of such talk.

"But I only gave him a room for a few nights!" Maggie

cried, although she saw how it must look to the rest of them. She, a middle-aged spinster, offering lodging to a young man off the road! What had they made of that?

With this awareness came the realisation that she had never properly belonged, although she had been born and brought up in the place. Some gulf separated her from everyone else. Perhaps it was this that had ultimately divided her from her father—an unconventionality and an unwillingness to conform.

"Anyway, I don't give a damn what they say," she added defiantly. "Let them gossip as much as they like."

"They'll do that right enough," Bateson agreed. "Look at the talk there was when the Lamberts first moved here."

"Yes, I know," Maggie replied. Her anger had subsided, leaving her subdued and depressed, and with this dejection came the first stirring of sympathy for the Lamberts. Until that moment, all her compassion had been directed towards Chris. She had remained relatively unmoved by the murder except as it affected him. Now she saw the dead girl as someone like herself—an outsider, an object of gossip and criticism, someone who didn't belong.

We're a trio, she thought sadly. Chris and Jess and me. Lambert, too, in a way, although she found it more difficult to identify with that silent, taciturn man.

"Mind you, it's Lambert I feel sorry for in all this," Bateson was saying, as if he had been aware of her thoughts. "He thought the world of that daughter of his and he's got no one left now, except the child. I've gotten to know him quite well; as well as anyone can, that is. He's not an easy man to get along with. But he's been rough-shooting with me a few times . . ."

"I didn't know that," Maggie broke in.

"It's no secret," Bateson said a little defensively. "I just haven't had any call to talk about it. But I speak as I find and I got to like him in a funny sort of way."

"Yes, he's a lonely man," Maggie said, distractedly. She was beginning to find the conversation disquieting and wanted to cut it short. Bateson's remarks had brought home to her the full implications of Jess Lambert's death; not just Chris's involvement in it, but what it meant for the others who were concerned, for Lambert and for the child who would now be motherless.

"I must go," she said hurriedly.

Bateson looked surprised.

"What was it you called about?" he asked.

"Oh, yes," she said, remembering that the whole purpose of the visit was to establish a reason for her being in the area in case she was seen. "It's about the gate to that field you're renting. I'll put in an order for a new one if you and Dick can put it up between you."

"I'll have a word with him," Bateson said carefully, giving nothing away.

It would probably lead to a row, she thought as she got on her bike and pedalled furiously up the road. Oh hell and damn! It was all collapsing round her, the safe, warm world she thought she inhabited. Or perhaps it had never existed except in her imagination.

Take Bateson and his son as an example. Or Vi and Ken Aston . . .

But her mind shied away from thinking about them. She still felt guilty about the hint she had dropped to Rudd about someone else seeing Jess Lambert, not that the inspector would know who she was talking about. She had said it without thinking, hoping to draw him off the scent. But if it wasn't Chris who had killed her, and Maggie was convinced that he had been speaking the truth when he had denied it, then who had?

It was a question she hadn't asked herself until that moment. Her mind had been too confused with memories of Chris's face and raised arm to think beyond them to another's guilt.

Oh, God, it just gets worse, she thought despairingly, and, pressing down on the pedals, tried, with the energy of desperation, to ride away from the new frightening thoughts that came crowding into her mind.

8

Following Deakin's directions, Rudd drove through the village to Aston's market garden and, parking the car on the forecourt, went off in search of Aston himself.

He found him in the yard at the back of the packing shed, supervising the loading of boxes and crates onto a lorry. For a few moments, Rudd stood unobserved, watching the activity. He had no difficulty in picking out Aston. He was the man obviously in charge who was standing at the tail board, checking off the crates from an order sheet he was holding in his hand.

He was a large, broad-shouldered, good-looking man, with an immediate animal attractiveness and the kind of easy, physical assurance that would be appealing to a certain type of woman. At the moment, though, he was surly and bad-tempered, shouting at the two men who were loading the lorry to get a move on, they hadn't got all bloody morning.

The fact was he was frightened. The news of Jess Lambert's murder had shaken him badly. He had heard it from Fraser, the man who had taken Deakin home, and he had passed it on with the slightly pleased air of someone bringing bad tidings.

The implications of it weren't lost on Aston. He knew there would be a police investigation, that people would be questioned and he was afraid that, sooner or later, his name would be mentioned in connection with the girl. Reg Deakin probably knew, or guessed, although Aston didn't think he'd talk. But there might be others.

He'd been a fool ever to get mixed up with her, he told himself. He should have known it would only lead to trouble.

As for Vi, Aston had pretty well convinced himself that

she knew nothing. She couldn't. She'd've made more of a scene about it if she had, like the time she found out about the woman from Watleigh he was knocking about with. True, she'd been a bit short with him recently but that was nothing new. She was always bloody griping on about something.

So the chances were it'd be all right, Aston thought.

Glancing up from the order sheet, he suddenly noticed a man standing at the corner of the packing shed; a stocky man, a bit round-shouldered, with a careless, rumpled look, and yet with an air of quiet, watchful authority that didn't suggest a customer or a caller. He was there on official business and Aston, with a great lurch of fear, guessed what it was.

Rudd, who was aware that Aston had seen him, saw the change of expression that immediately came over his face. It was a wary look, hostile and at the same time guilty, and Rudd knew that the man not only had something to hide but that it wasn't going to be easy to get him to admit to anything.

"Mr. Aston?" he asked pleasantly, stepping forward. "I'm Detective Inspector Rudd. I wonder if you would mind answering a few questions?"

"What about?" Aston asked in a churlish voice.

Rudd didn't reply but gave a significant look at the two other men. Aston, taking the hint, handed the order sheet to one of them and, telling them to carry on, jerked his head towards the packing shed, inviting Rudd to follow him inside.

"I've come about the murder of Jess Lambert," Rudd said, once they were out of earshot of the yard.

"Oh, yes?" Aston replied guardedly.

"Don't you know about it?" Rudd asked, surprised by his lack of response. He must know. Lambert was his foreman and Aston had surely asked why he hadn't turned up for work. Someone must have told him. There had been time for the news to circulate round the village.

"Yes, I'd heard," Aston said. "One of my men told me first thing this morning." There was an air of offhandedness about him that Rudd guessed was largely assumed. "What can I do to help you?"

The inspector hesitated. It had been his intention to confront Aston straightaway with the gossip concerning him and Jess Lambert. Now he wasn't so sure. It would be better, perhaps, to put the man more at his ease before asking the crucial question.

"I believe Mr. Lambert, the girl's father, works for you?" he said.

"That's right. He's not in today, though; not that I was surprised when I heard what had happened. . . ."

"I understand he's taken the child to his sister's in Norfolk," Rudd explained. "As a matter of fact, it's the child I wanted to check up on. I believe you took Mr. Lambert on as foreman just over a year ago?"

"Fifteen months," Aston corrected him. He was visibly relaxing, leaning against the long bench that ran the length of the shed with an almost negligent attitude.

"And the daughter was already pregnant when they moved here?"

"I suppose she must have been," Aston replied with a shrug that implied the unspoken comment, "So what?" "She had the kid about seven months later. Lambert hinted that something like that might be in the offing when he came here for an interview."

"What did he say?"

"Not a lot. He explained he was changing jobs because there'd been a bit of personal trouble and he wanted to make a fresh start. I tumbled to the reason soon after they moved here. Anyone could see she was in pod."

He grinned broadly.

"He came from Suffolk originally?"

"That's right. He'd been working at Babcock's; that's a nursery garden at Ashbourne, just outside Sudbury." He paused and then asked curiously, "What's all this leading up to?"

Why not tell him? Rudd thought. It would do no harm. Besides, it might lead Aston to think that the police were on to another line of inquiry unconnected with him.

"I wondered if the girl had kept in touch with the child's father. Lambert's not said anything to you about it, I suppose?"

Aston's expression brightened, although he shrugged and pretended indifference.

"Not to me. But he's not very forthcoming at the best of times. I suppose she could have done, though."

"No gossip about a man turning up in the village at any time?" Rudd hinted.

"Only that camper of Maggie's," Aston replied. His grin widened. "And I don't reckon it was him."

"Oh, why not?" Rudd asked, genuinely interested. It was clear Aston knew nothing about Lambert's accusation against Chris and didn't suspect that Jess Lambert might have had another boy friend other than himself. Protective egoism, Rudd thought. Aston would see himself as the only cock of the walk. It would be interesting, though, to find out his opinion of Chris Lawrence.

"A bit too la-di-dah, if you ask me," Aston explained.

"Not her type?"

"I wouldn't have thought so."

"You think she'd be attracted to someone a bit more—well, manly?" He paused fractionally before adding, "Someone more like yourself, Mr. Aston?"

It gave Rudd a lot of quiet satisfaction to see the grin wiped off Aston's face, although, to give the man his due, he made an effort to fight back.

"I don't know what the hell you're talking about. If anyone's been gossiping . . ."

"People always gossip," Rudd replied in a sad, philosophical tone which he followed up much more briskly with the question, "What were you doing last night, Mr. Aston?"

"Me? Why me?"

He sounded astounded.

"We're checking up on everyone's movements," Rudd said reassuringly.

"I was at home," Aston replied sullenly.

"All evening?"

Aston hesitated, wondering whether to lie or not and then deciding not to risk it. Too many people had seen him, at the Rose and Crown as well as the White Hart in Gossbridge. Then there was Vi. Not that Aston thought she'd let him down deliberately but, if Rudd questioned her separately, she might come out with the truth.

"No, I went out for a while," he admitted reluctantly.

"At what time?"

Rudd had produced a notebook with an official, businesslike air and waited, pencil poised. Aston eyed it uncomfortably and ran his tongue over his lips.

"About ten past nine, but I couldn't swear to it being exact."

Rudd made a note of it and then cocked his head inquiringly. "And where did you go?"

"I called in at the Rose for a short time."

"How long?"

"I don't know for sure; long enough to drink a couple of pints."

"Say half an hour?"

"Near enough, I suppose," Aston conceded grudgingly.

"And then?"

"I drove on to Gossbridge and had a few more at the White Hart."

"Did you have any particular reason?"

"I don't get you."

"I mean," Rudd explained patiently, "that you'd already had a couple of drinks at the Rose. Why did you leave there and go on to the Hart? Were you meeting someone?"

"No, I . . ." Aston stopped, realising the trap that was opening up at his feet. He daren't give the real reason why he had been out the previous evening—that he was hoping to meet Jess Lambert and have a talk with her—but it might look suspicious if he offered no explanation. "I decided to call on Maggie Hearn," he said quickly, "for a chat about a field I'm going to rent off her but she was out. So, instead of bothering to turn the car round, I drove on to Gossbridge."

"You're sure Miss Hearn was out?" Rudd asked. The information surprised him. She had said nothing to him about leaving the house the previous evening but there was a lot he suspected she hadn't told him.

"Yes, quite sure," Aston replied. "The back door was unlocked so I went inside to make certain. She wasn't anywhere about."

"I see," Rudd said noncommittally. It was something he'd have to check with Maggie later, along with a lot of other things.

"How long did you stay at Miss Hearn's?" Rudd went on, picking up Aston's account again.

"Only a few minutes; maybe five. Then I drove on to Gossbridge and stayed at the White Hart until closing time."

"Did you pass anybody on the way?"

"No, not that I noticed. It was getting dark by then."

"You didn't see Jess Lambert?"

"No, I've already told you, I didn't see anybody. Look, what is all this?" Aston suddenly burst out. "Some kind of third degree?"

"Not at all," Rudd said blandly. "I'm simply checking on the movements of anyone who knew the dead girl. You did know her, I assume?"

"Well, yes, in a way. I mean, she was Lambert's daughter and I'd seen her about the village . . ." Aston began. The old confident swagger had gone and he looked curiously diminished, as if he had shrunk up into himself.

"I think you knew her a lot better than that," Rudd told him with the assured manner of someone who has irrefutable proof. "I believe you were in the habit of calling on her. There's no point in denying it, Mr. Aston," Rudd added, "unless you're prepared to sign an official statement to that effect and that, of course, is a serious matter."

The implied threat worked. Aston ran a hand uncertainly over his hair and then came to a decision.

"All right," he admitted, "maybe I did a few times but I swear to God that's all."

"Did you see her yesterday dinnertime?"

"Yes, I dropped by her place for a short while. As a matter of fact, I told her it'd be the last time. I'd finished."

"How did she take it?"

"Take it?"

Aston looked round despearately as if searching for an escape. It had only just occurred to him exactly what he had let himself in for by admitting that he'd seen the girl on the day she was murdered. The half-veiled threats she had made and his own fears that the affair might be discovered gave him, he realised now, a motive for murder.

"She didn't say much," he muttered.

"She didn't make a scene?"

"No, she just said all right, she supposed it was for the best . . ."

He broke off, his eyes going beyond Rudd to the open doorway. Rudd, turning to follow his gaze, saw a woman standing just inside the shed. She was big-boned, like Aston, but unlike him had not kept her looks, although it was possible to see in the tired, coarsened features the vestiges, not of prettiness, but at least of a certain bold handsomeness that must have been striking when she was young.

She moved towards them walking with a heavy, flat-footed manner, the expression on her face changing quickly from suspicion as she looked at Rudd, to a hard, bright look of triumph that was directed towards her husband.

"The wife," Aston mumbled, feeling obliged to make some sort of introduction. "I didn't see you standing there, Vi," he added, addressing her. "Been there long?"

He glanced at her sideways with a strange, furtive appeal.

"Long enough," she said ominously. "What's he want?" she went on, indicating Rudd with an abrupt movement of her head.

"It's the police, Vi," Aston explained, shocked by her offhand attitude. "He's come about . . ."

"I know what he's come about," Vi interrupted him. She turned to Rudd. "It's about Jess Lambert, isn't it? Found murdered this morning—isn't that what you want to tell us? Well, it's old news as far as I'm concerned."

"You've heard about it?"

It was Aston who asked the question, rather to Rudd's surprise.

"Yes, the women told me when they knocked on for work this morning," she said briefly before returning to Rudd. "And I can't say I'm surprised or sorry. She probably asked for it."

Rudd suddenly understood the situation. It was evident in her shrill, angry voice. She knew of Aston's association with the girl although Rudd doubted if Aston was aware of it himself. Like many other good-looking married men who found it easy to have casual relationships with women, he had built up a protective shell against the humiliation of discovery by pretending it could never happen to him. But, underneath the self-assurance, Aston was a badly frightened man; afraid not only of his implication in the death of Jess Lambert but of his wife finding out about his relationship with her. That was why he hadn't shared the news of her death, leaving her to find it out from someone else. It was a stupid, ostrichlike attitude but, Rudd guessed, Aston was probably a stupid man, at least where his own self-gratification was concerned.

"Well," Vi was asking accusingly, confronting Rudd

with her hands on her hips, "What do you want with *him?*"

She had moved nearer to Aston, unconsciously implying where her loyalties lay, and had taken up a position slightly in front of him, like a mother defending her child from attack. Her tone of voice suggested the same attitude. It was angrily protective and yet, at the same time, a little contemptuous as if he were incapable of standing up for himself.

Rudd decided it was time he asserted himself.

"I'm checking up on Mr. Aston's movements yesterday evening," he told her bluntly and, so that she shouldn't miss the point, he added, "at the time Jess Lambert may have been murdered."

"He was home here with me," she said, as quick as a flash.

It was a brave attempt. She was quicker witted than he suspected, Rudd thought.

Aston, whose face had flushed up at this encounter between his wife and the inspector, stepped forward to intervene.

"It's no good, Vi. He knows I went out last night."

"Who told him?" she asked belligerently.

"I did."

"What the hell did you want to do that for?"

"Because there's no reason why I bloody shouldn't!" Aston shouted. Now that the attack had moved to him he seemed to recover some of his assurance. "I didn't have anything to do with the murder. I had a few drinks, that's all."

"Yes! Going off boozing! That's all you're fit for . . ."

Rudd, who could see a domestic quarrel brewing, moved off towards the door. He had found out enough for his present inquiry. To witness a row between husband and wife wouldn't add anything of much relevance.

"I may have to call again another time," he announced but he doubted if either of them heard him. They had turned to face one another like a pair of boxers squaring up in a ring.

Walking back across the yard, he considered what he had found out. Aston's confession that he had been having an affair with Jess Lambert and had been away from home at the time she might have been murdered put him in the running, next to Chris Lawrence, as a suspect. It gave him

a possible motive and opportunity as well. His story would
have to be checked, of course, at the Rose and Crown and
the White Hart and the times verified as far as they could
be but, by Aston's own account, they were only approxi-
mate. It wouldn't take more than five or ten minutes to kill
the girl and dispose of her body. Besides, on his way to
Gossbridge, he'd have to pass the Lamberts' bungalow. He
could have met her then as she was walking home from
her date with Chris Lawrence. The motive was obvious—
to keep her quiet, for Rudd didn't for a moment believe
that Jess had taken the ending of the affair as calmly as
Lambert had tried to make out. That part of his story
hadn't even begun to sound convincing. There had been
some sort of scene; of that he was sure. Had she threat-
ened him? It was possible.

But, in considering Aston's account. Rudd was aware
that two other suspects had now entered the picture: Vi,
Aston's wife, and Maggie Hearn.

Maggie Hearn he was less sure about. There didn't
appear to be any convincing reason why she should want
the girl dead but it was significant that she had been away
from home when Aston called. He worked out a rough
estimate of the timing. If Aston had stayed at the Rose
and Crown for half an hour, then he would have called at
the farm at approximately a quarter to ten, between the
hours of nine o'clock and midnight, which was when
Pardoe reckoned the girl had died. So Maggie had no alibi
to cover at least part of that crucial time.

Neither, of course, had Vi Aston and she had a better
motive for murdering Jess Lambert than Maggie Hearn.
He had seen enough during the interview to convince him
that she knew of the affair between her husband and the
girl and of her animosity towards Jess Lambert. It had
been too strong for Vi Aston to pretend even pity for
her. With Aston out of the house, it was possible she
had been left alone, with no one to check on her movements.

He paused halfway across the yard and, ignoring the
curious glances of the men who were still loading the
lorry, walked back towards the garage that faced the
packing shed. Its doors were open and a large blue
Vauxhall could be seen parked inside it: Aston's car,
judging by the man's jacket that was lying on the front

seat. Beside it stood a green mini, dusty and a little battered.

"Mrs. Aston's car?" he asked one of the men, who, after a surprised look at his companion, nodded in agreement. Without further comment, Rudd walked away.

So Vi Aston had transport, should she want to go out on her own, and it wouldn't take more than a few minutes to drive from the market garden to the far side of the village.

No, she certainly couldn't be ruled out, Rudd decided, which left five possible suspects: Chris Lawrence, the Astons, the child's father—whoever he was—and Maggie Hearn.

Aston's remarks concerning Lambert confirmed the story that he had already heard from Cookson: that Jess Lambert was pregnant when they moved to the village, so there was no likelihood that the father was a local man. But that didn't rule out the possibility that she had kept in touch with him. Although neither Cookson nor Aston had heard of a stranger being seen about, it was feasible that they'd met surreptitiously, without even Lambert knowing about it. After all, it was only an hour's drive from Sudbury.

But, out of them all, Chris Lawrence still led the field and it was high time, Rudd thought, as he got into the car and headed back towards the village, that he had another go at Maggie Hearn and got her to admit to exactly what Chris had been doing the previous evening. At the same time, he could try to find out if she could have any possible motive for the murder.

The quarrel that Rudd had seen on the point of breaking out between the Astons exploded as soon as he was out of earshot.

"You bloody fool!" Vi shouted. "What the hell have you been playing at!"

"I told you. I went out for a drink," he began.

"I'm not talking about your boozing," Vi retorted. "That's the least of it. It's the other things you've been up to."

She didn't dare say too much in case she gave away the fact that, after he had slunk out of the house last night, she had gone down to the Rose and Crown to check up on him. Although she had found his car in the car park, it hadn't altogether allayed her suspicions. He could have stopped for a drink before going on to meet the little bitch. Not that she dared admit it. He often argued that what he did in his spare time was none of her business.

"I don't know what you're talking about," Aston said contemptuously and began walking deliberately away from her towards the door. But Vi had no intention of being shrugged off in this way. Running after him, she grabbed at his arm.

"You'll bloody well listen to me for once!" she told him. "I'm not going to be taken in with a pack of lies this time."

Aston decided to lose his temper. It was a trick that usually worked. It gave him the advantage of attack and put her on the defensive.

"Lies?" he shouted, pushing his face toward hers. "You'd better watch what you're saying. One of these days you'll open that fat trap of yours a bit too far."

She stepped back to avoid him but instead of bursting into angry, frightened tears, which was what usually happened, after which he would put his arm round her and some kind of reconciliation would follow, she remained dangerously quiet.

"It's not lies," she said, "and you know it. You've been seeing that girl, calling in at the house while her father's been at work."

He felt his anger die down although he tried to keep it going.

"Who told you that tale? I'll bloody smash . . ."

"Nobody told me."

"You were listening at the bloody door, then."

"I knew long before that," Vi replied. She gave a little laugh that he didn't much like the sound of. It was dismissive, as if what he had been doing no longer had any importance for her. "You're not that clever, Ken, although you may think you are."

"All right, so I saw her a few times," Aston agreed, realising further denial was useless. "But it didn't mean anything, Vi—honest."

"Not to you, maybe."

"What d'you mean by that?"

He came closer to her, coaxingly, but she shrank away from the contact.

"Nothing. It doesn't matter anymore," she said, in a

tired voice. She felt too weary to dredge up the rest of it and, besides, what was the point? He wouldn't understand her feelings. It wasn't in him. She could see she'd be wasting her time explaining.

"What are you going to do?" he asked a little anxiously but, even so, with a cocky brightness in his eyes, not really believing she would do anything.

And he's probably right, Vi thought. She certainly couldn't leave him now, not with the police investigation hanging over his head. Some loyalty remained, if not to the man he was now, then at least to the man he used to be, who had come courting her with his hair combed flat and his cheeks freshly shaved, or who had creaked into the hospital the time she had her third miscarriage clutching a bunch of flowers, and who had cried with her when the doctors told them she could never have a child.

They would jog along somehow, she supposed, as they'd done for years and, from time to time, he'd find himself another woman. She didn't expect that to change. The most she could hope for was that he'd go about it a bit more cleverly. Perhaps he'd learnt that much.

"I'll make it up to you, Vi," he was saying. "We'll go over to Watleigh Saturday night and have a meal out at the Steakhouse. How does that suit you, eh?"

Buying me off, Vi thought. And, bloody hell, why not?

"All right," she agreed. "I'll take Friday afternoon off and have my hair done."

"Yes, you do that!"

He had put his arm round her and was squeezing her shoulder, laughing like a little boy because everything was all right again. Even Rudd was forgotten in his relief.

Christ, he's hopeless, Vi said to herself. But I'm bloody well stuck with him now.

9

Returning to the centre of the village, Rudd saw that the mobile canteen had arrived and had been set up on the wide grass verge outside the village hall. Boyce was already there, receiving reports from the men as they returned from the house-to-house inquiries. Rudd parked the car and joined him.

"Any luck?" he asked.

"Not so far," Boyce admitted. "But there's still a couple more to come in from the Gossbridge side. I don't get it," he went on in an aggrieved voice. "At eight o'clock it was still light and there were plenty of people about; kids even playing on the swings over there."

He nodded towards the small recreational field that ran alongside the hall, part of which had been equipped as a children's playground. "Unless, of course, he didn't come through the village but turned off before he got to it."

"Or unless Maggie Hearn was lying about the time," Rudd replied. And about a lot more else besides, he suspected. "I'm going to see her this afternoon to check on her story."

Another car drew up as they were talking and Boyce went across to speak to the occupants. He came back looking gloomy.

"That's the last of the men on the house-to-house and they've got nothing to report either. So what do we do now? Start searching the fields?"

"It looks like it," Rudd agreed.

Boyce's gloom deepened.

"It'll be a hell of a job."

"Not as bad as all that," Rudd told him. "We'll get Henty and the dog handlers in on it. They may be able to pick up a trail from the farm. Even if they don't find him, we may be able to get some idea of the general direction he took and that'll narrow the area down a little. Any response to the other question, about a stranger or a car seen about the place?"

"Nothing on that-either," Boyce replied. "If you ask me, that line of inquiry's a dead loss."

"Well, we'll see," Rudd said, and added, indicating the village hall, "Have they gotten set up in there?"

Boyce nodded.

"Yes, they've just finished connecting up the phones."

"Then we'll get ourselves something to eat and drink and work out a plan for this afternoon," Rudd said, moving towards the canteen. As they were being served with tea and sandwiches, more cars arrived, bringing Stapleton and the other men who had been searching the field. Stapleton joined them, looking as gloomy as the sergeant.

"Nothing," he announced shortly, "except for a lot of rubbish that's been lying about for longer than one night. You're welcome to look at it, if you want to. It's packed up in plastic bags in the back of the van. There's a lot of footprints up and down the field but that's all. No blood and no sign of a struggle that I could see."

"The prints are currant pickers', I expect. They were working in the field yesterday," Rudd explained, preceding them into the hall where a couple of constables were putting the finishing touches to the motley collection of chairs and tables that had been set up along the centre. Telephones had already been installed and a blackboard set up in front of the wooden staging that ran along the far end.

Rudd wrinkled his nose as he entered. It had the familiar smell of all public halls, a mixture of dust, floor polish and stewed tea that had seeped into the very fabric of the building. Pinned to a notice board just inside the door were details of the weekly activities: the Men's Club, the choir, the Youth Club, the Women's Institute, a dance on Saturday night to raise funds for the new cricket pavilion. Unless the case could be quickly cleared up, they would either have to be postponed or held somewhere else.

A small room opening off the main hall, used for committee meetings, had been set aside for Rudd's use. Having sent one of the constables to fetch Henty and the dog handlers, he led the way inside and spread a large-scale map of the area on the table. Boyce and Stapleton gathered round it.

"I want the men to be divided up into two groups," he told Stapleton. "The first is to follow any scent the dogs may find at the farm and spread out into the surrounding area, assuming they don't lead us straight to him. The other group is to make a wider search of the fields round where the body was found. I'm still certain she was killed somewhere else and taken there and, in the absence of any tyre marks in the gate opening, except for Aston's lorry, I'm going to assume she was carried to the field from somewhere relatively close at hand. If I'm proved wrong, we'll have to widen that part of the search later."

"That would fit in with her meeting the young chap from the farm," Boyce commented. "He'd be on foot and, if he'd arranged to meet her, it'd be somewhere fairly close."

"Agreed," said Rudd. "But don't forget we have only Lambert's word that Chris Lawrence had been seeing his daughter that evening, and we've only got that second hand through Cookson and Maggie Hearn. Maggie Hearn has denied it and, with Lambert still in Norfolk, we can't check his evidence. And anyway both Maggie Hearn and Cookson agree that Lambert had been drinking and was barely coherent. It's possible he got hold of the wrong end of the stick. As I said, I want to check her story this afternoon and I'd like you, Tom, to be in on it. I'm pretty sure she's lying but I've deliberately left her with the impression that I believe her story. However, I think the time has come to lean a bit more heavily on her." He turned to Stapleton. "As I said, I want you to work with Henty and the dog handlers, following up any scent the dogs may pick up at the farm but I'd like you to wait until we get back from interviewing her before you move in."

"Right," said Stapleton. "Meanwhile shall I get the other search started, of the area round where the body was found?"

"Yes, do that," Rudd agreed. "Take as many men as you need, although you'd better leave a couple here on duty in case anyone reports in by phone. And could you round up Kyle and get him to check on Aston's movements last night? According to him, he had a few drinks at the Rose and Crown here in the village and then went on to the White Hart at Gossbridge. Kyle's job is to check the times he arrived and left both places. Also I want him to find out if anyone saw Vi Aston driving through the village yesterday evening in a green mini. Can you see to that as well, Bob?"

Stapleton nodded and Rudd, swallowing down the last of his tea, got up and left, followed by Boyce.

Turning the car into the yard at the farm, Rudd noticed at once that Maggie's bike was propped up in a different place against the barn wall. When she had arrived on it earlier that morning, he remembered she had put it close to the door. Now it had been placed farther along towards the corner. He commented on it to Boyce as they got out of the car.

"Where do you reckon she's been off to?" Boyce asked.

"Looking for Chris Lawrence?" Rudd suggested. "It's a possibility that's only just occurred to me. This morning she said she'd gone into Gossbridge and I had no reason to doubt her then. Now I'm not so sure."

"Do you think we ought to have a man watching her?" Boyce asked. "I mean, if she's going off by herself, she might find him first and warn him."

"I don't think that's necessary," Rudd replied. "After all, we've got the big guns on our side. There'll be fifty men out this afternoon, not to mention the dogs. It might be as well, though, to have a Panda car patrolling up and down the road. At least, it'll make her think twice before she goes out for another trip on her bike."

"I'll have a word with Stapleton about it," Boyce promised and then broke off as the back door opened and Maggie Hearn came out to meet them, standing defensively on the doorstep as if to bar their entrance.

"My sergeant, Boyce," Rudd said comfortably. "Do you mind if we come in?"

Maggie looked from one to the other of them with rising panic. Two of them this time, she thought. There was an air of increased officialdom about this visit, although the inspector seemed the same as before, smiling pleasantly, with his tie loosened and his hands stuffed into his jacket pockets. The sergeant looked less at ease.

"All right," Maggie conceded reluctantly, standing aside so that they could pass into the kitchen. "What do you want this time?"

"Just a few more questions. It shouldn't take long," Rudd assured her. "Mind if we sit down?"

She nodded and they sat down at the table, the sergeant taking a few heavy glances round him as if to set the scene in his mind. Rudd crossed his legs easily, like a man who is already at home. Maggie remained standing, her back to the Aga, feeling that to join them at the table would somehow put her in a more vulnerable position.

"I'd like to go over what happened yesterday in a little more detail," Rudd was saying. "Now I understand Mr. Lawrence was working in the currant field?"

That was easy enough.

"Yes, that's right," Maggie replied. "I suggested it. Ken Aston was short of pickers and I thought Chris might like to earn himself a bit of money."

The explanation was unnecessary but served the purpose, Rudd realised, of placing the decision that he should be in the field at all on her shoulders. It was a small but interesting instance of how far she was prepared to go to protect him.

"He came back here for lunch?"

"Yes, about quarter to one."

Rudd watched her without appearing to do so, letting his gaze rest as if casually on her face. He was aware that she was relaxing as the first part of the interview proceeded. There was obviously nothing so far that caused her any anxiety.

The next question, however, caught her off guard.

"Did he mention that he'd met anyone in particular that morning?"

It seemed harmless enough but Maggie suddenly realised the hidden implications behind it. She was back in the morass of knowing or guessing more than she dared admit to. It was clear to her now the reason for Chris's evasiveness and unease during the midday meal. He must have already met the girl, as the inspector's question implied, and had decided even at that early stage to lie to her about it, although why Maggie could still only dimly guess at.

"No, he didn't," she replied. "In fact, he said the only person he'd spoken to was the driver."

"Yes, Reg Deakin. I've already had a word with him," Rudd said cheerfully. He offered no further explanation, leaving Maggie deliberately in the dark as to what information Deakin had given him. He saw her face change and a look of alarm come into her eyes.

Oh, God, she was thinking despairingly. What did Reg tell him? What happened in that damned field yesterday morning?

"So Mr. Lawrence didn't mention meeting anyone else that he'd spoken to?" Rudd asked, as if establishing the point.

"No, he didn't," Maggie replied with conviction.

So far, so good, Rudd thought to himself. She's kept to the truth up till now. Let's see what she makes of the rest of it. He nodded to Boyce, who took over the questioning while the inspector settled back in his chair.

"Mr. Lawrence went back to work in the afternoon?" Boyce asked.

"Yes, about two o'clock."

"And what time did he get home?"

"I'm not sure of the exact time but it was before five o'clock."

"I see."

A glance passed between the two men and Rudd resumed the questioning.

"Now, Miss Hearn, I'd like you to tell us in your own words what happened after that."

Maggie felt relief, as Rudd had intended her to. The short answer and question session, shared between the two men, although harmless so far, had begun to alarm her. If they kept up that method of cross-examination she would have no alternative except to lie. But left to tell it in her own way, it might be possible to blur the details a little and make the events seem perfectly ordinary.

"Well, he seemed very tired when he got back," she began, noticing that Rudd gave a little sympathetic nod. She wanted to build Chris up in the inspector's mind as someone sensitive and gentle, not particularly strong; the real Chris, not the young man suspected of murder—not even the person who had struck her last night. "He wasn't used to field work and I think he'd got a touch of sun stroke. So I made tea for him and then he had a bath and after that he went to his room for a lie-down."

She paused, realising that from now on she would have to be more careful about what she said.

"He came back into the kitchen for supper, which we had about half-past six. We ate, then he helped me wash up as usual."

"Yes, go on," Rudd said encouragingly. He was aware that the tempo of her account had slowed down. Maggie Hearn was choosing her words with greater care.

"After that he said he still felt a bit tired and he'd like to go to his room to read for a while."

Something in her tone made Rudd ask. "Did he usually do that?"

"Well, he's a student so he'd be keen on books," Maggie replied.

The first lie, Rudd thought, or more probably the first evasion of the truth. He got the distinct impression that Chris didn't usually spend the evening reading in his room.

"Did he leave it at any time?" Rudd asked.

"No," Maggie said firmly. Two patches of dull red had appeared on her cheekbones. "You can see for yourself, he couldn't cross the yard without me seeing him."

She turned to indicate the window, a movement that allowed her to avert her face with its telltale heightened colour.

Top marks for courage, Rudd thought, and intelligence. If a case should ever be brought against Lawrence, her evidence would be invaluable for the defence for it was obvious that, from the kitchen window, she had a clear view of the stable door. It would be impossible for Chris to leave without her being aware of it.

"You were in the kitchen all evening?" Boyce was asking.

"Yes. I was sitting where you are now, doing my accounts," Maggie replied. There was a more assured air about her now, as if she knew she had just played an important card.

Boyce and Rudd exchanged glances.

"I see. Go on, Miss Hearn."

"There's not much more to tell," she replied. "He came back into the kitchen a little bit later and said he thought he'd leave."

"This was just before eight o'clock?" Rudd reminded her.

"Yes. I told you that when you called this morning."

"So you did," Rudd said cheerfully. "And when he came into the kitchen to say he was leaving, where did he come from?"

"I don't . . ." Maggie began and almost too late saw the

trap he had prepared for her. Of course, she couldn't say she didn't know. She had to know. She had only just said that he couldn't leave the stable without her seeing him. So what direction could he have come from except from his room?

"From the stable," she said quickly.

"Are you sure?"

"Yes, of course. Don't you believe me?"

No, Rudd said silently to himself, I don't.

"You realise that you will be asked to make an official statement?" Rudd asked in his police officer's voice. It was intended as a warning, as she knew.

She looked down at her hands, which were tightly clasped in front of her.

"Yes, I realise that," she said dully.

"Now, to continue," Rudd went on in a brisker voice. "Mr. Lawrence came into the kitchen from his room. What happened then?"

"I told you. He said he was leaving," Maggie replied in the same dull tone. She felt drained now of all energy. All she wanted was to get the interview over as soon as possible.

"Wasn't that a sudden decision?" Rudd asked.

"Sudden?" she repeated, as if she hadn't understood the question.

"It was evening," Rudd explained with a patient air. "Surely it would have been better for him to wait until the morning?"

There was no real answer to that except to say, "I don't know. He just decided to go. He didn't say why."

"Was there a quarrel?" Rudd asked.

The heightened colour drained from her face, leaving a pallor against which the bruise under her eye showed up with a livid intensity.

"No. There wasn't a quarrel," she replied, aware that her voice had become too loud and strained. She saw the two men look at one another and knew that neither of them found her story convincing.

Oh, God! she thought desperately. What else can I say to persuade them that it wasn't Chris? She felt they must know everything already, even the fact that Chris had struck her, although she knew this couldn't be so.

But Rudd did indeed suspect it. Some disagreement must have taken place, otherwise why else had he left so

suddenly? Had they quarreled about Jess Lambert? It
seemed a possibility even though Maggie denied that
Chris had even met the girl. As he sat watching her, he
found himself speculating about the exact nature of the
relationship between Maggie and Chris Lawrence, an
aspect of the case that hadn't occurred to him before.
Although Maggie Hearn had said very little about it, he
got the impression that it was more than a casual acquain-
tanceship between lodger and landlady. She had taken him
in, given him a room, fed him. But, more than this, she
seemed prepared to lie to protect him; not very expertly,
for Rudd guessed that falsehood didn't come naturally to
her, but with an air of desperation.

If Chris had struck her, which seemed likely, then it
showed he was capable of violence, an important factor
with a girl found dead only a couple of hundred yards up
the road.

But would Maggie Hearn admit it? Rudd doubted it.
She seemed willing to perjure herself for his sake.

"And you have no idea where he went?" he asked,
repeating the question that he had already asked her
during the first interview.

"No," she replied. "I have no idea."

This time she looked him straight in the eyes with a
directness that seemed genuine until Rudd noticed the
opaqueness in her gaze that he had seen before in the eyes
of children who are lying by instinct, having disassociated
themselves entirely from the truth of what had happened.

"Well, if that's all . . ." Maggie was saying, walking
heavily towards the door and opening it pointedly.

"Just one more thing," Rudd said, remaining seated at
the table. "I believe you know the Astons?"

"Yes," Maggie replied, fearful of what was coming
next.

"Did you know that Mr. Aston had been seeing Jess
Lambert?"

So he knows about that, too! thought Maggie. She was
torn between relief for Chris, that the suspicion might
have been shifted to Ken, and guilt at this relief; guilt, too,
that the casual remark she had made earlier might have
put the inspector onto this line of inquiry. She was aware,
also, that she was too exhausted to go through another
cross-examination in which she had to think out the implications of everything she said. Protecting Chris was

enough. She couldn't take on the task of shielding Ken Aston as well.

"Yes," she admitted after a small pause. "I did know."

"How did you find out?"

Maggie remained silent.

"Did Mrs. Aston tell you?"

It was little more than a shot in the dark, although Rudd had guessed this might be the explanation. Vi Aston was an emotional and volatile woman who would need someone to confide in.

"Yes," Maggie said in low voice, "although she wasn't sure. She only suspected it."

"How did she seem to be taking it?"

"I don't know," Maggie replied flatly. She no longer cared that the inspector knew she was evading the truth.

"Was she angry?"

She didn't answer but from the look on her face Rudd knew he would get nothing more out of her.

"She was angry," he stated, as if she had answered the question, and took her continuing silence for agreement.

He had gotten up from the table, in company with Boyce, and the two men walked past her into the yard. On the threshold, Rudd stopped to add casually, "Oh, by the way, Miss Hearn, Mr. Aston called on you about quarter to ten last night and found you were out. Where had you gone?"

Maggie was too tired to be frightened or even startled by the question. In a strange way, she was almost relieved. At least, it was her movements he was checking on now, not Chris's.

"I went out for a ride on my bike."

"Towards the village?"

"No, up the road."

"Past Lambert's bungalow?"

"Yes."

She was answering the questions with a candour that surprised Rudd. Maggie Hearn wasn't a stupid woman by any means and yet she didn't seem to realise that, by her admission, she was placing herself in the vicinity of the murder at the time it might have been committed.

"Did you see anybody while you were out?"

"No."

"Why did you go out at that time of night, Miss Hearn?"

There was a brief silence and then, for the first time, she smiled. It was a small, tired smile but it was genuine enough to reach her fine, long-lidded eyes.

"Because I wanted to, Inspector."

Rudd smiled back. He preferred her this way, showing a touch of spirit. She seemed more true to what he felt was her real self.

"There's no law against that," he admitted comfortably, stepping out into the yard. "There's one more thing before we go. We'd like to take another look at the stable. You don't mind, do you?"

He had begun to walk towards it, followed by the sergeant, unaware of the look of sudden panic that crossed her face.

Oh, God! If he went up there, he might see that the camping stove was gone and then he'd know that she'd found Chris. She must stop him somehow. Could she refuse to let him go up there?

She broke into an awkward, loping run after them, holding up her bun of hair with one hand. But, when she followed them inside the stable, she found that, instead of mounting the loft steps, they had picked their way through the box where the hens roosted and were examining the small window in the back wall that opened out into the orchard.

It was a casement window with rusty metal fittings that hadn't, as far as she knew, been opened for years and yet Rudd was pushing against the dusty glass, his hand covered with a large, white handerchief. It opened stiffly on its hinges and Maggie knew at once that this was the way by which Chris had managed to get out of the stable yesterday evening without her seeing him.

"Unfastened," Rudd commented briefly over his shoulder to Boyce. He pointed to the cleaner patches on the hinges where the rust particles had dropped away, revealing the raw metal beneath. "And it's been opened recently."

"I did it," Maggie said breathlessly. "I was cleaning out the hens the other day and I pushed it open to let the dust out."

Anger had cleared her mind and given her the boldness of invention. The anger was directly mainly at Rudd, who stood smiling at her with a look on his face that expressed an odd kind of amused approval, as if he knew she was lying and yet admired her for her audacity. But part of it was directly also at Chris, a resentment that she was aware still lay dormant under her fear for him and her desperation to protect him.

Why had he lied to her? She still didn't understand.

Boyce had pushed the window still more widely open and was craning his head to look out.

"There's scuff marks on the wall," he remarked to Rudd in a low voice so that Maggie couldn't hear him, "and the grass just below is crushed flat. It looks as if someone climbed out."

And we can guess who that was, Rudd thought. No wonder Maggie hadn't seen him leave the stable. That much of her evidence, at least, might be true.

"I'd rather you didn't touch the window," Rudd said, addressing Maggie. "My sergeant will have a look at it later."

The two men, brushing off their hands, began to walk towards her. She backed away from them until she was standing at the bottom of the steps as if to bar their way up.

Rudd looked at her speculatively. It was clear she didn't want them to go up to Chris Lawrence's room. Was it worth making a fuss about? he wondered. Perhaps not. After all, he hadn't got a search warrant and he'd already looked at the room earlier that morning. But it might be worthwhile getting Boyce to give it a thorough going-over once the dog handlers had been.

"By the way," he added, "have you stripped Mr. Lawrence's bed?"

"He took his sleeping bag," she replied, "but the blankets and pillow are still there."

They had walked out into the yard where she stood facing them, her eyes screwed up painfully against the sun. Rudd felt a sudden stirring of compassion for her. She had put up a damned good fight to save the young man but there was too much going against her; not only the evidence that was beginning to mount up, but the whole complex structure of police procedure—fifty men combing the fields, and more if he wanted them; an incident room set up in the village; the experts he could call in at any time. She didn't stand a chance.

"I'll be sending over some police dogs and their handlers," he explained. "They'll want to pick up a trail from his room. You understand," he added, in a gentler voice, "that we have to find him?"

"Yes, I understand," she replied. Her mouth had fallen open slightly in a little, silent gasp that reminded him of the dead girl's face.

"If you find him first," he went on, "tell him to give himself up."

He touched her briefly on the arm, a small, quick gesture that was meant to convey some of the sympathy he felt for her, and a warning, too.

Then they had gone, walking briskly towards the parked car, neither of them giving a backward glance at her.

10

"What did you make of that?" Rudd asked Boyce. They were in the car driving back towards the village.

"It looks obvious to me," Boyce replied. "The young chap who was staying at the farm, whatsisname, Chris Lawrence, must have done it."

"The evidence certainly seems to point that way," Rudd agreed. "And yet I'm not convinced myself."

"Oh, come off it!" Boyce protested. "We know he met the girl yesterday morning in the currant field. We've got the lorry driver's evidence on that. According to Lambert, he met her again that evening and, while I grant you, we haven't checked that yet with Lambert himself, it seems pretty clear to me that it was Chris Lawrence who climbed through that stable window. Now why else should he do that except to keep a date with her on the sly? Added to which, he's disappeared. I don't know what else you want."

"We've got means and opportunity," Rudd conceded, "but so far no motive. Don't forget, she wasn't sexually interfered with in any way, so that can't be the reason."

Boyce shrugged.

"You probably won't find out what the motive was until you find him."

"And I don't just mean the motive for killing her," Rudd went on, pursuing his own line of thought. "I mean the reason behind why he acted the way he did yesterday evening before the murder was committed."

"I don't get you," Boyce said heavily.

"Well, take the window as an example. Why bother to climb out of it? Why didn't he go out by the stable door and across the yard?"

"He didn't want to be seen," Boyce replied, with the prompt air of someone stating the obvious.

"I know that," Rudd snapped. He was beginning to feel exasperated, not only by Boyce's obtuseness, but by his own inability to explain this aspect of the case that bothered him. Something was wrong; something in the relationship between Chris and Maggie Hearn that he felt was crucial to his understanding. "But why didn't he want to be seen?"

"Could have been a lark, I suppose," Boyce suggested without much enthusiasm. "You know what these students are like; always climbing in and out of buildings or sticking jerries on the top of them, that is when they're not sitting down in the road, protesting about something or other."

He sounded massively disapproving.

"I suppose so," Rudd said, appearing to agree. He decided to leave it there. "But even so we mustn't lose sight of the other evidence," he continued. "There's enough against Aston, for example, to keep him in the running. He had as much means and opportunity as Chris Lawrence, *and* motive. He's agreed he was having an affair with the girl. That might be enough reason for wanting to keep her quiet for good. We shall know better when Kyle comes back from checking on his movements. Then there's Mrs. Aston."

Boyce looked surprised.

"You haven't got much on her, have you?"

"Only what we learned from Maggie Hearn this afternoon—that she knew about her husband's affair with Jess Lambert, something I suspected when I saw her this afternoon; and that she probably has no real alibi covering the time the girl could have been killed last night. While Aston was chasing round the pubs, it's possible she was alone in the house. I want to have another talk with both of them this afternoon. There's a few points that haven't been properly explained. Why, for instance, Aston went visiting Maggie Hearn last night. It was a bit late for making a business call. Which brings us to our fourth suspect, Maggie Hearn herself. She was out, too, during the crucial times, looking for Chris, if my guess is right. So she, too, had the means and the opportunity."

"What about motive?" Boyce asked.

"I'm not sure," Rudd admitted. He was still turning that one over in his mind. "But supposing she met Jess Lambert on her way home from seeing Chris, there's a quarrel, perhaps even a bit of fisticuffs . . ." He broke off as an idea occurred to him. "It could have been then that she got the bruise on the side of her face. She picks up something handy, a stone, say, wallops the girl on the head with it, realises she's killed her, panics and dumps the body in the field. She's a strong, well-built woman. She'd be physically capable of doing it."

It might account for some of the lies, too, he thought. Maggie Hearn might be protecting herself as much as Chris, although this didn't strike him as very likely. Her anxiety seemed to be directed exclusively at him, which brought him back to the question he had already asked himself—why? What was so special about the young man that made her fight so desperately to save him? She could have grown fond of him, of course. She was, after all, a spinster living alone. He might have aroused some deep affection in her, although there was no way of judging their exact relationship. But, assuming she did deeply care for him, it could provide a possible motive for murder. She might have killed Jess Lambert because she was afraid the girl would take Chris's affection away from her.

They had arrived at the village hall and Rudd, still deep in thought, got out of the car and walked into the small committee room followed by Boyce, who, seeing the inspector's preoccupied air, kept quiet, knowing better than to interrupt it.

But that didn't altogether make sense, Rudd told himself, as he sat down at the desk. According to Deakin's evidence, Chris had met the girl for the first time on the morning before the murder. It hardly left time for great passions to build up. Or did it? He didn't know Chris Lawrence so he had no way of judging how he might react in a situation. As for Maggie, he had seen her only as a tired, haggard woman, at the end of her tether; emotionally on her knees, so to speak. But that wasn't to say she couldn't be capable of killing in a jealous rage.

Jealousy. Rudd found himself testing the word in his mind and realised, with a small shock of self-revelation, that what he had been dismissing from his consideration of the relationship between Maggie Hearn and Chris Lawrence was the possibility of any sexual element. It was sheer prudery on his part, as he now recognised. Some puritanical streak in his own nature made it hard for him to accept that a woman in her fifties might be in love with a young man thirty years younger than herself. Some ageing beauty, yes, he could accept that. But not Maggie Hearn, who gave the impression of common sense and, well he had to admit it, *decency,* although he had to smile as the word came into his mind.

"Something funny?" Boyce ventured but the inspector was spared the trouble of having to explain by a knock at the door.

"Come in!" he called.

A young constable entered.

"Inspector Stapleton and Sergeant Henty are outside with the dog handlers, sir," he announced.

"Right," said Rudd. "Tell them to wait a few minutes." To Boyce he added, "I want you to go back with them to the farm. Give that window in the stable the once-over for prints. You should be able to get Chris Lawrence's dabs from the loft room upstairs. He's left some stuff behind— books and a camping stove among other things. And while you're there, give the room a good going-over. I got the impression that Maggie wasn't anxious for us to go up there when we called this afternoon. You'll need her prints, too, for elimination. I know she said she opened that window but I don't believe her and I'd like it confirmed."

As Boyce made for the door, Rudd called after him, "And treat her gently, Tom. She's having a rough time of it."

Boyce nodded, keeping his expression noncommittal, and only raised his eyebrows after the door had closed between them.

When Boyce had left with the others, Rudd remained in the office long enough to write up his notes for the report on the second interview with Maggie Hearn before leaving again for Aston's market garden where he found Aston was out, making a delivery in the absence of Reg Deakin, the lorry driver. But Vi was there, working in one of the greenhouses, engaged in picking tomatoes for a late order.

At Rudd's suggestion, they went up to the house to talk. The presence of the other women made privacy impossible and, besides, Rudd found the greenhouse, with its hot, humid atmosphere and the dense, subtropical foliage of the plants, oppressive.

"What do you want this time?" she asked, turning on him as soon as they were inside the sitting room. She seemed angry and impatient but, Rudd guessed, it was probably a cover-up for fear.

In this assumption, he was partly correct. She was afraid. More intelligent than her husband, she had seen the interview that morning as only the beginning of an inquiry that might lead God knows where. How much more would come out? she wondered. If only they'd find that damned camper of Maggie's and arrest him, then the investigation would be over and Ken's part of it forgotten.

Her anger was genuine enough and stemmed from much the same cause. She hadn't been able to make Ken see any of this. He had gone off in the lorry quite cheerfully, convinced that his part in the case was now over and the police wouldn't be back. Everything would be all right. His stupidity and optimism had infuriated her. He was always the same, never seeing further than the end of his nose, always believing that things would turn out just the way he wanted them to.

"May I sit down?" Rudd asked. He wanted to avoid a standing confrontation, suspecting that, given half a chance, Vi Aston would unload some of her anger onto him.

"Please yourself," she said grudgingly.

He sat, taking the opportunity as he did so for a rapid glance round the room. It was furnished with expensive, contemporary, Swedish-style furniture but the room had a bleak, unlived-in feeling as if no one had bothered to turn the collection of chairs and tables into a home. It wasn't only apparent in the film of dust that covered every surface, the hastily pulled back curtains that were bunched untidily on either side of the window, the fallen soot that was scattered across the hearth, but in the absence of any books, flowers or personal objects that might have given the room life. It looked out over a garden to which the same minimal care had been given, being a mere oblong of lawn, which needed mowing, surrounded by conifers and evergreen shrubs. There hadn't been even any attempt at creating privacy for, at the end of the lawn, Rudd could see the yard and the back ends of the packing shed and greenhouses.

Vi sat down reluctantly opposite him, keeping to the edge of her chair, as if ready to jump up and join in battle at the first opportunity.

"There are a few question I want to ask," Rudd said soothingly. "Mainly a matter of checking and corroboration. What time did your husband go out, Mrs Aston?"

There was no ducking that one. Ken had already admitted leaving the house, and besides, Rudd would probably ask at the pubs. After the inspector's visit, she had grilled Ken on exactly what he had done the previous evening and gotten the truth out of him at last although, even then, he hadn't wanted to admit to anything.

"Can't you see, you fool," she had shouted at him in the end, "that I've got to tell them the same as you?"

It was only then that he had told her, with a sulky air, like a schoolboy forced into owning up.

"He left here soon after nine o'clock," Vi replied. "I know that because the BBC news hadn't long started."

"And what time did he get home?"

"About quarter-past eleven, give or take five minutes."

"So he was out of the house for roughly two hours and a quarter?"

"A bit less than that, I'd say."

"I see. Do you mind being left alone, Mrs. Aston?"

The question caught her unawares. Then she shrugged with weary resignation.

"I don't mind. I've got used to it. It's a case of having to."

The tone in which she spoke suggested a deep dissatisfaction but that wasn't what interested Rudd at that moment, although it implied the Astons' marriage wasn't a happy one, confirming his impression of earlier that morning when he had seen them together. But it confirmed, also, something much more important to the case: Vi Aston had been alone in the house when her husband went out.

"What did you do yesterday evening, Mrs. Aston?"

"Me?"

She sounded surprised.

"Yes, after Mr. Aston left?"

"I watched television," she answered, after a pause.

"All evening?"

"Most of it."

"Let's see." There were copies of the *Radio* and *T.V.*

Times lying on the floor under the television set. Rudd bent forward and, picking them up, turned to the pages that contained details of the previous evening's programmes. "You were watching the BBC news when Mr. Aston went out . . ."

"I didn't see all of it," she said quickly. "I went out to the kitchen to make myself a cup of coffee."

"And when you came back, what programme did you see then? The detective serial on BBC One or the film on ATV? Or perhaps you watched the concert on BBC Two?"

"I turned over for the film."

Rudd watched her speculatively. There was an uneasy defensiveness about her, although she met his eyes boldly enough. She makes a better liar than Maggie Hearn, he thought.

"You saw all of it?"

"No, I missed a bit at the beginning. I told you, I went out to the kitchen."

"Still making coffee?"

"No, I had a bit of a clear-up."

There was an air of quick improvisation about the statement that convinced him she was lying.

"You didn't leave the house at any time during the evening?"

"No, why should I?" she asked belligerently.

Rudd ignored her and put a question of his own.

"So if someone said they'd seen your car in the village about quarter-past nine, they'd be lying?"

It was pure bluff. No one had reported seeing anything of the sort. But her response was immediate.

"Oh, Christ!" she said in a tone of angry despair.

"Where did you go?" Rudd asked, pressing home the advantage.

"Only down to the Rose and Crown."

"To check that your husband's story that he was going out for a drink was, in fact, true?"

It seemed the only likely explanation.

"I was only there a few minutes. I could see his car was in the car park so I came home."

"You didn't go to the Lamberts' bungalow?"

"No, I bloody didn't!" she shouted. "Why should I? There was . . ."

She stopped abruptly.

"No need?" Rudd suggested gently. "Because yesterday evening, at least, you knew where he was?"

Her story, that she had come straight home, had the ring of truth to it and yet he could be wrong. It would take only a few minutes for her to drive a little farther through the village and, meeting Jess Lambert on the way, quarrel with her and kill her. Rudd had no doubt she'd be perfectly capable of it if she lost her temper. He remembered the atmosphere of physical violence that had crackled like an electric charge between her and Aston when he had left them confronting each other in the packing shed that morning.

If she had killed the girl, the motive was obvious. It was the same as he had ascribed to Maggie Hearn: jealousy, what the divorce courts used to call "alienation of affection," a bleak, official phrase that didn't even begin to hint at the howling waste of rejection and bitterness that can follow the loss of love.

It couldn't have been easy for her. The girl was young and pretty or, at least, she must have been when she was alive. To this fact was added the extra complication that she lived in the village and her father was one of Aston's employees.

"How long have you known that your husband was having an affair with Jess Lambert?" he continued in the same quiet voice.

Vi realised it was useless to deny it. In a strange way, she was almost glad that it was out in the open. There was no need for her any longer to try to hide the anger that lay too close to her heart to make pretence easy.

"Almost from the beginning," she admitted.

"Did he realise you knew?"

"Ken?" She laughed. "No, not him. When he's out on the loose, he seems to think he becomes invisible or I get too blind to notice what he's up to."

"Did Mr. Lambert know of the affair?"

"Him!" Vi said disparagingly. "No, I shouldn't think so. Ken went to see her when Lambert was working down here. It fitted in nicely."

The contempt and bitterness in her voice told him all he wanted to know about her reactions, not only to Jess Lambert but to the girl's father as well, and he wondered why he should be included in her dislike. But, as Deakin

had said, not everyone got on with him. Evidently Vi was
one of those.

"There's been some gossip," Rudd pointed out, wondering if she knew and watching for her reaction. Her
surprise seemed genuine.

"Has there? Well, I haven't heard anything. Nor has
Lambert or he'd've had it out with Ken."

"Is he outspoken?" Rudd asked. It was an aspect of
Lambert that neither Cookson nor Deakin had mentioned
and added another detail to his mental picture of the man
whom he hadn't so far met.

"He can be when he wants. I heard him once laying in
to one of the men. Most of the time, though, you can't get
a word out of him."

"How does he get on with your husband?"

"All right, I suppose," she admitted grudgingly. "Ken
always says he knows his job."

She glanced at the clock on the mantelpiece.

"Look, I don't want to rush you but we are short-
handed with both Deakin and Lambert off today . . ."

It was only partly true. She was anxious to get rid of
Rudd before Ken came back from making the deliveries,
which he might do at any moment, for God alone knew
what he might say in his present jubilant mood. He was
always at his most careless when in a good humour, acting
the fool, blurting out things he didn't really mean. A kind
of showing off, she supposed. Nor did she want Ken to find
out that she'd followed him down to the Rose and Crown
the previous evening. That would swing him the other way
into losing his temper.

If only we could have a bit of peace and quiet, she
thought wearily. That's all I really want. Things back to
normal. Ken too tired of an evening to do anything much
except watch telly with his feet up. Not that it'd last very
long. He'd soon get fed up and then he'd be off again,
nosing round for another woman and a bit of excitement.

Rudd, who had followed her glance, said, "I ought to be
off myself, Mrs. Aston." It was gone half-past five and he
wanted to have a look round the outside of Lambert's
bungalow before Lambert himself returned home. "There's
only one more question. When you were out last night, did
you see anybody?"

"No, I can't say I noticed."

"Not Miss Hearn?"

"No."

"Or the young man who's been staying with her?"

"I haven't met him so I wouldn't know him if I saw him."

"Well, did you pass a young man, dark-haired, with a rucksack on his back?"

"No. I told you, I didn't see anybody."

"What time did you go out?"

"I left soon after Ken, about quarter-past nine, and I got back in less than ten minutes."

"Thank you," Rudd said, getting to his feet. The question he wanted to ask Aston about the real reason for his visit to Maggie Hearn's would have to wait for another occasion when Aston was at home.

He walked back with Vi Aston as far as the greenhouses where he left her, returning to the gravelled forecourt where he had parked the car.

Driving back towards the village, he mulled over the interview. If Vi Aston had killed the girl, she was being remarkably cool about it, although he had been aware of an uneasy tension about her. But could it have been on Aston's account rather than her own? Did she suspect her husband of more than adultery?

She certainly made no attempt to cover up the bitterness towards both the Lamberts, father and daughter. Her attitude to the girl he could understand, but her feelings towards Lambert were less easily explained.

Passing Maggie Hearn's farm, he almost turned into the yard to ask her opinion of the relationship between Vi Aston and Lambert and then changed his mind. Instinct told him to leave her alone. The process of breaking her down would be better achieved if she were left alone to brood.

There was a rough drive-in at Lambert's bungalow, nothing more than a gap in the hedge with an area of grass beyond, worn down by tyres and marked with a big patch of black oil where presumably Lambert's van usually stood. Parking a little beyond it, Rudd got out and walked towards the bungalow.

The front door was locked and the small bay windows on either side were covered with net curtains and allowed him only a hazy view into the rooms. The letter box wasn't much better but did give him an oblong-shaped glimpse into the hall, gloomily decorated with a heavily patterned wallpaper and drab brown paint that had been grained to look like wood.

Having seen all that was possible of the front of the building, Rudd tramped round to the back where a narrow, concreted yard extended from the door to the high hawthorn hedge that surrounded the bungalow and its garden on all sides.

The two windows on either side of the back door, also locked, were not netted and he was able to peer through them quite easily. The room on the right was a bedroom, simply furnished with a single bed, a cheap wardrobe and chest of drawers in dark oak. A man's dressing gown hanging up behind the door suggested it was Lambert's bedroom.

The other window looked into a tiny kitchen of the type referred to in estate agents' jargon as a "kitchenette," meaning that it is too small for working in comfortably. The sink, the cooker and a tall cream-painted cupboard, the sort with a let-down working top, took up most of the space. Nevertheless, a table and a couple of chairs had been squeezed in as well.

Both bedroom and kitchen were, like the hall, painted with the same gloomy, simulated graining. In fact, the whole place gave the impression of some secret and isolated refuge, cut off from the outside world, where no laughter or sunlight ever penetrated.

All right, perhaps, for Lambert. But what about his daughter? Rudd remembered Mrs. Deakin's sudden and unexpected burst of pity for the girl. No, it certainly couldn't have been much of a life for her.

Not much of a death either, come to that, he added, lowering himself onto the back doorstep, in the absence of anywhere else to sit, to wait for Lambert's arrival.

11

Lambert drove slowly through the village, aware of nothing more than the stretch of road immediately in front of him. After the nightmare of the previous night, this limited consciousness had been his only means of survival during the hours that followed, a numbing of mind and body that enabled him to go automatically through a series of necessary actions and nothing more. He had said very little to his sister on arrival and it was lucky for him that she was, like him, a person of few words.

"Jess has gone," he explained to her, finding it impossible to tell her the truth. Indeed, he hadn't properly accepted himself the fact of her death. It had been blanked off somewhere in his mind; a loss; an emptiness; some great gap in his life that he hadn't yet been able to assimilate, let alone put into words.

His sister had said nothing, merely compressing her lips as she took the child from him, but her unspoken comment was as comprehensible as if she had voiced it out loud: "Run off, just like her mother."

Lambert had left it there. Let her think what she liked. It no longer seemed to matter.

He had gotten through the rest of the day somehow, unpacking the child's things from the back of the van, carrying the pieces of the drop-sided cot upstairs to the little spare bedroom where he reassembled them, going back for the mattress and the blankets. He even ate the dinner she cooked for him and slept a little afterwards in an armchair, a heavy, black sleep that, in its total oblivion, had been like a death.

The only time the numbness had lifted and he had been moved by anything like emotion was when he went to see the child before he left. It was lying awake in its pram in the back garden and he had stood a little way off, watching it, not daring to go too close. The sun was on its hair, turning it to a cap of fine-spun gold, like Jess's when she had been a baby and he remembered, with a sickening lurch of his heart, how it had felt under his fingers, as light and as soft as feathers.

Then he turned blindly and went away.

Even the sight of Rudd's car could not move him in the same way. He guessed why it was there. The police had come. Well, it was only to be expected, although he felt a dull sense of despair at the thought of the questions he knew he would be asked. They'd churn it all over, not letting any of it rest; not even her.

Rudd, who had heard the van turn off the road, got to his feet and stood waiting by the back door for Lambert's arrival. He heard his footsteps first on the concrete path, heavy and deliberate, with no sense of urgency about them, and then Lambert himself turned the corner of the bungalow.

He was a short man, grey-haired, grey-faced, with bowed shoulders and yet, in spite of the air of exhaustion and defeat, Rudd was aware of a strong, positive presence, held in check by a deliberate act of will. As Lambert stood confronting him, the inspector was reminded of a picture he had once seen of a dancing bear, muzzled and chained, standing on its hind legs, tamed and yet still savage. It was an absurd comparison, of course. There was nothing of the wild animal about Lambert. And yet something of the image was nevertheless valid. Like the bear, Lambert, too, was restrained but the curbs had been put there of his own choice.

"Mr. Lambert?" Rudd said pleasantly, stepping forward to introduce himself.

Lambert acknowledged his presence with a curt nod of his head adding, in the same abrupt manner as he unlocked the door, "You'd better come in, I suppose."

Rudd followed him into the tiny kitchen that he had so far only glimpsed through the window. In spite of the late-afternoon sun that still lay rich and heavy over the fields, the room was dark and cold. Lambert switched on the light, which illuminated it with a harsh, white brilliance from a central shade, only increasing the impression of chilly bleakness.

"I'm afraid I shall have to ask you a few questions," Rudd explained. He remained standing just inside the back door. There was hardly room for both of them inside the kitchen and Lambert already seemed to fill it with his heavy, brooding presence. Nor did Rudd offer any of the usual, polite expressions of official sympathy. It seemed to him that it would be an impertinence to intrude into Lambert's grief; for grief was certainly there, shut away behind the grim, taciturn face. "I need your account of what happened last night."

"There's not much to tell," Lambert replied, after a short pause in which he seemed to be collecting his thoughts. "I came home a bit later than usual."

"What time was that?" Rudd put in.

"About quarter to seven. Reg Deakin brought in the lorry with the afternoon's currant crop and that had to be weighed and packed ready for the morning."

"Go on," Rudd said encouragingly, for Lambert had stopped speaking. A brief shudder passed over his whole body as if remembering the events of the previous evening left him suddenly cold.

"Jess was here when I got home," he continued. His voice was slower now, almost slurred. He had turned deliberately away from Rudd and was staring out of the window into the yard as if he didn't want his face to be seen. "I had my supper and then she said she was going out for a walk."

"Did she say where?"

"No."

"Did she say if she was meeting anyone?"

"No."

Even these monosyllabic answers seemed to be torn out of him.

"I knew though," Lambert added.

Knew, presumably, that she was meeting someone, an impression that was confirmed by Lambert's next remark.

"I saw him through the window."

"This window?" asked Rudd.

Lambert turned towards the inspector with a look that was full of a strange irony.

"No, the sitting-room window. Want to look?"

Rudd nodded and followed Lambert through the narrow hall into a room that overlooked the front garden. Like the kitchen, it was dark and bleak, the high hawthorn hedge that fronted it cutting out most of the light. It was furnished in the style of the thirties, with a heavy, overstuffed suite in dark-red fabric with broad arms and wide seats.

"I brought my cup of tea through into here," Lambert explained. "I was just about to sit down when I saw him."

He had taken up a position by the window and Rudd, joining him, followed his glance. It was just possible for someone standing there to see through the net curtains and over the top of the hedge to the road beyond.

"He was climbing over the gate of that field," Lambert continued, "and then he walked a little way up the road and waited."

"He?" asked Rudd.

Lambert shrugged and moved away from the window.

"I don't know his name but I've heard of him. That young man from Maggie Hearn's."

It was said with a curious lack of bitterness, almost with indifference, as if Lambert had passed beyond the point of anger or the need for revenge and was looking back to something that had happened a long time ago and that left only an aching sense of loss.

"You're sure?" Rudd asked sharply.

Lambert merely nodded but the abrupt movement of his head was enough to convey his conviction.

Rudd remained standing at the window, looking out. The gate was clearly visible. It opened into a meadow adjacent to the currant field where Jess Lambert's body has been found. So, if Lambert's account was true, and Rudd had no reason to doubt it in the face of the other evidence, Chris Lawrence had not walked up the road to meet the girl but had come across the field from the farm after, presumably, climbing out of the stable window. This element of secrecy about his movements still puzzled the inspector. It suggested that they had been carefully planned beforehand but that didn't square up with the manner of the girl's death which was unlikely to have been premeditated. She had been killed by a savage blow to the head, suggesting a sudden rage that couldn't have been planned with coldblooded foresight.

He turned from the window to face Lambert, who was sitting in one of the armchairs, looking down at the floor.

"Did you see them meet?"

"No."

"Why not?"

He meant why hadn't Lambert stayed at the window watching, a half-expressed question that nevertheless Lambert seemed to understand.

"Jess came past," he said simply.

Past the window, as she'd have to do to walk up the path to the gate. It needed no further explanation. Lambert, no doubt anxious not to be seen spying, had turned away. Out of delicacy? It was possible. He was a dour, uncommunicative man but that didn't mean he was without all sensitivity. Or, perhaps, on the other hand, he had seen enough to convince himself that his daughter was lying, if not directly then by omission, for it was obvious she hadn't told him that she had a date with the young man from Maggie's.

"What time was this, Mr. Lambert?"

Lambert looked up briefly.

"I'm not sure exactly. Just gone half-past seven, I'd say."

"What happened after that?"

"I waited. She'd said she'd be back by half-past nine so I could go down to the pub. But she didn't come. It got dark. I went up the road a bit to see if I could see her but I didn't like to go too far and leave the child alone. In the end, though, it got so late, I went out in the van to Maggie Hearn's, thinking she might be there."

No word about his drinking. No real explanation about his reasons for supposing his daughter might have gone to the farm. It was all very unsatisfactory and yet Rudd hesitated to probe too far. It wasn't exactly nicety on his part, although he certainly didn't want to cause this silent, awkward man more pain than he had already suffered. But, in a strange way, it was as if Rudd understood without the words needing to be said.

Lambert had sat drinking because there was nothing else for him to do and because he was worried. It was as simple as that; so obvious that he hadn't seen the need to state it. The girl had met the young man from Maggie's. Where else could she have gone when she didn't come home except back with him to the farm? Lambert must have been drunk by this time or sufficiently fuddled in his mind for such an explanation to make sense. And with a kind of simplicity and directness he had gone out looking for her in the one place it seemed feasible he'd find her.

Not finding her there, he'd panicked and driven on to the village to report her missing to Cookson.

Now, faced with explaining this to Rudd, Lambert found it difficult to frame it into words. Shame was probably partly the cause, although Rudd doubted if Lambert was the type of man who was naturally articulate.

He tried to express it for him in a few simple questions.

"You thought she might still be with him?"

"Yes."

"That perhaps she'd gone back with him to his room?"

"Yes."

"And when you found she wasn't at Miss Hearn's . . . ?"

But Lambert didn't let him finish. The shudder that before had passed briefly over his body now returned more violently, convulsing his features, shaking his whole frame. Bringing his fist down on the arm of the chair, he cried out in a voice that was vibrant with grief and rage, "For God's sake, be done! She's dead! Isn't that enough?"

In the silence that followed this outburst, Rudd stood immobile and then he moved quietly towards the door.

"I shan't bother you any more for the time being, Mr. Lambert. But I'd like to look at your daughter's room before I go. May I?"

Lambert, who had slumped back in his chair and put a hand over his face, nodded, and Rudd, going out of the room, softly closed the door behind him before crossing the hall and just as silently letting himself into Jess Lambert's bedroom.

It was brighter and more attractive than any of the other rooms in the bungalow, newly decorated with pale-blue paint and a pretty wallpaper of blue and white flowers. Although the furniture was cheap, someone, perhaps Lambert, had painted it glossy white and trimmed the edges of the drawers and the wardrobe doors with strips of thin, gold-lacquered beading. An empty space alongside the bed indicated where the child's cot had stood.

Rudd moved swifly to the dressing table and began opening the drawers, lifting up the contents with deft, practised fingers, hardly disturbing the layers of clothes they contained. He knew what he was looking for—letters or photographs that might give him a clue to the identity of the child's father, a question he had hoped to put to Lambert but, in the face of the man's distress, it hardly seemed appropriate to ask it now, even if Lambert knew it, which Rudd was beginning to doubt.

He guessed, too, that if any evidence lay in the room it was likely to be hidden, for it was clear from Lambert's account that the girl wasn't in the habit of confiding in her father. She seemed to have met Chris Lawrence and Aston on the sly so the chances were she had kept any other liaison secret.

The drawers were full of clothes, jerseys, blouses, underwear, most of it cheap, chain-store garments but nevertheless in enough quantities to convince Rudd that she wasn't short of money to spend on herself and it crossed his mind that the child's father might be supporting her. Or could it be more of a form of blackmail? Pay up and I'll keep quiet? If that were true, then it could be a motive for murder. Supposing the man had gotten tired of paying up, had met her last night on her way back from her date with Chris, had argued with her about money . . . ?

It was pure speculation, he told himself, but a theory that was worth following up.

Finding nothing in the dressing table to interest him, he turned his attention to the wardrobe.

It contained more clothes: dresses, coats, skirts. A row of shoes was lined up beneath them but that was all.

Baffled, he looked about him. There was nowhere else in the room where she might have kept anything personal except for the two tiny drawers in the bedside table. Sliding the top one open, he looked inside. It contained a jumble of costume jewellery, mostly cheap coloured beads and pendants. The second drawer held make-up.

Rudd closed them quietly and stood irresolute. The room had yielded nothing in the way of any evidence of her former life before she had moved with her father from Suffolk and this struck him as odd. She must have had friends, gone to school, perhaps even had a job, and yet there was not even a snapshot or a holiday postcard to indicate what that life had been.

As a final throw, he even got down on his hands and knees and looked under the bed but the space beneath it was empty.

Moving across to the door, he took a last look round before going out. He had come to a decision. If Chris Lawrence hadn't been found and the case against him proved by the following day, he'd go to Suffolk himself to find out about that past life of Jess Lambert's that seemed to be so effectively and so intriguingly expunged.

Going softly through the hall, he paused for a moment to listen outside the sitting-room door but he could hear no sound from behind it.

Lambert would have to be interviewed again, of course, Rudd thought, as he let himself out of the back door and, getting into the car, drove back to the village. There were a lot of gaps in his account that would have to be filled in, although the basic story hung together satisfactorily enough. Chris had met the girl at a little after half-past seven and that was enough to give the lie to Maggie's story.

Passing the farmhouse, he slowed down, wondering whether to go in and confront her with it there and then. But, glancing at his watch, he decided against it. Boyce should be back from fingerprinting the window in the stable and, with any luck, the dog handlers might also have reported in, possibly with Chris Lawrence in tow. There would be time enough to interview Maggie Hearn when he had a few more cards in his hand.

It wasn't something he was looking forward to, although it would have to be done. Maggie Hearn had fought gallantly and Rudd admired anybody who showed that sort of courage. But the evidence so far looked fairly conclusive and, in trying to save the young man, she was playing a losing game.

Boyce was in the main hall at the incident room, looking tired and talking in a desultory manner with one of the constables on duty. They both got to their feet when Rudd entered and Boyce stepped forward.

"Henty and the dog handlers have gone back to headquarters," he informed the inspector as they moved into the small office. "They were wanted on another case out at Padfield—a child gone missing. But Henty's gone over what they found out with me and he'll be putting in a detailed report tomorrow. And if you're going to ask did they find Chris Lawrence, the answer's no."

"Damn!" Rudd said softly. "What happened?"

"The dogs lost the scent," Boyce explained in tones of

gloomy satisfaction. "They picked it up all right to begin with. The handlers let them have a good sniff round the stable window where we reckon he climbed out. By the way, I've checked it for prints . . ."

"Come back to that later," Rudd told him. "What about the dogs?"

"Well, they started off across the orchard behind the stable and followed a big arc through the fields. God knows what he was up to but it came out onto the road just above the bungalow where the girl lived."

That squared with Lambert's account, Rudd thought. He had seen Chris climbing over a gate a little distance away.

"They followed it up the road," Boyce continued, "to a cornfield about two hundred yards away where they found an area of grass at the side of the field flattened down as if a couple had been lying there."

His face had taken on a slightly stiff, puritanical look, as if he disapproved of such goings-on.

"Oh, don't worry," he added as Rudd opened his mouth to speak, "I've searched the area myself since with Kyle and a few others. There's nothing to suggest that's where she was killed—no sign of a murder weapon, not even one spot of blood. We went round the whole of the damned field on our hands and knees. Anyway, the dogs seemed to get a bit confused and weren't able to pick up his scent back from the field so Henty decided to call it off and took them back to the farm to start again. This time they picked up a second scent from his room. I've got Henty to mark it out," he added, taking a large-scale map of the area out of his pocket and spreading it open on the table. "It led out of the farmyard," he explained, pointing with a stubby finger at the pencilled line, "down the road a little way and then branched off here."

Rudd followed the line with his eyes. It led across the fields towards the village, running behind the houses and emerging again onto the road on the far side of the church; which would explain why Chris Lawrence hadn't been seen in the village, Rudd thought. It also suggested to him some guilty purpose. Why had he been so careful to keep his movements secret unless he had good reason for doing so?

"There's a footpath here," Boyce was saying, "just at the

top of the hill that leads to Dearden, the next village. They followed the scent across this field. . . ."

The pencilled line, after emerging onto the road, had continued along it for two hundred yards and then turned off to the left.

"Henty reckons he may have slept here for the night," Boyce added, jabbing a finger. "As you can see, there's a wood that runs alongside the lane for part of the way and the dogs followed the scent into it. They found an area of flattened bracken and this clinging to a bush nearby."

He took a small plastic envelope from his pocket and laid it on the table in front of Rudd, who, picking it up, saw that it contained two or three dark-blue fibres, fine and silky in texture.

"Terylene by the feel of them," Boyce explained, "and my guess is they came out of an anorak or a sleeping bag."

"Any sign that a tent was put up?" Rudd asked quickly. He could check later with Maggie Hearn to find out if Chris Lawrence owned a dark blue anorak or sleeping bag. Forensic, too, could tell them a lot more about the fibres once they'd been tested. .

"No. I've had a look at the place myself since but there's no holes in the ground where tent pegs were put in. He may not have bothered, of course. It was a warm, dry night. He may have simply kipped down in the sleeping bag. Anyway, to take up Henty's account, the dogs tracked the scent back into the lane and followed it along to this point."

His finger stopped at the junction where the lane joined a cart track that, according to the map, was wider and ran at right angles to it, leading back in one direction towards a farm that was marked in and named as Uplands Farm.

"And there they lost it," Boyce announced in aggrieved triumph. "The dogs ran round in circles trying to pick it up again but it was useless. Henty reckoned someone had driven a herd of cows down the lane from the farm earlier that morning and covered up the scent. There were plenty of fresh cow pats around to suggest it. Later, I checked with the farmer, a chap called Bateson, and found out that this, in fact, was what had happened. He told me something else that you may find interesting but I'll come back to that later. To get back to Henty and his hounds—he took them farther down the lane past the field where the cows were grazing; this field, by the way," he added, pointing to the map, "and tried to pick up the scent again but it was no good. The dogs had lost it."

"No chance he turned off the lane before that?" Rudd asked.

Boyce shrugged.

"He could have done, I suppose, but if he did, the dogs didn't pick it up. There's not all that number of places he could have turned off anyway. The lane's got high hedges on both sides and the only openings are here and here, into fields." He indicated a couple of points on the map. "This one leads into the pasture where the cows were grazing and this one into another meadow . . ."

"Wait a minute," Rudd interrupted him, bending over the map. "There's a quarry marked in here."

"Oh, that!" Boyce said dismissively. "Henty had a look at it while the handlers went on with the dogs. He said there's no chance anyone could be hiding there. It's completely overgrown and there was no sign that anybody had broken through the undergrowth. No, Henty reckons Lawrence went on down the lane towards Dearden, only the dogs got confused over the scent of the cows and couldn't pick up the trail again. Dearden's a couple of miles farther on and, as it's on a main road, he may have thumbed a lift from there. It's worth checking on."

"Where are the men now?" Rudd asked.

"Still searching the fields. I had a word with Stapleton before I came back here and he's called in his men to cover this area, between the point where the dogs lost the scent and Dearden. He's sent a group of them round by road to start a house-to-house in the village. Not that they're likely to finish tonight," he added, looking at his watch. "They've only got about an hour and a half before the light goes."

"I'll have a word with Stapleton later," Rudd said with an abstracted air. He stood looking down at the map, nibbling at a thumbnail. "It all looks straightforward," he went on, "and, added to what I've found out from Lambert, I think we've got a fairly clear picture of Chris Lawrence's movements."

"Oh, yes?" Boyce said, cocking his head inquiringly. "How did you get on with him?"

"Not as far as I'd hoped but far enough to get quite a

good idea of what happened last night," Rudd replied. "But let's go back earlier than that, to yesterday morning. According to Deakin, Chris Lawrence meets Jess Lambert for the first time in the currant field. At least, I'm assuming it was the first time. That was Deakin's impression and there's no other evidence so far to suggest they'd met before. They're seen talking together. The girl goes home, where Aston calls on her, as he's admitted. That takes us up to lunchtime. In the afternoon, Chris goes back to the currant field but Jess Lambert doesn't turn up again. Why, we don't know. She may have gotten fed up with it. What she does instead we don't know either. Chris Lawrence knocks off work and goes back to the farm. According to Maggie Hearn, and I've no reason to think she's lying at this point, Chris has a bath and a rest, comes back to the kitchen for supper, helps her wash up and then says he's going back to his room over the stable to read. It was about seven to quarter past by then. Now, Maggie Hearn said he came back to the kitchen again at about eight o'clock to announce that he's leaving. At this point she must be lying because Lambert swears he saw Chris Lawrence climbing over a gate into the road at roughly half-past seven, shortly before Jess Lambert leaves the house, presumably to meet him. And if we look at Henty's evidence, we've got a pretty good idea what route he took to get there."

"Through the stable window," Boyce put in. "I've lifted the prints from the glass and sent them off to headquarters by Langdon, together with a cup I found in Chris Lawrence's room and a sample of Maggie Hearn's prints. Langdon phoned through about ten minutes ago. The prints on the window are definitely not Maggie Hearn's but they match up with those on the cup, so I think we can assume they're Lawrence's. Besides, the dogs picked up his scent on the other side of the window."

"So that looks fairly conclusive. He takes a wide circuit through the fields, presumably so as not to be seen, although why isn't clear yet, and then climbs over the gate into the road where the girl meets him. They walk up the road to the cornfield where the crushed grass suggests they sat or lay down together, for a bit of rustic lovemaking, if my guess is right. But, the point is, what happens then? That's what interests me. You say you had the field searched and there was no sign of a struggle?"

"No," Boyce admitted. "Apart from the one place where the grass had been flattened, and that was perfectly neat if you get my meaning, there was nothing, no broken twigs, no torn leaves, not even a scuff mark in the ground to suggest there was any kind of a fight."

"And no blood"' Rudd added, "so she can't have been killed there because whoever struck her on the side of the head did it with sufficient force to knock her down and, in falling, some of the blood must have splashed onto the grass. Right?"

"Right," agreed Boyce.

"So whatever happened in that field between Chris Lawrence and Jess Lambert it wasn't murder. Not there. Not yet. Now we come to the tricky bit, the bit we haven't any evidence for at all. What happened next? Did he take her somewhere else and kill her? Or did he leave her still alive and some other person met her and killed her? That question leaves us with several possible suspects —Maggie Hearn, Ken Aston, Vi Aston or someone else we haven't got a name for yet."

"You're not still thinking of the child's father?" Boyce asked in a slightly disparaging tone.

"I'm keeping an open mind," Rudd replied equably. "But I found out a couple of things when I went to see Lambert that were interesting. Firstly, the girl had plenty of money to spend on clothes. The wardrobe and the drawers in her bedroom were crammed with things. Secondly, I found nothing that referred to her previous life, not a letter or a snapshot. Now, taken by themselves, neither need have much significance but added to the fact that the girl must have had a lover who got her pregnant, then they begin to add up."

"I don't see it," Boyce said stubbornly.

"Don't you? I think it suggests someone who gave her plenty of money to spend on herself; someone from her past life that she's careful to keep hidden."

Boyce shifted impatiently in his chair.

"Why should she want to do that?"

"Lambert," Rudd said promptly. "I don't think she wanted him to know who the father of the child was. Why we can only guess. Perhaps it was someone he would have objected to. Perhaps the man was already married. It's possible he paid her to keep her mouth shut."

Boyce began to look interested.

"A married man? Someone like Aston?" he suggested.

"It could be," Rudd agreed. The comparison struck him as valid. Someone like Aston might very well fit the description. A man of local standing who'd have a lot to lose if his affair with Jess Lambert ever came to light, who'd be prepared to buy her off. . . .

"Did you ask Lambert if he knew who the man was?" Boyce was asking.

"No. He broke down before I got that far. And I don't think I'm going to ask him, not yet anyway. If you and Stapleton can cope with the inquiry this end for a few hours, I thought I'd go to Suffolk and ask a few questions of my own. I may be able to turn up something that Lambert himself may not know, or may not be willing to admit to.

"But to get back to what I was saying—we've left Jess Lambert alive in that field soon after she meets Chris Lawrence. What happens after that is pure guesswork. What we do know is that shortly after nine o'clock Ken Aston leaves the house, followed soon after by Vi Aston, who tracks him down to the Rose and Crown to check if that's really where he's gone. I found that out, by the way, this afternoon, when she also admitted she knew he was having an affair with the girl. We also know from Ken Aston's statement that Maggie Hearn was not at home when he called there about a quarter to ten. So, even if we leave out the possibility of the child's father turning up, we've still got three suspects, in addition to Chris Lawrence, who had the opportunity to kill her. According to Pardoe, she died between nine o'clock and midnight and, if we take a middle estimate of, say, around half-past nine to ten, any four of them could have done it.

"Meanwhile Chris Lawrence—and I agree with you he seems to be the number one suspect—disappears. Going on Henty's evidence, he left the farm and made his way across the fields by the footpath. The fact of his disappearance is suspicious enough. When you add it to the other fact that Maggie Hearn's been covering up for him, it looks even worse. And I'm fairly sure she's been looking for him. Remember how I pointed out to you that her bike had been moved when we called there this afternoon?"

"I meant to mention that," Boyce broke in. "I told you earlier that I'd been checking with the farmer, Bateson, about the cows. Well, in the conversation, he let drop that

Maggie Hearn had been to see him about half-past eleven this morning."

"So she had been out a second time," Rudd mused.

"And there's another thing," Boyce added. "Before I went back to the farm, you mentioned Chris Lawrence had left some books and a camping stove behind in his room that I might get prints from. Well, the books were there all right but there was no sign of the stove."

"Are you sure?" Rudd asked quickly.

"Positive. I had a good look round, not that there's all that much up there to search, but it definitely wasn't there."

"Maggie Hearn must have taken it then," Rudd replied. "But where to?"

"Into the house?"

"Why bother? And if she did, why not take the other things as well? No. I think she's taken it to Chris Lawrence. After all, if he's hiding out somewhere, he'd need it."

"You mean she knows where he is?" Boyce asked, sounding scandalised.

"Possibly. Or she may have taken it on the off chance she'd find him."

He got to his feet.

"Are going to see her?" Boyce asked, rising too.

"No. Not yet. Knowing Maggie Hearn, she'll lie her head off about it," Rudd said grimly. "I want a bit more evidence first. I'm going to see Bateson. I want to know what direction she came from, whether from the village or across the fields, and if she had anything with her that looked at all like a camping stove."

He made for the door.

"I want you to come too, Tom. After we've talked to Bateson, we'll go on to Dearden and see how Stapleton's getting on with the inquiries that end. Then we'll have a chat with Maggie Hearn. There's a lot more I want to discuss with that lady besides what she's done with Chris Lawrence's camping stove."

12

Chris heard the men before he was aware of the dogs; a medley of voices some little distance down the lane that came to him in snatches:

"...nothing here ..."

"Try farther down ... the scent ..."

"...you take that side ..."

A single, yelping bark, quickly silenced, punctuated the last remark He was lying quietly in his little arena of close, rabbit-bitten turf, watching, through half-closed eyes, the shifting pattern of light and shadow on the leaves above his head. Seen veiled through his lashes, the points of light merged and coruscated into coins of gold, flickering in and out with the light breeze that stirred the tops of the trees.

"Danaë's shower," he thought sleepily.

He was in that pleasant, drifting half-world between sleep and waking that always followed the deep, black, drugged oblivion of the tranquillisers; a midway state in which his body felt light and only partly incarnate and the edges of reality were still soft and blurred.

The bark of the dog and the voices of the men jerked him into full consciousness. For a few seconds, he lay immobile, incapable of movement, and then, without any conscious effort, his reflexes whipped into action and he found himself rolling over onto his stomach and scrambling towards the overhang of the bushes where he crouched, his arms tightly hugging his knees, his ears straining to pick up the slightest sound.

He knew why they were there. They were looking for him. The dogs must have picked up his scent and traced him this far. But the confusion of orders and the exasperated note in the men's voices told him that they were still not certain where he was hidden.

He looked quickly across to the tent. Its bright-orange canvas showed up in garish contrast to the green foliage that surrounded it.

Oh, Christ! he thought in sudden panic. They'll see it.

He wondered whether to crawl across and take it down. It would take only a few seconds to dismantle it and bundle it away out of sight. He even started towards it, emerging on hands and knees from the bushes when a voice, frighteningly near, stopped him in his tracks.

"I'll have a look over here. You others go on down the lane."

Chris couldn't see the man but he could feel his presence only a few yards above him. His feet tramped across the grass and then stopped at the edge of the quarry. Then came a small, scratching noise that puzzled Chris at first until he smelt the smoke from the cigarette and the spent match, carelessly flicked away, fell through the leaves and lodged in a branch just above his head.

The feet shifted, moved on. There was a sharp crackle as the man trod on a dead twig, followed by quick rustling noises, as if he were searching the bushes that surrounded the rim of the quarry.

Oh God! Oh Christ! He'll see where Maggie came down, Chris thought wildly, remembering her blundering descent. Why the hell did she have to come?

He felt a surge of anger towards her, although he was too tired and frightened for the rage to take complete possession of him. It seemed the final betrayal.

Discovery was only a few seconds away and, after that, the rest would follow with the terrifying inevitability of a nightmare; the questioning; the hostility; the lurching sickness in his stomach; the futile attempts to explain and finding instead only a growing confusion in his mind until nothing made sense.

Perhaps I did kill her, he thought. He couldn't really remember anymore what had happened, except her face laughing into his and the rage bursting inside him and pouring out like a red flood. And then running, running, running. But surely he had heard her still laughing behind him? Or had he imagined it? Perhaps the redness that had seemed to come from within himself had been actual, not imaginary. Real blood pouring out.

He looked down quickly at his hands. They seemed

clean but was that any proof? Perhaps he had washed them, although he couldn't remember having done so. He began to examine them obsessively, minutely, turning them over to look at the palms and then the fingernails.

The sound of footsteps retreating brought him back to the present.

The man's voice shouted again, only this time it was farther off.

"Nothing here! Try the next field!"

Someone shouted back and the sounds faded to be followed by silence. But it was half an hour before he dared move. Crawling out from the shelter of the scrub, he took down the tent, rolled it up and put it into its waterproof bag, which he thrust away deep into the bushes. Then he retreated again, back to his leafy cave, where he crouched, his arms crooked round his knees, staring out, waiting for darkness to fall.

Maggie, too, sat and waited; not for anything in particular but in a daze of despair in which any activity was impossible.

They'll find him, she thought. They'll run him down like a frightened animal.

She remembered harvest times from her childhood—the reaper working its way round the field, section by section, until only a square of standing corn remained uncut in the centre round which the men had positioned themselves with cudgels, the dogs at their sides panting with a dreadful eagerness, waiting for the final, panic-stricken moment when the rabbits and hares and other small creatures bolted from this last refuge and the afternoon was made hideous by their screams. Blood on the bright stubble and the scent of death in the air.

She had not moved from the kitchen since the men left for the second time with the dogs. They had been polite enough towards her, even courteous, with that official, rather abstracted formality of men who have a job to do and intend carrying it out with the maximum efficiency. But she had been aware of a suppressed air of excitement about them as if the prospect of the hunt pleased them. The dogs, too, had the same look of anticipation; beautiful animals that she might have admired under any other circumstances with their well-groomed coats and bright, alert eyes. But the swiftness and eagerness with which they had set off down the drive, following Chris's scent, had terrified her.

She had learnt a little of the progress of the chase from the snatches of conversation she had managed to pick up as they conferred together in the yard. They had traced him to the cornfield on the far side of Lambert's bungalow and now they were back, taking the dogs up to the stable loft to pick up the scent again from the bedding.

The big sergeant was with them, the one who had come with Rudd on the second interview. He had taken her fingerprints, seeming embarrassed and ill at ease as he lifted each finger and rolled it across the ink pad before transferring the print to the paper.

As he left, he had tried to reassure her.

"It'll be all right, Miss Hearn."

She had said nothing but remained seated at the table, watching through the window as the men came clattering down the stable steps, the dogs leading the way, straining at the end of their leashes, to disappear down the road towards the village.

The sergeant left shortly afterwards, coming out of the stable with a furtive air as if he didn't want to be seen, clutching at the case that no doubt held his equipment, for Maggie could guess what he had been doing: checking the stable window for Chris's prints.

After he had driven away, silence had fallen, more ominous and menacing than the bustle and activity of the men.

Now, faced with what to do next, she realised she could do nothing. She daren't go back to the quarry to warn Chris. That would be madness. She couldn't even bring herself to go up to his room. The signs of his recent presence would finally break her.

Outside, the late-afternoon sun fell across the yard and the outbuildings, glittering dustily on the stable window. The hens pecked and scratched fussily about the cobblestones. There was a lazy, contented, fulfilled quality about the air that mocked her own inward, cold sense of dread.

A car went by on the road outside—Rudd on his way to Lambert's bungalow; not that Maggie knew this. And then another—Lambert on his way home.

Between the sound of the two engines, there was nothing, only the tiny noises that she was accustomed to and hardly heard.

The light slowly shifted. The shadows grew longer across the yard. The blue dusk deepened, heightening the colours, turning the leaves to a deeper, more vivid green. Behind the roofs, sharply etched now against the sky, a few last birds flew homeward, an urgency in their darting flight. Then the last of the light faded and the colours retreated, leaving only the shapes of things visible.

Maggie sighed and got up stiffly from the table, turning on the light, going out into the yard to shut the hens up for the night and put her bicycle away in the barn, making a pretence of action.

Chris crawled out from his hiding place and, moving like an automaton, began to gather up his possessions. The one patch of sky visible at the top of the funnel of leaves was purple now. Dusk had dropped over the countryside, although a little of the day's warmth still lingered in the quarry; he could feel it in the grass as he groped about for the tent, the sleeping bag and the things that Maggie had brought for him.

Sitting cross-legged on the grass, he began to pack them away into the rucksack, finding a certain satisfaction in the routine task of stowing them away neatly, rolling up the sleeping bag into its smallest possible compass before fastening it under the waterproof flap.

The task finished, he slipped the straps over his shoulders and looked upwards through the dense mass of leaves, more crowded than ever in the gathering darkness, to the invisible rim of the quarry. It was time to be gone.

Rudd switched on the light in the small committee room and looked at the cream-painted walls and ugly deal furniture that were now familiar to him. Boyce had gone home. Or, rather, Rudd had sent him home. The man had looked exhausted. Besides, there was nothing more he could do. The interview with Bateston and the conference with Stapleton had taken longer than either of them had anticipated and it was now too late to see Maggie Hearn. That would have to be left until tomorrow, together with the resumption of the search of the fields behind Bateston's farm and the house-to-house inquires in Dearden.

All Rudd could do was write up his own reports and read through the others that were lying on his desk; Stapleton's on the search of the area round the body; Pardoe's on his preliminary examination; Boyce's on the fingerprints on the window; Kyle's on Ken Aston's movements the previous evening; although God alone knew how any of them had found time to put anything down on paper; Boyce and Stapleton in particular who had been on their feet since the investigation first began.

He open Kyle's report and began to skim through it. It was thorough but, as Rudd had suspected, Kyle had been unable to verify with any exactitude the times that Aston had arrived at the Rose and Crown and left it. In short, it meant that Aston could have found the five or ten minutes which was all that would be necessary for killing Jess Lambert and disposing of her body. As a suspect, he was still in the running. The same applied to Vi Aston for, although Kyle had not found anyone who had seen her driving through the village, her own timetable was sufficiently vague for her to have met and murdered the girl.

He didn't bother with the others, knowing what their contents were, but putting them to one side for reading through later, he turned to his own report on the interview with Bateson.

Reports. Files. Papers. Rudd sometimes felt drowned in them and a lot of them were unnecessary and pointless. Take the interview with Bateson. What could he possibly say about that? The bald facts of it made uninspiring reading.

Yes, Bateson had said, Maggie Hearn had called on him that morning to see him about a gate that needed replacing. No, he couldn't say what direction she came from; he had been round at the back of the barn trying to get the tractor started. No, he didn't see if she had anything with her. She'd propped her bike up against the barn wall and he hadn't noticed if she'd got anything in the basket on front of the handlebars. She certainly wasn't carrying a bag or a parcel when he'd talked to her.

All very dull but a necessary routine inquiry that had added nothing to solving the case, at least on paper.

But what had interested Rudd and could hardly be written down as evidence was Bateson's attitude, apparent in the brevity of his replies and the manner in which his eyes failed to meet the inspector's but had rested, with a ruminative opacity, at some point just beyond Rudd's right shoulder. He wasn't exactly being unco-operative. It was more a natural caginess and a negative response to outsiders and, more positively, Rudd thought, a strong loyalty towards Maggie Hearn, almost a protectiveness which found expression in answering the questions put to him in as brief and unhelpful a manner as possible.

Rudd tested this out before he finally gave up and concluded the interview.

"I suppose you've known Miss Hearn a long time, Mr. Bateson?" he asked.

"Since she was born."

It was enough. The simple statement expressed all that was needed. Maggie Hearn, in his eyes, was as good as kinfolk and, as such, was included in the loyalty that must be extended to the family.

"Did you know the young man who was staying with her?" Rudd asked, wondering how Chris Lawrence would fit into this circle.

"No, but if Maggie was putting him up, he must be all right," Bateston said stoutly.

So a ripple of loyalty touched him, too, although Rudd doubted if Bateson would go so far as to shelter him. But one thing he was sure of: Bateson wouldn't turn him over to the police either. If he did find him on his land, it would be Maggie he'd go to first.

There was nothing Rudd could do about it, of course, short of putting someone to watch the farm and that was hardly feasible. He needed every man he'd got for the search and it was too long a shot to waste anyone's time on. Besides, he doubted if Bateson would actually go looking for Chris. His loyalty to Maggie would be expressed in doing nothing, stonewalling every inquiry and maintaining a totally negative attitude to the investigation.

None of this, though, could feature in a report, Rudd thought, as he jerked a piece of paper off the top of the pile and began to type out one of those stilted, official sentences that had become almost second nature to him:

"At seven-twenty approximately this evening, I interviewed Mr. William Bateson of Uplands Farm, having occasion to believe . . ."

Behind the closed door, one of the constables on duty in the main hall coughed and creaked his chair. Someone drove up to the Rose and Crown opposite. There were voices, car doors slamming, footsteps crunching across gravel. Normal, ordinary life was going on outside.

Meanwhile, Rudd typed on:

". . .but Mr Bateson could offer no help in my inquiries . . ."

Maggie heard the footsteps in the yard and got defensively to her feet, assuming it was the police who had come back to question her again. What right have they to pester me at this time of night? she thought with a tired anger that at least was better than the dull despair that had overwhelmed her for most of the afternoon.

Going to the door, she flung it open with something like her old briskness.

And suddenly, Chris was there, standing in the yard with his rucksack on his back, just like the time when he had first arrived.

"I've come back," he said simply.

The next moment, she was laughing and bundling him into the kitchen, incoherent with happiness and relief. It was only when the first flurry of excitement was over and he had taken off the rucksack and sat down at the table that she saw how deathly ill he looked. Immediately her happiness turned to concern.

"Have you eaten?" she asked sharply.

He shook his head.

"What about those cheese sandwiches?"

"I'm sorry, Maggie. I'm afraid I couldn't finish them."

"Well, you're going to eat something now, my lad," she told him, "and it's no good you shaking your head at me like that. I'll cook you an omelette and you'll eat every scrap of it, if I have to stand over you till you do."

It was said with teasing authority, as if she were mocking her own bossiness, but nevertheless she meant it for, even as she was speaking, she was bustling round the kitchen, getting out the frying pan and the mixing bowl, opening the fridge door to find eggs and butter.

Chris made no further objections but sat passively in his chair, watching her prepare the meal. The cosy, warm kitchen enveloped him. It was as if he had never been away and the nightmare of the past few hours was just that: a nightmare from which he had wakened to find Maggie standing reassuringly over him.

She was speaking to him as she busied herself at the stove and he roused himself to reply:

"I'm sorry. What did you say?"

"I said, go and have a bath before you eat. A quick one, mind. I'll have your supper ready when you come down."

He trailed off obediently, too tired to argue. Besides what else could he do except put himself in her hands?

When he came back to the kitchen, he was aware of a subtle change in her. She was quieter, more thoughtful, as if the immediate excitement and concern had died down and she had her mind on other things.

"Which way did you come?" she asked as he sat down and she put his plate in front of him. There was a deliberately offhand air about her.

He looked up into her face.

"Across the fields."

"Did anyone see you?"

"No."

That was all right, then, Maggie thought with relief. If the police didn't know he was here, they'd hardly come looking for him, although she had taken the precaution of locking the back door and drawing the curtains while Chris was out of the room.

She let him eat in silence. It was only when he had finished and she took his empty plate away that she spoke again.

"What are you going to do, Chris?"

There was a long silence before he answered.

"I don't know."

"You realise the police are looking for you?"

"Yes. They came with dogs this afternoon quite near the quarry. For an awful moment, I thought they'd find me." His hands trembled at the memory of it. "But I didn't kill that girl, Maggie."

"I know that," Maggie replied. She didn't have to be told. Having him close to her again was all the proof she needed. Any doubts she might have felt were dispelled the moment she saw him standing in the yard. But would the police believe him?

"I thought . . ." he began hesitantly. It was difficult for him to put into exact words what was in his mind. Sitting under the low trees and bushes in the quarry as the light faded, he had come to certain decisions, all of which, he realised now, had been emotional and not rational.

He couldn't go on hiding; that much was definite. The thought of walking on in the darkness, of sleeping rough for another night had filled him with despair. Instead, he had thought of the kitchen at Maggie's, the round-faced clock on the wall, the warm smell of cooking, the cat asleep in front of the stove; of his own room, too, above the stable, full of shadows and yellow lamplight. They had drawn him back as inexorably as if he had a cord attached to his wrist.

Beyond the point of coming back—coming home, he realised—he hadn't really thought, except to trust in some vague, confused way that Maggie would sort it all out for him and everything would be resolved.

"I don't know!" he repeated, his voice rising. "I just don't know, Maggie! Tell me what to do."

She sat down opposite him and spoke to him as she might have done to a child.

"Look, Chris, I can't hide you here. You realise that?"

She waited patiently until he nodded his head in confirmation.

"It's not that I don't want to or that I mind for myself. But it just wouldn't work. Sooner or later someone's bound to see you and report you to the police. It'd make things worse instead of better. You see that, don't you?"

Again she waited for him to signal his agreement. All the time she was speaking, he kept his eyes fixed on her face, reading its expression, as if he were searching for something more than the mere meaning of the words. He looked so ill, so dreadfully vulnerable, that it took all her courage to go on and not put her arms round him, drawing him to her, as every part of her cried out to do.

"You've got to go to the police and tell them exactly what happened," she went on. "Do you understand? If it's the truth, they'll believe you. They'll have to."

She wasn't sure she believed it herself. Mistakes had been made before and the wrong people arrested. But what else could she do, she thought sadly, except offer him this childlike faith in the absolute power of truth to solve everything?

He nodded again and she got to her feet.

"I'll go and tell them now," she said.

He caught her by the arm.

"Maggie," he said urgently, "when it's all over, when

everything's all right"—his mouth twisted wryly at the word—"you'll let me stay here with you? I could work for you . . ."

"No, Chris," she said quietly.

"I'll get a job in the village, then, or in Watleigh. I'll pay for my keep and help you around the place in the evenings and weekends . . ."

"No, Chris," she repeated more firmly.

The expression on his face cut her to the heart and she knew it would be easy, fatally easy, to give way and agree; not just for his sake, she realised, but for her own.

Oh, God! how much she wanted to have him here all the time, to hear his voice, his footsteps on the stairs, to cook for him and wash for him and see him sitting, as he was now, across the table from her and know he would never go away from her again.

"No," she said again, more softly this time. "Chris, it wouldn't work, believe me. I don't know what happened before you came here or what the answer is for you but you've got to find it on your own. Don't you see? You won't find it here with me; not a proper answer, that is."

She wanted to say that there was much more that she now understood and for which she blamed herself. He had been right when he shouted out that she wanted to tame him. I would lap him round with love, she thought, until there was no room left in which he could be himself. I would turn him into a dutiful son in the same way that I was turned into a dutiful daughter. And look what happened to me, for God's sake. It was only my father's death that released me; but too late, too late.

With gentle fingers, she removed his hand from her arm and walked across the room to fetch her cardigan that was hanging up behind the door.

"I'm going to fetch the inspector," she told him as she put it on. "You'll wait here, won't you, Chris, until I come back?"

He nodded obediently, too distressed by her rejection of him to be able to speak.

Like a good child, Maggie thought sadly, as she wheeled her bike out of the barn. God knows what will become of him. It was like throwing someone into the deep end of a swimming pool and watching him flounder out of his depth. Sink or swim. It was a hard lesson but one she thought he'd survive. There was a hard, bright centre to him that she felt she recognised. At least, she could do nothing more than trust to her own judgement that it did, in fact, exist.

13

The sight of Maggie Hearn being ushered into his little office by one of the constables took Rudd completely by surprise. It wasn't just her unexpected arrival at that late hour which caught him unawares but some subtle change in her pesonality as well. She still looked tired but the haggard, haunted look had gone from her face to be replaced by an expression that was much more strong and confident.

"Chris has come back," she announced quietly. "I want you to come and talk to him."

"I lied to you," she added a few minutes later as Rudd handed her into the passenger seat of his car, leaving the bike to be brought back later by one of the men on duty.

He gave her an amused sideways look as he got in beside her behind the wheel.

"I thought you might have done," he replied cheerfully.

"I was afraid of telling the truth," she confessed.

"Afraid for Chris?"

She nodded.

"It was stupid of me, of course. I knew deep down he hadn't killed her but everything got so muddled up and confused. I wanted"—she hesitated—"to protect him but that was silly of me, too. He's quite old enough and intelligent enough to look after himself."

It was the nearest she could get to explaining to the inspector the intensity of her feelings for Chris and the decision she had made a little earlier that she must let him go, for both their sakes.

"I see," Rudd said blandly.

He could only guess at what had happened by the change in her demeanour and by even more subtle signs— the way her hands, for instance, lay quietly clasped together in her lap—that she had passed through some crisis and emerged with a new-found assurance and serenity.

"I've been looking for him ever since he left last night," Maggie continued. "I lied about that too, by the way. It was nearly a quarter to ten before he went and you were right, there was a quarrel; not over Jess Lambert, I didn't know then that he'd met her, but because he'd gone out without telling me. It shouldn't have mattered, of course. It was none of my business."

She made no further attempt to justify herself, Rudd noticed, but accepted the blame for Chris's sudden departure. Nor did she make any reference to the fact that Chris had climbed out of the stable window. In a sense, he realised, she was still protecting him, making it look as if his actions were perfectly acceptable and it was only herself who had behaved badly.

Perhaps Chris Lawrence would be able to give a better explanation of his motives.

"I went out again this morning," Maggie went on. "That's why I wasn't at home when you first came. And later, after you'd gone, I tried looking for him on the other side of the village, along the Dearden footpath, and I found him."

"Where?" Rudd asked with interest.

"In the old quarry."

I'll have to have a few words about that with Henty, Rudd thought grimly. He said he'd searched the area and there was no sign of him.

"Did you take the camping stove to him?" he asked.

For the first time Maggie showed signs of distress.

"You knew about that?" she asked quickly. It was only a small point but it made her realise how close Rudd had been to discovering the truth and how stupidly dangerous her own behaviour. Instead of helping Chris, she might very well have betrayed him.

"I mentioned it to my sergeant and he noticed it was missing from Chris's room," Rudd explained.

"Yes, I took it with me, hoping I might find him."

"Which you did," Rudd remarked encouragingly.

And a damned sight quicker than any of us, he added to himself.

"He was camping, as I said, in the old quarry. I told him Jess Lambert had been found dead and it upset him dreadfully." Some of the fear and tension of that meeting showed in her face and voice. "He didn't know about it. He couldn't have done. He said when he left her she was still alive. But, don't you see, if he had known, if he had killed her, he wouldn't have been so shocked?"

"Yes, I see" Rudd said soothingly.

There was a lot more, though, that he wanted to ask, but of Chris Lawrence, not of Maggie. Why, for instance, if he were innocent hadn't he gone straight to the police when he heard from Maggie that the girl had been murdered? Why had he stayed in hiding? Henty and the dog handlers must have been within yards of him that afternoon when they traced his scent as far as the lane and yet, even then, he had made no attempt to give himself up.

"Then this evening, he came back," Maggie concluded. The rest of it she had no intention of explaining; the fact that he had returned secretly across the fields; that he had half hoped she would hide him; and more important still that he had asked to stay on with her and she had rejected him. None of that could be spoken of. It lay too close to her heart. ·

"Well, we'll have a chat with him now he's back," Rudd said with an offhand cheerfulness as he turned the car into the gateway of the farm.

They found him sitting at the table in the kitchen, waiting their arrival, his hands clasped tightly in front of him and a set tension about his shoulders as if he were bracing himself for the ordeal in front of him.

To Maggie, his presence was a relief. Throughout the drive to the farm with Rudd, there had lain at the back of her mind the unspoken fear that he might have run off again.

I was right, she thought happily, smiling at him as they came in. He *will* survive. It was a beginning.

Rudd smiled too, one of his pleasant, avuncular grins that put people at their ease while, at the same time, he took in, with one sharp interested, almost imperceptible glance, the young man who sat looking at him with such obvious apprehension. Rudd's smile, however, seemed to reassure him because he visibly relaxed as the inspector drew out a chair opposite him and seated himself, crossing his legs in the comfortable manner of someone settling down for a pleasant chat.

Maggie's description of him had been accurate as far as physical details were concerned, Rudd thought. What she hadn't described, perhaps deliberately, perhaps because she hadn't the words, was the air of quick sensitivity and vulnerability that was apparent, not only in his features but in his whole personality. As they entered, he had looked rapidly towards Maggie and the inspector had been aware of an unspoken interchange between them; on his part, inquiry and entreaty; on hers, sympathy and reassurance.

Chris now turned to the inspector and Rudd could feel the same silent appeal for understanding, as if the young man were reaching out and trying to touch some answering chord. It was disarming. It had the effect of calling up Rudd's compassion and forebearance as a man but, as a professional policeman, he remained unmoved. Although he doubted if Chris was aware of this ability or used it deliberately, he knew enough about the human personality to realise that it could be a dangerous flaw. Too much sensitivity, too much dependence on the mercy and tenderness of others left the individual desperately exposed to suffering and betrayal.

"Well, Mr. Lawrence," Rudd said with a bright, friendly air, "you've led us a bit of a dance, you know."

"Yes I do know," Chris replied in a low voice. "I'm sorry."

He had again looked across at Maggie, Rudd noticed, but she had turned her back and was occupied at the Aga with making tea.

Was it a deliberate withdrawal? he wondered with interest. Certainly, Chris seemed saddened by her lack of response, even a little bewildered by it.

"I shall have to ask you for a full account of what happened yesterday," Rudd continued, drawing the young man's attention back to himself.

"Of course." It was said in a polite, almost formal tone; the decent young man doing the decent thing—owning up to authority, making a clean breast of it. Good, solid, middle-class morality, Rudd thought a little sardonically. Well, we'll see. All the same, he didn't think it was a pose. "Where do you want me to begin?"

"What about yesterday morning, when I believe you met the girl for the first time?"

A small nerve jerked at the corner of Chris's mouth, pulling it sideways into the travesty of a smile that made

Rudd realise the degree of strain from which he was suffering and the struggle he was having to maintain his self-control.

"Yes, I met her yesterday morning," he replied. "I talked to her when we had a break at about eleven o'clock. I didn't know anybody there to speak to, apart from Reg, the lorry driver, and she didn't seem to know many people either. She said as much, in fact. I didn't see her again until I was leaving at lunchtime. She was trying to push the pram over the grass but the wheels were stuck so I helped her carry it out onto the road."

So, far, so good, Rudd thought. Up to now, it agreed with Deakin's account.

"I stood talking to her for a few minutes and then I asked her for a date," Chris went on. He hesitated and gave Rudd a shy, embarrassed smile. "I—I was attracted to her. She didn't seem keen at first. Then she said all right, she'd meet me at half-past seven at a stile a little farther up the road from where she lived."

No word of Aston arriving in the middle of this tête-à-tête, Rudd noticed, although Chris Lawrence was probably unaware of the fact that Aston was having an affair with the girl. His arrival, though, could account for her reluctance to see Chris again but that was purely speculative now. She was dead and there was no way of knowing what had gone on in her mind as they stood together talking in the road.

There was a silence and Rudd cocked his head interrogatively at Chris.

Chris was debating with himself whether or not to describe how he had walked past the bungalow and then decided to leave it out. It would add nothing to the facts and he supposed this was what the inspector wanted to hear about. Besides, he felt reluctant to express his feelings in front of Maggie. Her refusal to let him stay had at first shocked him. He had been counting on it. It had never occurred to him that she might refuse. When she had left to fetch the inspector, he had sat alone in the kitchen, trying to reconcile himself to her rejection, which he still couldn't fully believe in or accept.

Her quick smile of reassurance as she returned had come as a relief to him. It was going to be all right, he told himself. She had given way and would agree to him staying at the farm. All he had to do now was to tell the truth, as she had advised him, and the inspector would check the facts and let him go.

Now he wasn't so sure. Maggie had turned her back on him, and Rudd, in spite of his friendly, twinkling air, was watching him with a sharp and disconcerting interest. He began to feel resentful towards both of them.

"She wasn't there when I went back to the currant field in the afternoon," he continued, his voice betraying his increased tension. "From something she said later, I gather she'd got a bit bored with it. Anyway, I finished at about half-past four when I came back to the house, had supper with Maggie and then went out to meet her as we'd arranged."

"Via the stable window," Rudd said pleasantly.

In the silence that followed this remark, both of them turned to face him, Chris with shocked eyes, Maggie with angry abruptness. It wasn't what either of them were expecting, he realised. He had broken some pact that the two of them, perhaps unconsciously, had worked out between them. Chris was to make a statement, a nice, bald brief statement that covered all the facts but nothing more. No word about his motives. No word either about his real feelings except perhaps for a few trivial explanations: "I was afraid," "I panicked"; and he was supposed to be satisfied with that.

Now he came to think about it, Rudd realised that Maggie had set the style for the interview with Chris during the talk he had had with her in the car. She had been careful to make no reference to her own reactions, an omission he hadn't paid a lot of attention to at the time.

Damn the pair of them, he thought angrily, I'm not going to be fobbed off with this!

"Look," he said with a patience he didn't really feel, "don't waste my time, Mr. Lawrence. I know and you know and *she* knows," nodding at Maggie, "that when you went to meet Jess Lambert you were very careful to cover your tracks, but not careful enough. Now, I'll be straight-forward with you. I'll put all the facts on the line. Firstly, I have proof that you climbed out of that stable window. My sergeant's found your prints on the glass. Secondly, I know exactly what route you took. The dogs traced your scent. You went through the orchard at the back of the stable, over the fence into the field, beyond which you skirted on the far side. You then went round the edge of the currant field, through a gap in the hedge into the adjoining meadow where you climbed over the gate that leads into the road. Jess Lambert's father saw you, by the way, and the time was about half-past seven. You then went up the road, presumably in the company of the girl because her father said she left the house shortly after you arrived, and climbed the stile into the cornfield where the pair of you sat down, or possibly lay down, in the long grass at the side of the field. It's all written down in reports, Mr. Lawrence; reports from the sergeant in charge of the dogs; reports from the plainclothesman who checked the window for prints and later searched the cornfield where you and Jess Lambert kept your date. But what isn't written down but which I intend to find out, either here or at headquarters, is why you bothered to go to such trouble to conceal the meeting from Miss Hearn. Why you lied. Why she lied. And why Jess Lambert lied as she undoubtedly did to her father. A lot of lies, Mr. Lawrence, but I'm sure both of us are intelligent enough to realise that no normal person tells lies without good reason—unless it's too inconvenient, too embarrassing or, perhaps, too dangerous, to tell the truth. Maggie's lies I think I understand." He turned to her briefly, unaware that he had used her Christian name and for a second, caught an odd expression on her face. Relief was it? "Jess Lambert's I'm still working on. But yours I don't know anything about, although I intend finding out. A girl is dead, Mr Lawrence, and, quite frankly, I don't give a damn about anything else except arresting the person who killed her."

Throughout this speech Chris hadn't taken his eyes from the inspector's face. Suddenly, unexpectedly, he laughed. It was a short, bitter laugh but not without a certain wry humour in it.

"I should have met you before, Inspector," he said, "because you've just given me what I realise I should have had a long time ago—the equivalent of a bloody good clip round the ear. You're right, of course. All that matters is the girl's death. I didn't murder her. I don't know whether you believe me or not but it's the truth. I don't deny I met her and I don't deny either that at one point I was angry enough to kill her. But I didn't. I came back here and hit Maggie instead. No, don't interfere," he said sharply, as she stepped forward with a little cry of protest. "Don't try

to protect me anymore. That's all finished and done with."
He made a gesture with one hand, dismissive, almost
contemptuous. "Pour out the tea. Do something, for God's
sake. The inspector wants the truth and I'm going to give
it to him unvarnished, penny plain, right from the bottom
of the well."

He turned back to Rudd, ignoring her. His eyes were
very bright with a feverish excitement in them that, at first,
Rudd took for a look of madness until he saw the quick
glint of intelligent awareness at the back of them. All the
same, he's worked himself up to a ferment of confession,
Rudd thought. He had experienced it before: the sudden
outpouring as if a dam had broken and there was nothing
to hold back the flood of words. He never liked witnessing
it. Something fastidious and controlled in his own nature
recoiled. It was too self-indulgent, too self-dramatising.
All the same, he recognised the fact that there were
people, too many of them perhaps, who like Chris needed
this catharsis and, at least, Chris was intelligent and
educated enough to make it articulate and sufficiently
self-aware to give it an edge of irony.

But still too self-absorbed to be aware of Maggie, Rudd
noticed. Since his dismissal of her, she had effaced herself,
quietly setting out cups and pouring tea for them with a
subdued air. As she stood beside him and placed his cup
on the table, the inspector glanced up into her face and
saw a bright, liquid shine in her eyes that told him she was
close to tears.

"I don't suppose you'll be interested in a long account
of my childhood," Chris was saying with a self-mocking
air. "The psychiatrist who was treating me has it all down
on record if you want to read the details. But, to sum it
up, I was an only child. My father left us when I was four
years old and I was brought up by an anxious, overprotective mother; a neurotic woman in many ways, although
that's not her fault. She's the product of her own upbringing. A circle, you see, Inspector, that's difficult to break
out of." For a moment, the glint of humour showed again
in his face. "I don't blame my father either. I expect he
had to leave her in order to save himself. I've been trying
to do the same for the past year but perhaps I've left it too
late. Too many little threads have been spun to bind me to
her and, besides, I'm what she made me—polite, clean,
tidy, nicely behaved, programmed to do and say the right

thing. And don't get me wrong. I wasn't unhappy. I accepted it. In fact I rather enjoyed it. The whole household revolved round me and it's not unpleasant to be the centre of so much devotion.

"The problems came for both of us when I went away to university. I chose London, largely to please my mother. I wasn't too far away and I could get home by train most weekends. She found me lodgings through the local church that were clean and comfortable and as near a home from home as you can expect. For the first term it wasn't too bad although I realised I wasn't like a lot of the other students. I didn't have the same freedom for one thing. But I might have jogged along in my comfortable rut, attending lectures, going back to my room to study, catching the train home every Friday evening, if I hadn't met Kate.

"Like me, she was studying English and she came up to me at the end of a tutorial one day and asked if I'd like to go to a party. I don't know why she singled me out. She said afterwards that she thought I looked lonely.

The old vulnerable look working its spell, Rudd thought, although Chris's comment seemed to suggest, as the inspector had guessed, that he was unaware of its appeal.

"I had never met anyone like her before," Chris continued. "She was a lively, attractive girl, with lots of friends; very positive. She seemed to take me over."

Maggie, who was standing against the dresser behind Chris, made a small involuntary movement that she quickly covered up but not before Rudd had noticed it. Had the remark relevance for her? he wondered.

"Of course, it meant I couldn't go home so often at weekends," Chris went on. "I made excuses, ringing my mother up and telling her I had a lot of work to do but I could tell she was bitterly disappointed and hurt and it made me feel as guilty as hell."

"Why didn't you tell her the truth?" Rudd asked.

"That I had a girl friend?" Chris laughed. "Because it would have hurt her even more. She could accept up to a point that I had to study but she would never accept sharing me with another woman. Then Kate and I became lovers and I moved into the flat that she was sharing with another girl and her boy friend. I didn't dare tell my mother what I'd done. I knew she wouldn't approve and, in a way, I felt ashamed of it myself. The psychiatrist explained it later. He said she had never accepted the fact of my sexuality and, because of it, neither had I fully. I didn't understand that at the time. All I knew was that I was becoming more and more involved in a mesh of lies, pretending to her that I was still living in my old lodgings, writing to here from that address and calling round to collect my mail.

"Of course, she found out. She began suspecting that the excuses I was making weren't the truth and she wrote to my former landlady and found out that I'd moved from there. The next time I went home, she confronted me with it.

"There was a terrible scene. I said a lot of things I shouldn't have said and she became hysterical. In the end, I had to send for her doctor and she was put to bed with a nervous collapse."

"Real or assumed?" Rudd asked.

"Oh, I think real enough," Chris replied. "But it had the effect, of course, of making me feel even more guilty and keeping me tied to her again every weekend. Kate saw through it, as I did, too. She was very angry. 'It's a form of blackmail,' she told me. 'Why the hell haven't you the guts to finish with her?' She was right. I should have had the courage. But she was my mother. She was ill. She needed me. Besides, I had had a lifetime of conditioned responses in duty and obedience. So I trailed up and down between them, trying to please both and feeling torn to pieces by the two of them."

He paused, staring straight in front of him, as if silenced by the memory of that double confrontation.

"Finally, I had a nervous breakdown. But it was Kate I turned on, not my mother. I'd come back one Sunday evening to the flat and Kate said something about a paper I should have prepared for a seminar the next day which, of course, I hadn't done. I suddenly went berserk. It all seemed too much to cope with; my mother, my work, Kate herself. I started screaming and throwing things at her. The other students in the flat managed to hold me down and a doctor came and gave me an injection but it was obvious I needed treatment. I was given a term off and was sent to a clinic on the coast, near Frinton, where I was having psychiatric and drug therapy as a voluntary patient. I suppose I should have stayed on and completed the treatment but I found it too much to take. All I wanted was to be left alone and yet they made me talk about it. I can see now that they wanted me to face up to my inadequacies but it seemed at the time to make it worse. In the end, I walked out, drew what money I had left out of the bank, bought some camping gear in the town and simply disappeared. That was just over a week ago."

He glanced into the inspector's face as if looking for some sign of sympathy.

"I'm sorry it's been such a long story but you had to hear it in order to understand why I acted the way I did. It was the reason why I didn't give myself up when I knew about the murder. I was afraid to. I had this history of violence, you see, and I thought the police would assume I'd killed her. The lies, too, I can explain." He turned to Maggie, addressing her for the first time since he had begun the account. "I didn't tell you I was meeting her because I thought you'd disapprove like my mother. Besides, I was so used to lying about my private life that I did it almost instinctively. I'm sorry, Maggie."

"Oh, no, Chris, I understand!" Maggie cried. "It was partly my fault, anyway. I was becoming too . . ."

"It doesn't matter anymore," Chris interrupted her. His voice was gentle, quite different from the dismissive tone he had used before.

Rudd watched this exchange with interest. A lot was still unsaid but he thought he could read into the situation some of the unspoken aspects of their relationship. Chris's attitude he could understand. Maggie's part was less clear but it seemed evident that, in Chris's eyes at least, she had become identified with his mother, a role that she seemed prepared to accept some responsibility for. It made sense. Maggie, kind-hearted, warm, generous, would be likely to see in Chris someone to love and cherish as a son. He should have realised that before. It explained her protective attitude towards him. The tragedy was that, out of all the roles she might have played, it was the one that Chris was the least able to accept.

"You already know part of what happened later that evening," Chris was saying, addressing Rudd. "I lied to Maggie about going up to my room to read. Instead, I climbed out of the stable window and went a long way round by the fields so I wouldn't be seen. I met Jess Lambert and we walked up the road to the cornfield. I wanted . . ."

He stopped and darted a rapid, oblique glance sideways at Maggie. It was embarrassed and guilty and Rudd realised that he still looked on her as the disapproving parent.

His own mother, Rudd thought, had a hell of a lot to answer for.

". . . to make love to her," he continued in a low voice.

He stopped again and the nerve just above the corner of his mouth began to jump again, pulling the lip upward in series of little spasms.

"But you didn't," Rudd remarked in his blandest voice. "The medical evidence proves that."

"No, because I bloody couldn't!" Chris burst out with a vehemence that startled both Maggie and the inspector. "I went to pieces. I started shaking. . . .Oh, God, it was . . ."

He began to tremble again now, turning away and putting a hand over his face. Maggie started forward as if to go to him, her face distraught, but Rudd stopped her with an abrupt gesture.

"She laughed," Chris was saying, his head still averted. He had fixed his eyes on the window sill that ran behind the sink, cluttered with familiar household objects that, in their very ordinariness, seemed to deny the existence of so much remembered pain and rage.

"I could have killed her," he went on. "I had gone beyond the point where I was acting rationally. But I didn't. Physically I hadn't got the strength, or the sense of purpose. Instead, I ran away."

It had the ring of truth, as Rudd had to admit. It fitted into a pattern. He had, after all, run away from the clinic and then from Maggie's. On the other hand, violence also formed part of the pattern. He had admitted striking Maggie and attacking the girl with whom he had been living in London. He could have killed Jess Lambert as the final act in another intolerable situation in which he had lost control.

"Where did you go after you left her?" Rudd asked coolly. His very matter-of-factness of voice seemed to steady Chris.

"Nowhere much," he replied dully. "I remember she called after me. I ran up the road and then I climbed over a gate into a field. I went quite near to a farm at one point but I can't tell you exactly where I went."

It was impossible to put into words the nightmare of

that journey. It had all the half-remembered, confusing details of a frightening dream; the sensation of running, of hearing a voice crying and realising, with a sense of shock, that it was his own; of slipping and stumbling over unseen obstacles in the dusk. And behind it all, like a crazy sound track, the disjointed scraps of thought that seemed too audible to be merely in the mind, keeping up a commentary. You're no good.... You're only half a man.... You'll never be free....

"It started to get dark," Chris continued. "I found I was about two fields away from Maggie's and I thought I'd go back, collect my things and leave without seeing her. I didn't want to face anybody." He addressed her directly. "I'd've left a note for you, Maggie, or written later to say thank you for all you'd done."

"Instead of which, I came out when I heard you in the yard and said all those awful things about you telling lies. Oh, if only I'd known, Chris!"

"But you didn't, so I couldn't expect you to understand. When I struck you, Maggie, it wasn't you I was hitting. Please believe me. For a moment, standing there in the dark, you looked like ... someone else."

Like his mother, Rudd supposed, although Chris seemed incapable even now, after pouring out so much, of admitting to the fact that it was her he wanted to punish.

"So you left," Rudd said. "What time was this?"

Chris looked at Maggie.

"About twenty to ten," she replied. "I went out looking for him about ten minutes later but I couldn't find him. That must have been when Ken Aston called round."

"Where did you go?" Rudd asked her.

"Up the road towards Gossbridge. I turned back at the crossroads."

"Did you see anybody while you were out?"

Maggie shook her head.

"No."

Rudd turned back to Chris.

"What time did you leave Jess Lambert?"

"I'm not sure. I met her just after half-past seven. She was a bit late coming to meet me; say about five minutes. I waited for her a little way up the road from the bungalow. We must have been in the cornfield for about an hour, I suppose. It could have been longer."

Rudd made a quick, mental estimate of the time. If he

accepted Chris Lawrence's account as being the truth, then Jess Lambert was still alive at about nine o'clock, give or take a quarter of an hour, perhaps even more. And that meant that both Vi and Ken Aston were still possible suspects. Or Maggie Hearn, come to that. Rudd looked at her speculatively.

Of course, there was one other possibility. . . .

"What's going to happen now?" Maggie was asking a little fearfully.

Rudd roused himself.

"I'm afraid both of you will have to come into headquarters to make statements," he replied. "In your case, Miss Hearn, it shouldn't take too long."

The evidence against her was, after all, not very strong, although he couldn't entirely dismiss her from the case; not yet. But he certainly didn't have enough against her to detain her.

"And Chris?" she asked anxiously.

"I'm sorry but we may have to keep Mr. Lawrence a little longer," Rudd said blandly.

Chris met his eyes and nodded as if in acceptance of this fact. It was Maggie who gave a little cry.

"Don't, Maggie," he told her sharply. To Rudd, he added, "I'll bring my things with me."

It was clear to Rudd what he was implying as he watched the young man gather up his belongings. Whatever happened to him, he wasn't coming back. Maggie helped him with a bustling practicality. Only the unnatural brightness in her eyes and the faint trembling of her chin revealed her true feelings.

"You've left some books in your room," she said. "I'll fetch them."

She had gone, picking up the torch from the dresser, before either of them could stop her.

In the stable room, by the light of the torch, she collected up the books and then looked round. The camp bed still remained and the chair pulled up in front of the trestle table that faced the window. The magazine pictures were still pinned to the wall.

Tomorrow I must come up here again and take it all down, she thought. Then there'll be nothing left of him except what I remember and no one can tidy that away.

They were waiting for her when she returned to the kitchen with the books in her hand.

"There you are!" she said with a terrible false cheerfulness, handing them over to Chris.

"Maggie," he began but she couldn't bear to let him say anything.

"Well, we're ready," she said brightly. "Shall we go?"

They didn't speak to each other on the journey to headquarters. From time to time, Rudd glanced curiously into his rear mirror and saw that they occupied separate corners in the back of the car, both gazing out of the windows as if oblivious of each other's presence.

In the brightly lit entrance where Boyce, roused from his bed and heavy-eyed with sleep, met them, they finally parted.

To an outsider it seemed casual enough; two people briefly saying good-bye. They didn't even touch hands. For a few seconds, they stood facing each other. Then Maggie gave a brisk, almost curt, little nod of her head, Chris smiled fleetingly and they both turned and walked away in different directions.

14

"So that's it, I reckon," Boyce stated.

It was three o'clock in the morning and they were sitting in Rudd's office in headquarters which, like all rooms however familiar, looked oddly strange seen at that unaccustomed hour, as if by entering it unexpectedly, they had surprised it in some secret life of its own.

The formalities were over. Maggie Hearn had made her statement and been driven home. Rudd had seen her briefly just before she left. She had been walking slowly towards the door, her cardigan pulled on anyhow, wrinkled across her broad shoulders. Seen from the back she seemed to symbolise for Rudd all women after the moment of departure, turning away, the final wave completed, the farewell smile gone, no longer needing to keep up the pretence.

Chris Lawrence, too, had made a statement that had only just been completed and had been committed to the cells "pending further inquiries."

"What further inquiries?" Boyce had asked.

He had an exasperating habit of becoming more and more argumentative as the night wore on. Stimulated by cups of tea and the little areas of bright light in an otherwise empty building, by voices heard in empty corridors and the darkness pressing against the windows, he had a tendency that Rudd had noticed before to turn belligerent.

"I want the exact time of death verified for a start before I make a charge," Rudd replied. "And for that I need Pardoe's report."

He didn't like to add, with Boyce in his present mood, that there were other aspects of the investigation that still bothered him. The small hours of the morning tended to have the opposite effect on him than they did on the sergeant, turning him inward, making him feel depressed and on the defensive.

Now, sitting hunched up in his chair while he listened to Boyce once more put the case again Chris Lawrence, he wished to God he would go home.

"Means, opportunity," Boyce was saying, ticking them off on his fingers to emphasise the points, "and now motive. I don't know what else you want. He tries to cover up the fact he's meeting her; he admits himself he had good reason to kill her; he comes back and acts violently; he runs away. Added to which, you've got his previous history of a mental breakdown. If you ask me, he flipped his lid, clobbered the girl and . . ."

"All circumstantial evidence," Rudd retorted sharply, stung into reaction "We haven't got a scrap of positive evidence against him yet; no murder weapon with his prints on it; no witness to what happened; no proof even as to where he killed her, if that's what he did. It wasn't in that cornfield, that's for certain. You went over it yourself and found nothing; not a bloodstain or a sign of a struggle. And yet it seems the logical place to kill her. Look at it from his point of view, Tom. He's attracted to her and makes a date. They meet and walk up the road to the cornfield. He admits he wants to make love to her but when it comes to the actual moment, he goes to pieces. She laughs at him. Now, allowing for the fact that he's a highly strung, emotional young man, who's had treatment for a nervous breakdown, what ought he to do if he's guilty of murder?"

"Ought?" Boyce asked, looking confused.

"Yes, ought," Rudd repeated. "What pattern of action would he follow if, as you say, he flipped his lid and clobbered her?"

Boyce stirred uneasily in his chair.

"Well, I suppose he'd do just that."

"Exactly. But he'd do it there, at that moment, as she was laughing at him. He'd pick up something handy and smash it down on her face. But that didn't happen, otherwise there'd be bloodstains on the grass. It was a hell of a wound. The blood must have poured out. And if for some extraordinary reason none of it fell on the grass, why didn't he leave the body there? Why hump it a couple of hundred yards down the road to the currant field? Remember, he had to pass Lambert's bungalow to get there. I can't see him carrying the dead girl past the very place where she lived."

"All right, I can see your point," Boyd conceded grudgingly. "I agree it's not very likely he killed her there. But supposing he starts to attack her and she runs away? She gets as far as the road where he catches up with her and kills her. He then realises he can't leave the body there. It would be found too quickly. So he dumps it just off the road in the nearest field."

"That's possible," agreed Rudd. "But if she knew he was going to attack her, she'd've screamed and put up a struggle and there's no evidence of either. The body wasn't marked, except for the wound in the head and Lambert didn't hear any screaming otherwise he would have said something about it. He was sitting, according to his statement, in the front room of the bungalow, waiting for her to come home."

"So you don't think Chris Lawrence did it?" Boyce asked.

"I didn't say that," Rudd replied. Getting up from his chair, he went to stand at the uncurtained window, looking out at the night. Beyond the dark, mathematical shapes of the buildings opposite, all triangles, squares and oblongs, softened by the cylinders of chimney pots, the sky was lighter in tone, softly barred with clouds turned milky by an unseen moon.

"I'm only pointing out," he continued, "that we haven't enough yet to make a charge, except circumstantial evidence and, if it comes to that, we've got almost as much against Ken and Vi Aston. Both of them, on their own admission, were out and about in the village at the time the murder could have been committed, roughly quarter-past nine. That's one of the reasons I want Pardoe to confirm the time of death more exactly. It's too vague at the moment. Chris Lawrence isn't sure when he left her. It could be any time between a quarter to nine and a quarter past, perhaps even later. Assuming for the moment that we believe his story and that she was alive when he ran away, then she'd take possibly five minutes to tidy herself up, another five to start strolling down the road. Now Kyle's checked Aston's movements and, according to the landlord at the Rose and Crown, Aston turned up there at roughly twenty past nine. He left home, or so he says, soon after nine. So his timetable's flexible enough to give him a few minutes in hand to drive up the road, meet Jess Lambert, quarrel with her, kill her and dump the body in the field, for the same reason that you gave for Lawrence—because the body was lying at the side of the road and might be seen too quickly. Oh, I know the objections to that theory," Rudd went on as Boyce opened his mouth to protest, "why choose his own field? He knew Reg Deakin would arrive the next morning with the lorry so it wouldn't remain undiscovered for long. But he may have panicked and chosen that field for the very reason that it was familiar to him. He's not a very intelligent or imaginative man and I can't see him working things out in a logical sequence. His affair with Jess Lambert proves that. If he'd stopped to think, he could have seen it was a crazy idea from the beginning. She was his foreman's daughter and she lived in the same villge. He couldn't have hoped to keep it secret for long. As it was, gossip was beginning to circulate.

"There's another objection, of course, to the theory that Aston killed her; the body was left lying too tidily and that doesn't suggest Ken Aston to me. He'd be much more likely to dump the body down and clear off as soon as he could. But, apart from these objections, the circumstantial evidence is still fairly strong.

"Then there's Vi Aston, also out and about in her car, checking on exactly what her husband was up to that evening. Almost the same theory could apply to her. She drives up to the Rose and Crown, sees her husband's car is safely installed in the car park but decides to have it out anyway with Jess Lambert. She drives on up the road, meets the girl on her way back from the date with Chris and exactly the same thing happens as I've described for her husband. There's a quarrel, she kills the girl and dumps the body in the field. In some ways, it makes better sense. She chooses the currant field because it's rented by Aston, as much as saying, 'There you are. There's your mistress dumped on your property.' She may even have wanted some suspicion to attach itself to Aston, but I'm not too sure about that. When I saw her yesterday, she seemed prepared to stick up for him. But she might very well lay the body out decently."

"What about Maggie Hearn?" Boyce asked.

"Oh, I think we can now rule her out," Rudd replied with conviction. "If she'd murdered Jess Lambert, she'd've confessed, if only to save Chris Lawrence, although I agree she had the same opportunity as the Astons."

Rudd had already considered the implications of this during the interview at the farm and later while her official statement was being taken down. Why hadn't she confessed? He had been half expecting it. After all, even if innocent of Jess Lambert's murder, it seemed the sort of gesture, emotional and irrational, that she might have made, in view of her other desperate attempts to protect him. And yet she hadn't done so. It wasn't lack of courage. It wasn't even too fine a regard for the truth for although Maggie was a woman of strong principles, Rudd suspected that when the chips were finally down, she'd sacrifice truth for loyalty and love.

No, the answer lay in the change in their relationship that he had been aware of earlier in the evening. She was prepared now to let him go; to let him step out from behind the shelter of her love and face the future on his own, even if it meant a murder charge. A harsh decision, perhaps. Certainly one he felt that she hadn't reached without personal sacrifice and pain, but one that had been possible because she loved him. *And because she didn't believe he was guilty*. That was vitally important.

It was a consideration that had partly caused Rudd to hesitate in charging him; an illogical decision perhaps, but one he could defend on more rational grounds such as the lack of hard evidence. But, nevertheless, Maggie's utter faith in Chris Lawrence's innocence had made him instinctively wary of taking too final a step himself. It was, of course, something he couldn't explain to Boyce. Indeed, he felt a little shame-faced about it himself. All the same, people counted as much as facts—if not more. They presented their own kind of evidence; not the sort you could submit to forensic tests or send up to the path. lab for analysis. But nevertheless they had validity.

"I suppose you'll be charging her, though, with obstructing the inquiry?" Boyce hinted. "When all's said and done, she told quite a few lies, hoping to put us off the scent."

"I had a word with the super about that," Rudd replied, "and we've decided not to proceed, under the circumstances. Her intention wasn't criminal; only misplaced loyalty. And she did persuade Chris Lawrence to give himself up when he came back to the farm. I don't think justice would be served by making her a scapegoat."

"So who are we left with, if she's counted out?" Boyce asked rhetorically. "The Astons and Chris Lawrence. And my money's on him, even though the evidence is only circumstantial."

"There's one other possibility . . ." Rudd began.

"You're not still thinking it could be the child's father?" Boyce interrupted.

"I'm not sure," Rudd admitted.

"But there's nothing in the way of evidence to show that anyone outside the village was involved." Boyce sounded argumentative again. "It's one of the questions we asked on the house-to-house and came up with nothing. No strangers seen about. No suspicious cars parked anywhere."

"Nobody saw Chris Lawrence either," Rudd pointed out, "for the simple reason that he took good care not to be seen."

Boyce set his chin stubbornly.

"I still think it's a nonstarter. You've got one perfectly good suspect; two more if you count the Astons. Why go chasing after someone we don't even know exists?"

"Because he must exist," Rudd snapped. "Someone must have fathered that child and it's almost certainly someone in Ashbourne where they lived before they moved here."

Someone, he added to himself, who probably paid Jess Lambert good money and of whom she had kept no memento.

"I'm going to Suffolk tomorrow anyway to check," he added. "It shouldn't take too long. The owner of the market garden where Lambert used to work may know something."

"Why not ask Lambert?"

"Because I don't think he'll tell me even if he knows. And I'm not sure that he does. But I'm certain I won't get a straight answer out of him. He'll cover up and I think I know why—to protect his daughter's reputation."

"A bit late in the day for that," Boyce commented.

"Perhaps he feels even more need to do it now she's dead," Rudd replied. He looked at his watch. "Come on, Tom. Let's get a few hours' sleep in before we have to start again."

"Right." Boyce got off his chair and began to yawn hugely. "Now that you've mentioned the word 'sleep,' I've suddenly realised how tired I am. Anything special you want followed up while you're in Suffolk?"

"Yes. You can chase Pardoe up for that report for a start and tell Stapleton to call off the inquiry in Dearden. That won't be needed anymore. Instead, I want the men to concentrate on the area round where the body was found —the grass verges along the road and all the nearby fields for the murder site. If nothing turns up, we'll have to think again."

Boyce nodded and left, still yawning. Lingering in the office before he turned off the light, Rudd felt the building settle down again into its normal nighttime routine after the bustle and activity of the past few hours. The main actors in the drama had all left the stage. Chris Lawrence was downstairs in the cell block. Maggie Hearn was presumably back at the farmhouse. He doubted if either of them were asleep.

He slept badly himself in spite of his tiredness; perhaps because of it. His body dozed but his mind hardly rested. It seemed to scramble feverishly round and round like a squirrel in its wheel, while scraps of remembered conversations came disjointedly to him: Vi Aston saying bitterly, "She probably asked for it"; Lambert crying out, "For God's sake, be done!" and striking the arm of the chair with his fist. Somewhere in the background he seemed to hear a child crying, on and on, in an ecstasy of grief. Even in his dream, he knew it was Jess Lambert's child and knew also that, although he had never seen it, it was significant in a way he couldn't understand.

At seven o'clock he got up, made tea and drank it standing at the kitchen window. The garden, even his suburban patch, was beautiful at that time of the morning with a freshness that hadn't yet been touched by the day's heat.

The night voices had receded but something of their memory lingered on.

A man, a woman and a child. The phrase came unexpectedly to him when, later, he started the car and backed it out of the garage. Of the trio, he could name only one: Jess Lambert. The child's name hardly mattered. In fact, he preferred not to have it too closely identified. Better perhaps that it should remain unknown, unnamed. As for the man: well, he hoped to find the answer to that one in Suffolk.

He drove at a reasonable speed, keeping to just under fifty miles an hour, and in little over an hour and a quarter had reached the village of Ashbourne, a few miles east of Sudbury. That part of the inquiry was satisfactory enough and proved that it was perfectly possible for someone to drive over to meet Jess Lambert without much inconvenience.

The village was nondescript: a double row of council houses and brick cottages facing the road, with a small, new development of detached bungalows set in a private estate that had been carved out of a field.

Babcock's nursery was easy to find. It stood on the outskirts of the village, with a large, double-sided board painted with the firm's name at the entrance, from which a long gravel drive led up, past lawns and flower beds in which garden statuary and furniture were displayed, to a shop and display area for pot-grown shrubs and roses. Behind it and on both sides stretched greenhouses and cultivated fields.

It reminded him of Aston's place, only it was much bigger and more ambitious.

Having parked the car, he went into the shop and asked the woman who was serving if he could see Mr. Babcock. She showed him into an office opening off the back of the shop where presently Mr. Babcock joined him.

Rudd looked him over with interest as he came in, wondering if he could be the man he was looking for, the third of the trio. At first sight it seemed unlikely. Babcock was in his sixties, almost bald, with a broad, mottled face and huge hands; not the type to appeal to an eighteen-year-old girl but Rudd had known stranger relationships.

As Rudd introduced himself, Babcock nodded and asked him to sit down.

"I'm here to make a few routine inquires about Mr. Lambert," Rudd began.

"About Lambert?" Babcock asked, looking surprised. "Surely he's not in trouble with the police? He always struck me as a steady sort of chap when he worked here."

"It's that I wanted to ask you about," Rudd replied,

nimbly sidestepping the question of the exact nature of the investigation. "I believe he was with you for quite a long time?"

"Over fifteen years. I was sorry when he left."

They had reached the heart of the matter more quickly than Rudd had dared hope. With careful casualness he put the next question. "Did he give any reason for leaving?"

Babcock looked at him shrewdly for a few seconds before replying.

"I suppose it's important otherwise you wouldn't have asked. No, he didn't give any reason. Not a real one, that is. All he said was he felt he needed a change. It didn't strike me at the time as being very likely. He'd worked here, as I said, for over fifteen years without any complaint and he'd never seemed to me the sort who changed jobs for the sake of it. He was well paid. In fact, I offered him a rise to try to persuade him to stay on but he wouldn't accept it. He had a good house that went with the job. His daughter worked here, too, part-time in the garden shop. Both of them seemed well suited. I've often wondered why he asked for his cards."

"Jess Lambert worked here?" Rudd asked. He was watching Babcock carefully for any reaction but the man seemed unmoved by the mention of her name.

"Yes, I took her on after she left school. Lambert asked me if I could find her an indoor job. He didn't want her working out of doors and I could see his concern. It's hard work for a woman and he wanted the best for her."

"No gossip about her?"

"Gossip?" Babcock repeated sharply. "No. Why should there be?"

"Jess Lambert was pregnant. That's why Lambert wanted to change jobs," Rudd explained.

"Pregnant? Good Lord, I had no idea!" His surprise seemed genuine. "Well, I can understand it now. He wouldn't want to face the gossip, not a second time. You see, his wife left him for someone else when Jess was about three years old. A pretty woman as I remember. Jess takes after her in looks. Not exactly flighty, but the type who liked dressing up and going out. My wife always said it was Lambert's fault she left him and I can see her point, although women tend to stick up for each other in these cases. You've met Lambert, have you? Well, then, you'll know what I mean. He's a quiet man, not much given to enjoying himself. Anyway, whoever's fault it was, she cleared off, leaving him to bring Jess up on his own."

"Difficult for a man to cope," Rudd suggested.

"He managed very well, considering. He paid a woman to look after her when she was small, and then, when she started school, the same woman used to take her to the gate and meet her afterwards. He was more careful about her upbringing than a lot of mothers would be. Almost too careful, in some ways. My wife's words again, not mine. She could see he was going the same way with Jess as he had with his wife; no fun; no outings . . ."

"No boy friends?"

"Not that I know of," Babock replied. He suddenly became more cautious. "Look here, Inspector, I don't know what your inquiries are about but Lambert was my foreman and a damn good one at that and I don't like the idea of gossiping about either him or his daughter behind his back."

"It's a murder investigation, Mr. Babcock," Rudd told him quietly. "Jess Lambert was found dead yesterday morning."

There was no question of Babcock's shock and consternation being anything but real. Not even the most skilful actor could have feigned his expression or the futile way in which his mouth opened and closed before he could even begin to frame a sentence. No, Rudd decided, he'd have to look elsewhere for her killer.

"Jess murdered? But that's . . . I mean, she was always so . . ."

Alive? Rudd wondered if that was the word he was looking for. Certainly, even in death, she had given the impression of health and youth, the hair still glossy and thick, the body plump and well formed.

"I'm making inquires about anyone in the area she might have had a close relationship with," Rudd explained. "I particularly want to trace the child's father. It could be important."

"I see, I see," Babcock was saying hurriedly. "Well, the person to talk to is Mrs. Ritchie. She's been here for several years. Jess worked with her in the garden shop. She'd know, if anyone does, who the girl was friendly with." He walked to the door, pausing to add before he opened it, "You don't mind if I break the news to her myself?"

Rudd nodded permission and Babcock left the office to return in a few minutes with the midde-aged, dark-haired woman to whom the inspector had spoken when he first arrived. She was still a little shocked and clutched a handerchief in one hand.

"You knew Jess Lambert fairly well, I believe?" Rudd asked, giving her a reassuring smile to set her at her ease.

"Yes, she served in the shop with me. Of course, I'd known her before that, in the village, but not so well."

"Did she ever talk to you about herself?"

Mrs Ritchie hesitated.

"At first she did. Later on she wasn't quite so free with what she said. That was in the weeks just before they left."

"Did you get the impression she was hiding something?"

"Not exactly. She just became quiet and not so ready to chat. I felt she had something on her mind."

"You didn't know she was pregnant?"

It was clear Mr. Babcock hadn't given her this piece of information. Her eyes opened wide.

"No, I had no idea. She said nothing to me." She turned to Babcock. "I feel terrible now that I complained about her."

Babcock shook his head at her as if to reassure her that it was of no consequence.

"Why did you do that?" Rudd asked. It was an aspect of Jess Lambert's past that he was interested to hear about.

"It was nothing much," Mrs. Ritchie explained, anxious to justify herself. "She was a bit slow in serving people. Didn't rush herself, if you see what I mean. Took her own time about it. 'You'll have to brighten up your ideas,' I said to her. 'Customers won't want to stand about waiting for you.' She just shrugged. In the end I had a word with Mr. Babcock about it."

Rudd turned to Babcock, who cleared his throat. He, too, seemed embarrassed that this small incident that put him in a bad light had been seized on by the inspector. After all, the girl was now dead; murdered. He didn't like to think anyone knew he had once rebuked her.

"I warned her about her attitude," he said. "I told her I'd be sorry, for her father's sake, if I had to sack her. She improved after that, didn't she, Mrs. Ritchie?"

"Oh, yes. She was a lot better," Mrs. Ritchie assured him.

Rudd looked at the pair of them speculatively. The implications in Babcock's remarks were interesting. He had used Lambert as a threat against the girl and Rudd wondered why.

"Was she afraid of her father?" he asked.

"Not exactly afraid," Babcock replied. He turned to Mrs. Ritchie. "Not afraid, would you say?"

She shook her head a little hesitatingly, as if not exactly sure, but offered no other explanation.

"In awe of him, then?" Rudd suggested.

"Yes, I suppose she was, in a way," Babcock answered. "He was a strong-minded man. He had"—he paused, searching for the right word—"authority. I noticed it with the men who worked under him. Very few would cross him and yet I've rarely seen him throw his weight about. That's why he made such a good foreman. I've met his type before in the army; long-serving noncommissioned officers mostly. They could walk into a barrack room full of soldiers all shouting their heads off and silence them by simply standing in the doorway."

Rudd nodded in agreement. He had seen Lambert only once and then he had been diminished by grief but he could appreciate Babcock's description of him. The man certainly possessed presence and that weight of silent authority that Babcock had spoken of.

He turned back to Mrs. Richie.

"Did Jess Lambert ever speak to you of a boy friend?"

"Oh, no," she said promptly, as if it were entirely out of the question. "Her father wouldn't hear of it. She said to me once, 'He treats me as if I was ten years old.' She used to go to the Youth Club but Mr. Lambert was always waiting for her on the doorstep to take her home. It frightened the boys away, you see. None of them dared show interest in her with him around. Mind you, I think it was silly of him. Sooner or later she'd kick over the traces. She was sixteen then and you can't treat a girl of that age like a child, not these days. I always say they're worse in the long run than the ones who have been given a bit of freedom."

"Yes," Rudd agreed. "They often are."

If they don't finish up dead, he added to himself.

He rose to go.

"Thank you both very much for letting me take up your time."

"You've finished?" Babcock asked. He seemed surprised at the abrupt ending to the interview. Nothing very much had come out of it that he could see.

But Rudd had heard enough.

The way we love, he thought, as he walked back to the car, is as much a conditioned process as any other human activity. It was only the popular songs that made it sound romantic, a question of losing your heart to the right person.

A man and a woman. The ancient duality. But the question was what sort of man and woman? Look at Chris Lawrence. His habit of loving had been learnt in childhood and he would possibly never escape from the mother-child relationship. Or Maggie herself, come to that. What conditioning had taught her that men were sons to be fussed over and cherished? Although, she at least seemed to have learnt better. The Astons too, were another example. He doubted if Ken Aston would ever be anything more than an adolescent in his wife's eyes.

Man, woman and child: the phrase came into his mind again. Roles that seem separate and yet the boundaries are a lot less fixed than we imagine. And it was when those boundaries became too fluid that people like Jess Lambert went under, victims to a habit of loving that could end only in tragedy.

15

"Lambert!"

Boyce sounded outraged. He was in the car with Rudd, who had picked him up in the village.

"I don't know why you're so shocked," Rudd said equably. "Plenty of it goes on. You've seen cases yourself in court."

"But all the same," Boyce protested. Words seemed to fail him. "What put you onto him?"

"Several things," Rudd replied. "None of them very important in themselves but added together they made sense. In the first place, Lambert had a good job at Babcock's; more responsibility and, I suspect, better pay than he's getting at Aston's. So by changing jobs, he lost out quite considerably. That in itself wouldn't have mattered. He might have been prepared to sacrifice his career for his daughter's sake. But neither Babcock nor Mrs Richie, who worked with Jess in the shop, knew she was pregnant or even so much as suspected it. Lambert must have known, though, and fairly early on in the pregnancy, too, which implied that the girl must have told him. Again, that didn't of itself signify a great deal although I'd have thought, in view of her secrecy about Aston and Chris Lawrence, that she'd have tried to keep it from her father for as long as possible. But the really important fact that Mrs. Ritchie told me was this—she was quite sure Jess Lambert didn't have any boy friends. In fact, Jess had complained to her about her father's attitude to her going out with boys and, besides, as Mrs. Richie pointed out, with Lambert playing the heavy father, they were all scared off the girl. It was then that it occurred to me that there was only one explanation that made any sense of the situation."

Boyce shook his head in condemnation.

"I can see what you're getting at but it's still something I've never understood."

"Isn't it?" Rudd asked. "I don't think I do; not properly, that is. But I think I can see how it happened from Lambert's point of view. His wife runs off, leaving him with Jess to bring up. According to Babcock, Mrs. Lambert was a good-looking woman who liked to enjoy herself. As I can't imagine it being much fun being married to Lambert, she may have been forced into running away simply to save herself, although why she left the child behind we may never know."

Like Chris Lawrence's attempt to break free from his mother, either his real one or Maggie, Rudd thought. The more emotional the relationship, the more violent the final break. Perhaps in his marriage, Lambert had tried to play the jealous father figure even towards his wife.

"So Lambert's left with a little girl to bring up and a memory of a wife who must have seemed to him unreliable if not downright immoral. Some of this attitude must have coloured the way he treated Jess as a child. Babcock suggested he was overprotective as a father. Possibly he only meant to make sure she didn't grow up to be like her mother. Or it might have been something more destructive even than that."

"What?" asked Boyce.

"An attempt to create her in his own image," Rudd replied. "A replica of himself. Only he failed. But whatever was in his mind, it's clear he was building up a thoroughly unhealthy relationship with the girl; jealous, overprotective, demanding. Too much of the wrong kind of love, in other words. It was almost inevitable that something would go badly wrong. The only thing we don't know are the exact circumstances and how often it happened."

They had arrived at the bungalow and drew off the road behind Lambert's van, which was already parked on the grass.

"How are you going to prove all this?" Boyce asked. "He's only got to deny it and you've got nothing, except for a theory."

"I don't know," admitted Rudd.

He looked about him. The sun had set but, although a pale wash of lemon light was still visible in the sky, here in

Lambert's garden, between the high hawthorn hedges, the darkness was already beginning to settle.

"I've only got one card to play and if I muff that I could lose the game. Anyway, it looks as if Lambert is at home so we can but try."

They followed the concrete path round to the back door where Rudd knocked. After a few minutes, a light sprang up in the kitchen, the door opened and Lambert appeared on the threshold. It was clear to both of them that he was drunk. Even with the light behind him and his face almost invisible, it was apparent in his swaying stance and the shambling awkwardness of his head and arms. Rudd was reminded more forcibly than ever of the figure of a chained bear.

"What do you want?" Lambert asked. His voice was louder than usual, the edges of the words slurred. But, even so, there was still an air of dignity and authority about him.

"May we come in?" Rudd asked pleasantly. Lambert gave a curt movement of his head which they took for assent and he and Boyce crowded into the tiny kitchen.

"The pair of you had better come through into the living room," Lambert remarked, looking them up and down. Now that he could see him in the full light, Rudd noticed that he was unshaven and his face had a leaner, more shadowed look. But, more than this, there was an air of exultation about him; an excitement that was possibly due to the whisky he had been drinking, which they could smell on his breath, although the inspector didn't think this was entirely the explanation. Something else had happened to give Lambert this heightened, glittering quality, this feeling of coiled tension.

He watched Lambert's back warily as they followed him through the narrow hall into the sitting room where the curtains were drawn and the lights switched on. An armchair had been drawn up to a low table on which stood a whisky bottle, nearly empty, and a glass. Although there was nothing tangible to prove it, Rudd had the impression that the room had been like this all day. It had the atmosphere of a place that has been shut away from the sun and light for many hours.

"Sit down," Lambert said abruptly. He himself took up a position in front of the empty hearth, standing with his feet apart and his head thrust forward, as if he were in charge of the situation, as indeed he might very well be.

"If you went looking for me at Aston's, I wasn't there," he announced. "I took the day off"

He looked deliberately at the whisky bottle as if to draw their attention to it. Only Boyce followed his glance. Rudd continued to look steadily into the man's face.

"I haven't been to Mr. Aston's," he replied. "I went to Suffolk instead."

The answer clearly caught Lambert off guard. For a moment, he looked nonplussed. Then he laughed, an odd laugh that had an unexpected quality of triumph in it.

"Oh yes? What did you manage to sniff out there?"

"Not a lot," Rudd admitted. He was sitting very upright in one of the armchairs, not daring to relax. Beside him in the other chair, just out of his line of vision, he could feel Boyce's presence, heavy, embarrassed, still hugely disapproving.

Should he play his last card now? Rudd wondered. Or would it be better to wait, to go through the interview step by step and save it for a final throw?

Instinct told him to wait. Lambert was preparing himself for some kind of climax, he decided, watching the man speculatively; probably in much the same way that he had worked himself up on the night his daughter hadn't come home and he had finally gone storming round first to Maggie's and then to Cookson. Rudd guessed he was in a similar mood tonight; an established pattern, possibly, of waiting and drinking until a culmination was reached. Perhaps it would be better to match Lamber's high point with his own. He got the impression, too, that Lambert had been expecting them.

All the same, he couldn't help remarking, "All I heard was some old gossip."

Lambert didn't reply to this, only lowered his head still farther, looking at them from under his brows and shifting from foot to foot like an athlete testing the flexibility of his legs before a race.

"We came to check through the statement you made yesterday," Rudd continued in his colourless, official voice. "We've since been in touch with Mr. Lawrence . . ."

"So you managed to find him at last?" Lambert interrupted to ask in a jeering tone. "What did he have to say for himself?"

"He doesn't deny meeting your daughter on Monday evening but he insists she was still alive when he left her at about quarter-past nine. If I accept his account as being true, that leaves me with two possible alternatives. Firstly, that she started to walk home and was met by someone else on the way who murdered her and carried her body to the field to get it off the roadside. I had several possible suspects who fitted this theory." He paused briefly, wondering how much, if anything, Lambert knew of his daughter's affair with Aston but Lambert did not give him time to finish.

"And the other alternative?" he was asking.

Rudd decided to let the interview follow the course that was being set by Lambert.

"That she came home," he replied simply.

A total silence fell on the room. Boyce sat quite rigid. Rudd, too, sitting upright in the low chair, didn't move. Lambert remained straddle-legged in front of the hearth, staring down. Then his eyes shifted, first to Boyce, then to Rudd.

"So you reckon I killed her?" he asked suddenly.

"I think you sat here waiting for her to come home," Rudd replied. "I think, too, that you were angry and also drunk. I think when she finally did come home there was a quarrel in which you struck her on the side of the head. You then took the body to the field just down the road because you couldn't leave it in the house and then made up the story against Chris Lawrence in order to lay the blame on him."

"And that's what you reckon happened?" Lambert asked.

"Yes," Rudd said quietly. "I do."

Lambert fixed his eyes on him for a few moments without speaking. Then he said abruptly, "I'll show you something."

He turned and began walking out of the room. Boyce and Rudd, after a quick exchange of puzzled glances, rose to their feet and followed him.

Thinking about it afterwards, Rudd was to blame himself for not being aware of what Lambert had in his mind. And yet how was he to know? Lambert's remark, although curt, was offhand, almost conversational. There was nothing in his voice or expression to prepare the inspector for what was to happen.

Ahead of them, Lambert had flung open the door that led into the bedroom at the back that he occupied. It was in darkness, the curtains drawn, and he switched on the light only as he ushered them inside.

As the light sprang up, Rudd saw that the room was in total confusion. Clothing was strewn everywhere, across the floor and the bed. Mixed up with it were the cheap necklaces and pendants that he had seen in the little drawer in the bedside table.

At first, his vision was too stunned to take in the details, except for a general impression of disorder. It was only after a few seconds that he was able to see that the clothes had been deliberately ripped to pieces: sleeves torn from dresses, skirts and underwear slit into tatters, the cheap jewellery broken and scattered. Covering it all was a film of spilt face powder and spatters of black eyeliner from the smashed bottle and jars of make-up that lay on the top of all this ruin, together with fragments of what looked like letters, photographs and birthday cards.

"You see," Lambert was saying, trampling past them over the jumble of torn fabric and loose beads that lay on the floor, "I thought I'd have done with it for good and all. It's been pressing on me here." He put both hands against his chest. "I couldn't bear with it any longer. Yes, I killed her. I thought it would be enough but it wasn't. There was too much of her left."

He's mad, thought Rudd, and yet there was a terrible sanity about Lambert as he stood among the chaos, looking from one to the other of them, searching their faces for some glimmer of understanding.

"You don't believe me?" he went on, as neither of them responded but stood silent in the doorway. Kneeling down, he began patiently to clear away some of the torn-up clothes that lay on the floor beside the bed. "Well, I'll show you. That's where she fell. You can see it on the carpet. I covered it up with a rug but it wouldn't stay hidden. Not even when I put her things on top of it. I still seemed to see it. Blood burns, you know, like acid. . . ."

He had turned back a corner of the bedside rug revealing a large, blackened patch that had spread across the cheap cotton carpet that lay beneath. Strangely enough, it looked burnt to Rudd, as if some dark, corrosive liquid had been poured onto it, or perhaps he was seeing it with Lambert's eyes.

"What did you kill her with?" Rudd asked. He used the same conversational tone as Lambert.

"I'll show you," Lambert replied eagerly. He turned quickly and, opening the wardrobe, fumbled inside. A warning voice sounded ineffectively in Rudd's mind to be followed a split second later by Boyce's shout of "Look out!"

He was standing a little to the left of the inspector and had a better view of what Lambert was holding in his hand. Then the man swung round and Rudd, too, could see what it was: a double-barrelled shotgun. He saw also that the glitter had come back into Lambert's eyes.

"I hit her with this," he told them in the same offhand voice. His lips had parted slightly and they could see his teeth showing white against the dark stubble. "I heard her come in the back door and I went into the hall to meet her. I knew she'd met this boy and what they'd been up to. I didn't need telling. She started to shout at me and I pushed her in here so that she wouldn't wake up the child."

It was hopeless trying to interrupt him to tell him that, in fact, nothing had happened between Jess and Chris Lawrence. Lambert's voice was rising. The excitement that Rudd had seen before was returning more strongly. He could almost feel it in the room like a powerful current, running through the man, stretching his lips into a grimace, gripping his hands round the stock of the gun until the knuckles seemed about to burst through the skin.

"Like her mother!" Lambert shouted. "Like the whore she was! They took my love, everything I had to give, and then they spat on me. Look at this lot—this *trash!*" He swung the gun round until it was pointing at the scattered heaps of torn clothing. "Everything she wanted! Everything! She took and took and then gave herself to the first boy who came along."

His finger moved to the trigger so swiftly that neither Boyce nor Rudd were prepared for the report that followed. In the confines of the room it sounded like an explosion. Deafened by the noise, confused by the hanging bulb that, caught in the blast, gyrated madly, sending light and shadow chasing up the walls, and by the scraps of blackened fabric that, shredded by the force and heat of the detonation, whirled up into the air, Rudd staggered back against the door. He was aware that someone thrust past him; was aware, too, that it wasn't Boyce, who had flung himself onto his knees and covered his head with his arms.

"Are you all right?" he shouted, and as Boyce nodded and scrambled to his feet, shocked but unhurt, Rudd plunged out into the hall.

The back door was open. Lambert had gone that way. Yelling at Boyce to follow, Rudd raced out through the kitchen and into the yard in time to see Lambert making off across the garden.

If he had intended using his van to make a getaway, he was baulked, for Rudd's car was drawn up behind it, effectively blocking it in. For a second, he seemed to hesitate before plunging on towards the far corner of the garden where a gap in the hedge gave him easier access to the field beyond.

He cleared the surrounding ditch in one stride and, by the time Rudd and Boyce had gotten to the opening, he was already half-way across the meadow, running like a bull, his head lowered, his shoulders hunched, his feet pounding the grass.

As he took up the chase, Rudd realised it was a final burst of rage and despair that Lambert wouldn't be able to maintain for long. Whatever had broken inside him, whatever long-pent-up emotion, finally freed, had given him the strength for this last act of defiance, the climax that he had been building up towards, that the murder of his daughter and the destruction of everything she possessed had not appeased, it would not be long before he reached the end.

A small wood ran along the farther side of the field, a mere copse, consisting of a few standing trees and a thick undergrowth of low bushes made darker and denser by the fading light.

Ahead of them, Rudd heard Lambert crash into the scrub and then there was silence. The bear had gone to ground.

Dragging Boyce back by the arm, for the sergeant showed every sign of plunging in after him, Rudd halted a few yards from the edge of the field.

"He's armed, don't forget," he warned him, crouching and drawing Boyce down with him.

"Christ alive," Boyce said, wiping his face on the sleeve of his jacket. "I thought we'd bought it back there when that bloody gun went off. What's the matter with him? Is he mad?"

"Not so much mad as maddened," Rudd replied.

He was peering through the dusk, trying to fix his eyes on the dark mass of leaves in front of him and to pick out from it the darker mass that would be Lambert, at the same time straining his ears for the smallest movement that would betray the man's exact position. But he must have been standing stock-still for Rudd could not even discern the rustling of leaves.

Kneeling upright, he glanced quickly about him. There was no chance of taking Lambert by surprise. Without the benefit of cover, such as Lambert had, it would be impossible to move forward across the grass without being seen. Besides, such light as was left was behind them. Unless they lay perfectly still, he would be able to pick them out quite easily.

Lambert was also armed, which gave him another advantage. Assuming the gun had been fully loaded, there was still one cartridge left in it and no way of knowing if Lambert had brought more with him in his pockets. He could blast a hole in both of them before they'd even reached the spinney.

Nor was there any chance of flushing him out. The copse, though narrow, ran the length of the field. Boyce and himself on their own couldn't possibly cover the whole of it. Lambert could break out at any point and be away across the fields before either of them could catch him.

He could, Rudd realised, send Boyce back for more men but that would take time and he had the feeling that Lambert wouldn't lie doggo for long. And, anyway, Lambert would see them coming long before they could get the place surrounded.

That would be his final move, he decided. But first he'd try persuading the man to give himself up.

"I'm going to talk to him," he whispered to Boyce, who grunted in reply.

Rising to his knees, Rudd made a megaphone of his hands.

"Lambert!" he shouted.

There was silence. He tried again.

"Lambert! Don't be a fool, man. Throw down the gun and come out."

Again silence, except for a bird that, disturbed by his shouts, called aloud and fluttered in the leaves.

There was one argument left that had occurred to Rudd before when they had confronted Lambert in the bedroom and that he hadn't then been able to make. He decided to use it now.

"Listen, Lambert. Chris Lawrence didn't make love to her. The doctor told me that when he examined her. She hadn't been touched."

The silence continued for a few seconds but Rudd was aware of a difference in its quality. It was impossible to say exactly how it changed but, with every nerve straining, he seemed to pick up a greater listening intensity from the massed shadows in front of him.

Then Lambert spoke.

"Is that true?"

"Yes, I swear it. You can read the medical report if you like."

As he spoke, he edged forward on hands and knees, Boyce following him, covering a few more yards towards the spinney.

"Why did she lie to me then?"

About meeting Chris? Was that what Lambert meant? Or was there something else he had in mind? It was impossible to tell. But the important thing was to keep him talking.

"Perhaps she didn't mean it," Rudd replied, still crawling forward in the direction of the voice. At the same time, he made a circling movement with one hand to Boyce, who, understanding the gesture, nodded. Once they had Lambert's exact position, it might be possible for the sergeant to approach him unseen from the side, taking him by surprise before he had time to aim the gun.

"She meant it all right."

Lambert's voice was quite close now. He no longer had to raise it to make himself heard. It came somewhere to Rudd's left and he inched cautiously towards it, Boyce meanwhile crawling off to the right, moving with surprising agility for a man of his bulk.

"She told me he loved her," Lambert was saying. "She said he loved her better than I ever could."

He must be speaking of the time after Jess had returned, Rudd realised, just before the murder. God alone knew what had prompted her to say such a thing. Was it to taunt him? Was it to show him that someone nearer her own age could find her attractive? Or was it because she had no other defence against him except the one weapon of rousing his jealousy?

Rudd half rose to his feet. He could see Lambert now over the top of the low bushes. He was standing in a small clearing, his back against a tree, a man at bay, the gun cradled across one arm, his head bowed.

Rudd was reminded of some lines that he had read once in a play at school. Shakespeare, wasn't it?

> They have tied me to a stake; I cannot fly,
> But, bear-like, I must fight the course.

A reference to bearbaiting, of course. It had been explained to the class. The creature was fastened to a post and had to defend itself as best it could from the dogs that were set loose against it. The picture that it had evoked in his mind had affected him powerfully at the time.

Lambert raised his head. It was doubtful if he could see Rudd, who was now lying beneath the overhang of the bushes. His face, anyway, was tipped too far back. He was looking at the sky.

"Oh, Christ! Oh, Jess love! I never meant you any harm. When I came to you that night, I was drunk but I thought you wanted me. I never knew you took me because you were afraid."

The second explosion was almost as loud as the first. It reverberated through the spinney like thunder, rousing the birds that took flight in a great flurry of startled cries and beating wings that whirled away above the trees, recalling to Rudd's mind the fragments of charred cloth that had burst upwards in the same mad ascent.

In contrast, Lambert fell slowly, first to his knees, then forward again onto his face, with the slow, deliberate, downward descent of a great tree toppling and crashing to the ground.

He must have died at once. The cartridge from the barrel of the gun that he had placed under his chin had taken half his face away. The one eye that remained was still open, gazing upwards with the terrible expression of fixed eagerness, as if he were still searching.

Taking off his jacket, Rudd covered up his head. There was nothing else he could do. Lambert had reached his climax, the closing scene to his tragedy for which he had been preparing himself during the past few hours. It seemed a better ending than any Rudd could ever have devised for him.

16

"Was she afraid of him?" Boyce asked.

He and Rudd had returned to the bungalow and were standing in Lambert's bedroom, regarding the confusion that, so far, hadn't been examined, although the experts had been called in. The rest, Lambert's body and the gun that had been used for the double killing, had been taken away.

Rudd picked up a scrap of torn fabric: underwear by the look of it, pale pink nylon with a fragment of lace along one edge, while he considered the question. It was the same one he had asked of Babcock and Mrs. Ritchie and the answer he had gotten then had seemed satisfactory at the time. Certainly Lambert had died believing it. Perhaps he had killed himself because he believed it. But Rudd wasn't quite so sure himself anymore. It wasn't as simple as that.

It was obvious that she had been sufficiently afraid of him not to admit to Aston being her lover. She hadn't dared go that far. But she had admitted instead to something she knew couldn't be true: that Chris Lawrence had loved her. Had she wanted to believe it? Or had she chosen him to taunt her father with simply because it was untrue and Chris Lawrence was the most vulnerable out of the men who desired her? Had it been, perhaps, her way of paying him back for having failed sexually? Chris had said she laughed at him. That was a woman's weapon. Rousing her father's jealousy had been another but one she obviously hadn't realised would be fatal. There, at least, she had shown her inexperience.

But whether or not she had been too afraid of him to repulse his advances when he came drunk to her bed was another matter. The question would go unanswered with Jess Lambert to the grave, if indeed she knew the answer to it herself. Afraid? In awe of? Or just too young to know how to handle the situation? Easier, perhaps, to give in than to put up a struggle. Plenty of girls got caught that way.

The other possibility was that she had welcomed it secretly but Rudd wasn't enough of a cynic to believe that, although she evidently hadn't had too many scruples in accepting Aston into her bed.

"I don't know, Tom," he replied, sounding more irritable than he intended.

Stepping inside the room, he contemplated the hole in the carpet blasted by Lambert's shotgun. The bloodstain had gone, obliterated in the charred fragments of cotton fabric and splintered floor boards. Lambert had succeeded finally in destroying it, burning out blood with fire.

"He had a rare old time in here," Boyce commented following Rudd into the room. "Every stitch she possessed torn to pieces."

"He'd paid for it," Rudd replied. And so had she, he added to himself. He felt in a sour mood. What a hell of a mess in every sense of the word! Two people exacting payment from each other for that one mistake; she in dresses and cheap jewellery; he in duty and obedience; a debt that was only finally settled on both sides by death.

He stooped to pick up two torn halves of a photograph from the top of the heap of scattered clothing and fitted them together; Jess Lambert and some classmates, boys and girls, taken at a school's sports day, judging by the shorts and running vests they were wearing. Some of the other scraps of paper were also photographs. A few were torn-up birthday cards, one inscribed "Love from Sandra." A couple of Valentines were among them, unsigned of course, no doubt from the boys she had known who daren't come too close because of her father.

No wonder he hadn't been able to find anything relating to her past life when he had searched her bedroom, Rudd though. Why had Lambert taken them? Was he jealous of any contacts she had apart from him? Or had it been a futile attempt to cover up the past, knowing that, after her death, the police would come asking questions?

It was another aspect of the case he'd never know the answer to, he decided, letting the scraps flutter to the floor again.

Of one thing he was certain though; Lambert had removed them from the girl's bedroom before his own visit the previous evening, although how long before he could not guess. But the destruction had come afterwards. Apart from that one burst of rage when he had struck the arm of the chair with his fist, Lambert had been like a man stunned. It must have been later, after he had sat brooding and drinking, that he had worked himself up to a pitch of fury that had sent him bursting into her room where he had gathered up the things he had bought her and gone about his orgy of devastation.

Rudd had looked briefly into the girl's bedroom on their return to the bungalow. It bore mute witness to this, the wardrobe doors open, the drawers wrenched out and scattered about the floor.

"There's a couple of things I still don't understand," Boyce was saying. "First of all, why did Lambert make it look as if Chris Lawrence had killed her?"

"Because he thought he'd made love to his daughter and therefore he ought to be punished," Rudd replied. "I think, too, in some odd way, Lambert may have really believed it was his fault. If Chris hadn't met her, none of it would have happened. He was drunk as well which can't have helped him to think very clearly."

"And how did Lambert find out that she was meeting him? After all, Chris Lawrence was very careful not to let on he had a date with her. Look at the way he climbed out of the stable window and came round by the fields."

"According to Lambert, it was pure chance. He just happened to be standing at the window when he noticed Chris climbing over the gate. I believed him at the time. Now I'm not so sure. I think he already suspected she was up to something and made damn sure he could watch her as she went out. Of course, it was stupid of her to arrange to meet him so close to where she lived. She knew her father's attitude to her having boy friends."

"Why did she then?" Boyce asked.

"She didn't realise Lambert could see over the hawthorn hedge in front of the bungalow. That seems the only explanation. She probably couldn't but then she was shorter than he was. So she went off for her date, thinking her father knew nothing about it. It must have come as a shock to her when she got back and Lambert confronted her with the truth."

"Could you have caught him if he hadn't given himself away? You remember, your winning card?"

"Card?" Rudd asked. For a moment, the question meant nothing to him. "Oh, that. I doubt it. It wasn't a very good card anyway. I don't think it would have persuaded Lambert into making a confession if he hadn't been ready to do so. It was something that occurred to me in Suffolk, while I was talking to Babcock and Mrs. Ritchie. Neither of them knew Jess Lambert was pregnant. Neither, come to that, did Aston when he took Lambert on as foreman. Lambert simply told him he was changing jobs for personal reasons. But, as I've pointed out already, Lambert must have known, otherwise why did he give up a good job at Babcock's to move here. And yet he did nothing about it. At first I thought he might not have known who the child's father was or perhaps it was someone he preferred to keep quiet about, taking his daughter away rather than cause a scandal. And then it struck me that couldn't be the reason. Jess Lambert had only the one date with Chris Lawrence and yet Lambert knew about it and, when he didn't come home, he'd been prepared to make a scene, going round to Maggie's and then Cookson's getting them both out of bed.

"We know now, of course, that this was merely a blind. The girl was already dead—murdered by Lambert. But nevertheless he was acting in character, playing the part of the anxious father. Both Babcock and Mrs. Ritchie said he was overprotective. But if, as I've said, he knew she was pregnant, why didn't he make the same sort of fuss about finding out who the child's father was? He didn't though. He simply gave in his notice and moved out of the district, hushing everything up. It wasn't the way he normally behaved in relation to his daughter and it made me realise that he knew only too well who the child's father was— himself. He couldn't stay at Ashbourne. The gossip really would have been flying. It was bad enough here but at least no one knew anything about their past life. Jess was regarded as an unmarried mother who had had a child presumably by some young man in the village where she used to live. As long as both of them kept quiet about it, the truth would never come out."

"When do you reckon he got rid of the body?" Boyce asked.

"Again, it's pure guesswork but I imagine on the way to

Maggie's. He went in the van so it would have been easy enough to put the body in the back, stop at the roadside, which was why we found no tyre marks in the gateway except for Aston's lorry, and carry the body into the field. The fact that it was laid out neatly fits in with Lambert, too. I thought at first that it suggested a woman but it was the sort of thing Lambert would have done. After all, she was his daughter and he loved her. So he put her down carefully and straightened the clothes. Whether or not he chose the currant field deliberately because it was the place where Chris Lawrence and Jess first met is another point we'll never resolve. He may have chosen it simply because it was nearby."

"We could have the van checked for bloodstains," Boyce pointed out. "If the body was put in the back, there's bound to be some evidence. Do you want me to see to it?"

"Yes. We might as well get all the pieces we can together," Rudd replied. He looked at his watch. "It's getting late, Tom, and I'd like to have a chat with Maggie Hearn before she goes to bed. McCallum and Pardoe will be along soon to photograph and examine this lot. Will you wait and let them in? I shan't be long but you can send Kyle down in the car to fetch me from the farm if they arrive before I'm back. I'll walk."

As he went to the gate, he stood for a few minutes in the garden. It was quite dark now and the sky was clear and very high, thickly scattered with stars that were losing their brilliance as the moon rose over to his left, lifting itself above the dark rim of trees which was all he could see of the copse where Lambert had died.

It seemed to follow him as he walked the short distance to Maggie's place and, by the time he had reached the farm, it had floated free of the horizon and was clearly visible, a pale, round disc marked with its own strange pattern of shadows.

The kitchen light was on and, through the uncurtained window, he could see Maggie at the table, reading glasses on the end of her nose, turning over the pages of a newspaper with the desultory air of someone merely filling in time. But her senses must have been alert because, before he reached the door, she glanced up and seeing him, got up to let him in.

"Something's happened," she said, before he had time to speak.

"It's Lambert," he told her. "He killed himself tonight after confessing to his daughter's murder. I thought you'd want to know."

"Lambert? But why?"

She sounded bewildered.

Rudd shrugged. He didn't want to tell her too much. It was better to blur over the truth.

"I think he was jealous."

"Of Chris?"

"Possibly."

"So Chris was to blame in a way?"

"Oh, no," Rudd said in quick protest, catching sight of her expression. "You mustn't think that, Miss Hearn. If it hadn't been Chris, it would have been someone else sooner or later. As you said yourself, she was young and pretty. Some other young man would have wanted to take her out and the same thing would have happened. If anyone was to blame it was Lambert, but I suppose he couldn't help being stupidly jealous."

Any more than Chris's mother, he added to himself. He realised for the first time how alike Jess Lambert and Chris Lawrence were; both had been deserted by one of their parents while still young children and had been brought up in an atmosphere in which too much had been demanded of them; both had struggled in their own ways to escape and find the essential freedom in which they could be themselves.

Jess had died because of it. As for Chris Lawrence, Rudd could only hope that he might at last escape.

"Besides," he went on, "I think the girl taunted Lambert when she got home and the quarrel got out of hand."

"But why should he feel so . . . ?" she began and then stopped. "You look tired," she said instead. "Would you like some tea?"

It was typical of her, Rudd thought. But, at least, she was acting in character.

"Yes, I'd love some," he replied, sitting down at the table and watching while she put the kettle on to boil and set out cups. The task had given her some animation. Even so she looked tired herself, he thought. Or rather weary, with that dulled expression that comes not just from physical exhaustion but from some inner loss of light and purpose.

"What will happen to the child?" she asked, her back to him as she poured boiling water into the teapot to warm it and swirled it round before carrying it over to the sink to empty it.

"Jess's child, you mean?"

"Yes."

Glancing over her shoulder as she stood at the sink, she caught a glimpse of the look on his face before he had time to change it into something more bland and non-committal.

"I believe it's with Lambert's sister in Norfolk. She'll have to be told, of course. I don't know whether she'll keep it or want to have it adopted."

She had guessed the truth. He could tell that by the way she met his eyes briefly before she turned back to the task of making the tea. But he knew the secret would be safe with her. She wouldn't say anything. What would be the point? They were all gone now, father, daughter, child. Besides, he knew she had her own integrity.

"I really came," Rudd went on, "to tell you that we'll be releasing Chris Lawrence."

Maggie was silent for so long that he wondered if she had heard him. Then, as she carried the teapot to the table and sat down opposite him, she said quietly, "What will happen to him?"

"After his release? I don't know. That's up to him."

Rudd knew she was looking for further reassurance that he couldn't give her. Although he doubted if she expected or even hoped that he would come back, she still hadn't quite let him go. She still wanted news of him, some idea of where he might go and what he might be doing. Rudd felt that he couldn't leave it there. He had to offer her something.

"He may go back to university," he said, "although, if he's sensible, he'll finish the treatment he was having first."

He paused and, as she still said nothing, he added, "I think he'll be all right. He's young, you know. They recover easily."

"Yes, of course they do," Maggie said quickly. She had to believe it, she told herself, otherwise it had all been nothing more than a tragic waste.

"What will you do now?" he asked, curious to know her reactions although it was better, he realised, not to probe too far.

"Me?" she sounded surprised. "Oh, I'll potter on as usual. There's always something to do."

Rudd had finished his tea and he stood up.

"You're not going?" she asked.

"I'm afraid I must, Miss Hearn. There's quite a lot still to finish."

"Well, I mustn't keep you then," she replied with a show of briskness.

All the same, he felt he was walking out on her, as Chris had done, as he went to the door.

"You'll see him before he goes?" she asked on the doorstep.

"Yes. There'll be certain formalities to go through before he's released."

"Then give him my . . ."

Was she about to say love? Anyway, she stopped and began again.

"Give him my best wishes for the future."

"Of course," he assured her. "I'll do that."

He waited for a few seconds, wondering if she would add anything more, but as she didn't, he nodded good-bye to her and went away.

An unsatisfactory ending, he thought as he walked up the road. Too much left unsaid. Too many futures unresolved: Maggie's, Chris's, Jess Lambert's child.

But that's the way it went. A case nicely sewn up as far as the dead were concerned but a lot of loose ends left for the living. However, that wasn't part of his job.

All the same, it was a long time before he was able to get out of his mind the picture of Maggie Hearn sitting alone at the table, turning over the pages of a newspaper; a glimpse through a window that seemed more poignant than it ought to be.

ABOUT THE AUTHOR

JUNE THOMSON's previous Detective Rudd novels include
A Question of Identity, Death Cap, Case Closed and *The
Long Revenge*. She lives in the beautiful Essex country-
side outside of London.

INSPECTOR RUDD
Books by June Thomson

June Thomson is a highly praised British mystery writer whose series of books features Inspector Rudd, a likeable policeman who cleverly but without a great deal of flash, investigates and solves unusual murders in English towns. The following are the first American paperback appearances of Ms Thomson's books.

DEATH CAP

In the quiet Essex village of Abbots Stacy, Detective Inspector Rudd of the local CID becomes involved with murder—someone has slipped a poisonous mushroom in Rene King's food. Rudd is at his wits end until he discovers a piece of village gossip that had long ago been swept under the carpet.

THE HABIT OF LOVING

This time Inspector Rudd's case involves a bizarre triangle —Maggie Hearn, a middle-aged spinster who has befriended handsome young Chris Lambert and Jess Lambert, a beautiful young girl who has a date with death.

A QUESTION OF IDENTITY

When the local archaeological society asks permission to excavate a meadow they hope to find bones. They do. However they are the badly decomposed remains of more recent vintage. The only clue is a corroded cross on a chain. Rudd's investigation leads to a man who had disappeared several years before.

Read these Bantam Books by June Thomson, available wherever paperbacks are sold.

Ross Macdonald
Lew Archer Novels

'The finest series of detective novels ever written by an American . . . I have been reading him for years and he has yet to disappoint. Classify him how you will, he is one of the best novelists now operating, and all he does is keep on getting better."
—The New York Times

☐ 12249	THE BARBAROUS COAST	$2.25
☐ 12443	THE DROWNING POOL	$1.95
☐ 13963	FIND A VICTIM	$2.25
☐ 10979	THE IVORY GRIN	$1.75
☐ 13234	MEET ME AT THE MORGUE	$2.25
☐ 12926	THE MOVING TARGET	$1.95
☐ 12914	THE FAR SIDE OF THE DOLLAR	$1.95
☐ 10987	THE WAY SOME PEOPLE DIE	$1.75
☐ 12771	THE GOODBYE LOOK	$1.95
☐ 12544	THE UNDERGROUND MAN	$1.95
☐ 13789	THE BLUE HAMMER	$2.25
☐ 12120	THE WYCHERLY WOMAN	$1.95
☐ 12119	ZEBRA-STRIPED HEARSE	$1.95

Buy them at your local bookstore or use this handy coupon for ordering:

Bantam Books, Inc., Dept. RM, 414 East Golf Road, Des Plaines, Ill. 60016

Please send me the books I have checked above. I am enclosing $_____ (please add $1.00 to cover postage and handling). Send check or money order —no cash or C.O.D.'s please.

Mr/Mrs/Miss_____

Address_____

City_____ State/Zip_____

RM—4/80

Please allow four to six weeks for delivery. This offer expires 10/80.

WHODUNIT?

Bantam did! By bringing you these masterful tales of murder, suspense and mystery!

☐	10706	**SLEEPING MURDER** by Agatha Christie	$2.25
☐	13774	**THE MYSTERIOUS AFFAIR AT STYLES** by Agatha Christie	$2.25
☐	13777	**THE SECRET ADVERSARY** by Agatha Christie	$2.25
☐	12838	**POIROT INVESTIGATES** by Agatha Christie	$2.25
☐	12458	**PLEASE PASS THE GUILT** by Rex Stout	$1.75
☐	13145	**TROUBLE IN TRIPLICATE** by Rex Stout	$1.95
☐	12408	**LONG TIME NO SEE** by Ed McBain	$1.95
☐	12310	**THE SPY WHO CAME IN FROM THE COLD** by John LeCarre	$2.50
☐	12443	**THE DROWNING POOL** by Ross Macdonald	$1.95
☐	12544	**THE UNDERGROUND MAN** by Ross Macdonald	$1.95
☐	13789	**THE BLUE HAMMER** by Ross MacDonald	$2.25
☐	12172	**A JUDGEMENT IN STONE** by Ruth Rendell	$1.95

Buy them at your local bookstore or use this handy coupon for ordering:

Bantam Books, Inc., Dept. BD, 414 East Golf Road, Des Plaines, Ill. 60016

Please send me the books I have checked above. I am enclosing $_____ (please add $1.00 to cover postage and handling). Send check or money order —no cash or C.O.D.'s please.

Mr/Mrs/Miss_____

Address_____

City_____State/Zip_____

BD—4/80

Please allow four to six weeks for delivery. This offer expires 10/80.